I0691648

Tenderhearted Cowboy

By Barbara Baldwin

Print ISBN 978-1-77362-578-2
Amazon Print ISBN 978-1-77362-579-9

A quality publisher of genre fiction.
Airdrie Alberta

Dedication

For my long time friends and co-conspirators,
Mickey Teel and Linda Denning.
How dull my life would have been
without you.

Prologue

Camino, Texas, 1870

"You can't take my kin," Joe shouted, struggling against the deputy who had pinned his arms behind his back. His sister, Mary Elizabeth, was crying. Seth, his five-year old brother, jiggled baby Jessica in his arms, trying to quiet her. The two-year-old twins stood silent as statues, each with a thumb in his mouth as they were wont to do when they were troubled.

"Sheriff, they don't understand. What's it hurt if we stay here on the farm and fend for ourselves?" He had been asking the same question ever since they buried Pa, and the sheriff made it clear that homes would be found for Joe and the others.

Joe felt he was man enough to take care of them. At fifteen, he had been fending for his brothers and sisters pretty near a year, anyway. His pa did more drinking than working and Rebecca, his step-ma, was too sick with child to do much of anything.

"Joe, you ain't got the know-how to take care of these little ones," the sheriff answered. "Times are tough and there ain't nobody going to take in five young'uns. 'Sides, your pa owed money to just about everyone in town and the bank owns this farm."

The sheriff was right. Rebecca died a month ago giving birth to little Jessica. Then their pa, damn his hide, got drunk once too often and fell down a ravine and killed himself.

"Tomorrow morning Preacher Burke is going to take y'all up to the mission orphanage at San Antonio." The sheriff looked at Joe with pity, which only made him angrier.

Joe stiffened his spine. Eyes burning, his gaze flickered over the freshly turned graves under the gnarled mesquite tree. He hadn't cried when pa died and he wasn't about to do it now in front of the sheriff.

"Tell you what," the sheriff said. "Seeing as how I'm a family man myself, I'm going to let you say your good-byes. Get on into the house and do what you gotta do."

Joe herded the little ones toward the house. The door slammed behind him. He looked at his brothers' and sister's stricken faces in the dim light from the only window. How could he keep them all together?

The only way he could be any good to them at all was if he were free. He'd follow the preacher and ambush him along the route—far enough away from Camino that the sheriff wouldn't come looking for them.

He gathered supplies, rolling them up in a bedroll and tying it with a section of rope. Taking a tin from the top shelf, where he always kept it hid from his pa, he dumped the contents onto the table where the young'uns sat staring, wide-eyed. Two silver dollars spilled out, along with six silver conchos Rebecca once used as buttons on a dress. She had cut them off one day, telling Joe to trade them for food if need be.

Raw anger welled up inside him. When Rebecca was alive, she repeatedly told them to respect their pa. Joe had tried, even if he didn't much deserve it. But what kind of sonofabitch would leave…? He bit back an oath as he looked at the faces watching him.

What would become of them? How could he leave them even for a short time?

Yet how could he help them if he didn't?

He stuffed the money in his pocket before sitting down at the table. Taking the knife he had hidden in his boot, he cut six short lengths of sinew, slid a concho onto each, then tied the ends together. Still, the children watched without saying a word.

He placed a sinew necklace around Mary Elizabeth's neck and then one on baby Jessica, where he shortened the

6

sinew so it wouldn't slip off. He whispered to Mary Elizabeth, "Try to stay with the baby."

"Joey." She began to cry. Mary Elizabeth was small for eight years old, hardly more than a baby herself. Joe held her tight, feeling much older than his fifteen years.

"Shh, I gotta do this. I'll find you down the road a piece." He kissed her forehead and slid a finger down the baby's soft cheek, hoping never to forget how that innocence felt.

He knelt on the floor and gathered Seth, Michael and Matthew to him. "You boys mind your sister, now." He slid a necklace over each of the boys' heads. The twins didn't understand the gravity of the situation and grinned as they studied the shiny engraved concho at the end of the sinew. Joe closed each little hand around the silver, clasping them in his big ones, his eyes on Seth as he spoke.

"*Never* take these off. They're talismans that will protect each of you until I can find you and we can be a family again." He took the last necklace and slid it over his own head, dropping the concho inside his shirt.

"I promise," he whispered as he slipped out the back of the cabin.

He hadn't gone more than twenty feet before a hand grabbed him.

"Where you think you're going?" One of the deputies jerked him around.

All of Joe's pent up frustration poured forth as he swung a fist at the man. He only got in one punch before he found himself flat on his back in the dirt, the deputy looming over him, revolver in hand.

"Week or so in jail will cool that temper of yours, boy." The deputy hauled him roughly to his feet, twisting his arm cruelly behind his back.

Joe's heart plummeted. Just like his own ma and Rebecca and Pa, he had failed to protect what was his.

Chapter One

Sky stood on the porch of the Double T ranch house, shaking her head as heat waves rippled upward from the landscape. The sky was brilliant blue, not a cloud in sight, particularly not any that might contain rain. It was only early spring, but *it was hotter than hell*, according to Patch. While she might not repeat the cuss word out loud, she most assuredly agreed with the old bunkhouse cook. Even the adobe walls of the ranch house didn't do much to keep the afternoon sun from baking the air to just below stifling. She had come outside hoping for a breath of breeze, but there was none.

She had overheard William Cazneau from the Circle C ranch say that if this drought didn't end soon, he'd be thinking of selling out. There had always been water available to the ranches because they bordered the Rio Grande, but the Double T was fortunate that several smaller creeks cut diagonally through the vast ranch. That didn't mean the several thousand head of cattle her daddy owned could survive if they didn't get rain soon.

Besides, with no rain to fill the slowly shrinking creeks, there also would be no grass for grazing. She had lived in West Texas all her life, and couldn't remember it ever being this bad. She lifted her gaze to heaven in prayer when a movement caught her eye.

Shading her eyes against the bright Texas sun, she watched a lone rider canter up the lane. As he drew closer, she suddenly recognized the black attire, broken only by a brightly colored bandana around his neck. Not a day had gone by in the past three years when she hadn't thought of him. She knew the set of those shoulders, though they appeared wider than she remembered.

Joe Dawson.

No matter how long he had been gone, her heart still pounded and her stomach clutched like it had the very day he left. Her blood rushed to warm her cheeks and hands.

Hands that wanted to caress him…and strangle him.

The hand on her forehead trembled. From the day Joe first set foot on the ranch, he had done this to her. He created an upheaval of her emotions when she didn't even understood what the rapid heartbeat, sweaty palms and ringing ears meant. By the time she did understand and want to explore those emotions, Joe left without a word.

Now, two days before her twentieth birthday, he came riding back to the Double T, big as you please. Actually, Sky revised that opinion as he rode closer. He looked much, much larger than life.

"Howdy, ma'am." The slow drawl rippled across her like heat waves on the baked, West Texas plains. The sun at his back created a halo, leaving his face shadowed beneath the broad Stetson he tugged in greeting.

Sky gasped. The voice was deeper, stronger, but she couldn't mistake the shiver that ran down her spine at hearing it.

"Is your husband around?"

He didn't recognize her. Now that made Sky downright mad. It didn't matter that she had changed dramatically in the time he had been gone; that she had finally grown into her long legs and had filled out considerably. She had never forgotten him. The least he could do was remember her.

She decided not to tell him for the moment. Instead, she put her hands on her narrow hips, her breeches clad legs spread in a determined stance.

"Who is it you wish to see?" She spoke in an icy voice, dripping disdain as she glared at him from beneath the hat that shaded her face. Even if he couldn't see her expression, she felt better. His eyes narrowed.

"Cooper Tate." He took off his hat and ran a hand through his hair.

Sky almost lost her composure. Hair, black as midnight, fell in unruly waves across his forehead and over his ears. A dark shadow of a beard gave him a dangerous look. Even though she couldn't see them clearly, she easily remembered silver gray eyes full of mystery.

Sky straightened her shoulders but didn't trust her voice to speak. She wasn't about to let him know he still affected her. She nodded to the right, indicating her daddy was around the back of the house.

Joe reined away from the porch, wondering at Miss Tianna's attitude. When he worked for Coop before, his wife had been reserved but cordial until she got to know a body. And regardless, she always displayed the hospitality for which Texas was famous. Just now, she had been downright rude. Letting his horse plod around the side of the house, he lifted his hat and wiped a sleeve across his sweaty brow. It came away wet and dirty. It was no wonder Miss Tianna didn't acknowledge him with more than a nod. He looked like a drifter and no doubt smelled worse.

Kneeing Critter in the side, he turned towards the corral where he saw activity. He drew along the fence and swung a leg across the neck of his horse, hooking his knee over the saddle horn. Several hands sat along the railing. A couple of men were on the ground inside the corral with coils of rope and one sat atop a bronc that was determined not to give up without a fight.

"Doesn't look like you've improved any," he yelled, laughing as the cowboy flew by on the snorting horse. Seconds later, the man was tossed from the back of the sorrel and landed in the dirt. He got slowly to his feet, bent to pick up his hat and slapped it against his thigh, all the while looking around the corral.

Joe grinned when the man's eyes lit on him.

"Damn, you broke my concentration," Cooper Tate hooted as he ambled over, his rolling gait speaking of long years in a saddle. "Hell, boy, I thought some outlaw got you for sure!" Light blue eyes looked him over from head to toe.

"No, sir," Joe said with a chuckle.

"Come on up to the house." Coop climbed the fence like a man half his age and hopped to the other side. "Matt, take care of his horse."

"I prefer doing that myself," Joe interrupted.

Coop shrugged. "Suit yourself, but I'll be one cool drink ahead of you."

Joe laughed. "You always were, sir."

"What's this *sir*, bullshit? I'm not the law or the local minister."

Joe just shook his head. Some things never changed. "I'll meet you at the house."

He took his time unsaddling Critter, rubbing him down and giving him an extra ration of oats. He went over in his mind what he would say to Cooper Tate now that he was here. He hadn't thought about where he would end up when he left San Antonio, other than it wouldn't be back to the dirt farm of his youth. The Double T was the only home he cared to remember. Coop had taken him in, taught him well, and gave him a second chance. Joe guessed he really shouldn't have been surprised when he headed for the only family he had at the moment.

* * *

Coop hollered at Bonita before entering the house to tell her to ready a guest room and set an extra place for supper. He washed the dust off at the water bucket on the back porch, wondering why Joe had returned. He had been the son Coop never had, and seeing him again brought back a lot of memories.

Seven years ago, Bonita found a skinny, scraggly boy trying to steal a loaf of bread off the kitchen windowsill. When Coop confronted the boy, he saw something in the youngster's eyes that wrenched his heart—loss and hopelessness. He was hungry, mistrustful and as full of anger as a bear woken up in the middle of winter, and

11

wouldn't tell Coop more than his name. Even so, Coop put the youngster to work instead of turning him over to the sheriff.

His wife, Tianna, had tried to teach the boy to read and do figures but for the most part he worked with the men and slept in the bunkhouse. Regular meals and hard work quickly filled out Joe's slight frame and turned skin and bones into muscle and brawn. Never once did he take advantage, and in most cases he worked twice as hard, as though trying to prove something. Joe Dawson turned out to be something else, taking to ranching like a duck took to water.

It took two years after he first got to the ranch before Joe trusted Coop enough to tell him a little about his life. Two years after that, Joe said he was joining the Texas Rangers to protect Texas and bring peace to the frontier. Coop thought it more likely Joe would use the badge to hunt for his brothers and sisters, stolen from him years before.

Coop shook his gray head. That boy had gone through some kind of hell growing up, and Coop was sure he didn't know the half of it. He poured himself a drink in the study, then poured another when he heard Bonita squeal. Joe must have come in the back way.

He turned to the door, then laughed. Joe was biting into a hunk of bread smeared with blackberry jam. The smile on the boy's face almost had Coop overlooking the severe limp that hampered his walk. He handed him a drink, then waved him over to a chair by the hearth, not missing the way he grimaced when he sat down.

"Didn't take you long to find your way to the kitchen."

"Bonita always did have the best bread and jam in Texas."

"From the sounds of things, she didn't mind giving you any of it, either."

Coop settled into the other big leather chair, feeling every one of his fifty-six years. He couldn't prevent the groan as his knees cracked.

12

"You're too old to be busting broncs," Joe said, a frown dipping his dark brows as he licked the last of the jam off his thumb.

Coop opened his mouth to tell him he'd better mind his manners, but realized when he met Joe's gaze that the boy had become a man. Oh, he had the same features, like those gray eyes that sparked with keen intelligence that had allowed Joe to soak up learning faster than the parched ground during a summer storm. But he had filled out his tall frame and the boyish face was now chiseled into hard angles by the wind and weather, not to mention the years that had gone by.

"Sky would have hollered at me good if she'd seen me on that bronc, so don't you be telling on me. But hell, I can't let the boys have all the fun."

"Sky? I haven't seen her, though I did see Miss Tianna on the porch when I rode up."

A frown crossed the man's face. "My Tia died almost three years ago, Joe, close after you left."

Joe remembered the petite, soft-spoken woman who was the complete opposite of Cooper Tate. Though she had tried to teach Sky and him numbers and reading and manners, she just as readily laughed at their antics. A sense of loss pricked his heart, but he quickly tamped it down. He couldn't spend his life grieving for losses and what might have been in circumstances he couldn't control. He had enough of his own worries.

"I'm sorry to hear that, Coop," he said out loud, knowing he needed to say something. "But then, who was...?" He let the sentence die, unable to believe the beautiful woman he had seen earlier was once the scab-kneed girl with braids who always trailed after him. He was sure the surprise was evident in his voice as he said, "She's the spitting image of Miss Tianna."

Coop nodded. "Yes, she is. If only she had her mother's sweet, gentle nature."

Joe laughed. "She never did cotton to taking orders, as I recall."

13

"Some things never change, son, but some things do. I never thought to see you back at the Double T. You always had your eyes on the horizon," Coop said, then took a sip of whiskey. "What happened to your leg?"

Joe shrugged, trying to make light of the wound that had nearly cost him his life. "A stray bullet."

Coop said nothing but continued to stare and frown. Joe squirmed, knowing he wanted the whole story.

"You ever hear of the Horrell brothers?"

"Hell, yes. They've been making trouble since '72. Didn't they get to feuding with Pink Higgins?"

Joe nodded. "All they *do* is feud with Higgins. If it were up to my captain, he'd just let them shoot it out and kill each other off, but every time there's a gun fight, the law is obliged to step in."

"And you stepped in at the wrong time?" Coop nodded in understanding. "Can't see why there's got to be some damn range war when Texas itself is big enough for anybody that wants to work hard. Hell, there's more country in these United States now than there are people to get it all settled."

"That may very well be, but some people aren't happy unless they're fighting," Joe added.

"How long ago did this happen?" Coop asked, nodding to indicate Joe's injury.

"Four months, give or take. I've been recouping in San Antonio, but Captain Armstrong decided to retire me." Joe was sure Coop could hear the bitterness in his voice. Being a Texas Ranger had given his life purpose, and he didn't know if he was ready to give that up. "Anyway, I'm looking for work while this leg heals."

"You're welcome to do your recouping here," Coop said. "It'd heal faster if you stayed off it."

"Yeah, well, you know I can't do that, Coop." Joe had quit taking Coop's charity years ago. He wouldn't accept his hospitality if he didn't work for his keep.

Coop shrugged. "All right, if you want to be stubborn. Paul has been wanting to step down as foreman. Claims he's too old to be roping and branding." He snorted. "Hell, he's not any older than me."

Joe shook his head at the offer. "I'll start wrangling."

"Like hell," Coop muttered, slapping his free hand on the wide arm of his chair. "I trained you to take over this ranch, Joe, whether you realized it or not. I always thought…well, never mind what I thought. If you want a job, the only one available is foreman. Take it or leave it."

Joe had to grin. Cooper Tate hadn't changed a whit over the years, still crusty and hell-bent on having his own way. No wonder his daughter was so stubborn. "I'll take it on one condition." At Coop's nod, he continued, "I have to be able to take off if I get word about…." Even after so long, he had a hard time talking about his lost brothers and sisters.

"You got it," Coop interrupted, reading his mind and agreeing without hesitation.

Joe blew his breath out in a sigh. "I'll put my stuff out in the bunkhouse."

"You can stay right here. Paul and Bonita have the foreman's house and Sky and I just rattle around in here. Bonita's already opened a room for you down the hall."

* * *

Sky started to enter her daddy's study when she overheard their conversation. She stopped, not too proud to eavesdrop, as she had always wondered about Joe's background. Now she scuttled down the hall as fast as she could without letting her boot heels touch the hardwood floors. So, Joe was going to work for her daddy. She wondered what Daddy meant about him taking over the ranch. Being his only heir, the Double T would be hers someday and no two-bit cowboy, even one with smoky gray eyes that could turn her inside out, was going to prevent that.

She slammed out the back door of the kitchen and ran to the barn. Not bothering with a saddle, she swung up on

15

Stormy and galloped out of the yard. She didn't think of anything except the wind on her face until she got to the pond. She dropped the reins, letting her horse drink as she jerked off her boots, shimmied her pants down her hips and tugged her shirt over her head.

The pond was small and edged by mesquite trees, which helped create a secluded bathing pool. Two steps into the water and she dove, holding her breath as long as she could and coming up in the middle of the cool, clear water. She treaded water, turning her face to the hot sun. Only then did she try to make sense of her jumbled emotions as she thought back over the years when Joe had been part of life at the ranch.

Sky was an only child, and as much as she loved her parents and the other cowboys on the ranch, she always longed for a brother or sister. Joe arrived when she was thirteen and she viewed him as her own personal companion, especially when her parents allowed him to take lessons with her. She often coerced him into leaving his chores, becoming her reluctant conspirator in escapades around the ranch.

By fourteen, though, her feelings subtly changed. His compelling gray eyes, full of laughter one minute and pain the next, tugged at her tender heart. He was handsome and strong but seemed so alone. She never could comprehend why he'd ride off for days at a time, preferring the loneliness of the land to her company. Her daddy wouldn't tell her where he came from and Mama wouldn't say why Daddy favored him over the other ranch hands.

At fifteen, she was hopelessly in love. Her heart did funny little flip-flops whenever he smiled at her. One day they even experimented with kissing in the barn, but he ended up telling her she didn't know anything and he wasn't going to waste time on a girl.

"Well, I've grown up since then, Joe Dawson, and I know a whole lot more," she muttered. Granted, her experience with men was limited, but she had been kissed and the ones doing it must have liked it. Otherwise, they wouldn't have tried to get her shirt out of her pants. She never allowed things to go too far and often wondered why. Now, she began to suspect the reason.

Floating on her back, she tried to imagine what it would be like kissing Joe now. Heat coiled low in her belly at the thought. Something about him had always drawn her, but now that she'd seen the man he'd become, Sky knew she wanted more than a kiss from Joe Dawson.

Lordy, I still love him, she thought, even when she told herself over and over she didn't after he left the ranch without a word.

"Skyla Tate, you still haven't learned a whit of restraint, have you?"

Sky jackknifed in the water at the sound of his voice and immediately went under. She came up sputtering to his laughter.

"Joe Dawson, you should be ashamed, sneaking around a lady's bath." Her cheeks burned with heat that he might have seen her naked. That heat quickly shot throughout her body and Sky knew it wasn't embarrassment.

"A lady wouldn't be taking a bath in a pond, now would she?"

She watched as he bent over, pulled a long stem of grass from the edge of the bank and put it between his teeth. He stood, legs spread, towering tall and solid against a backdrop of blue Texas sky.

He had taken his hat off and the breeze tossed his black hair across his forehead and along his shirt collar. All Sky could think about was running her fingers through it. His broad shoulders more than filled out the shirt he wore and she imagined the muscles that stretched across his chest and down that flat stomach.

"You could come swimming with me." She surprised them both by suggesting.

Joe ran a hand through his hair as a stab of heat sliced straight to his groin.

"I don't think so." He managed a strangled-sounding chuckle.

"We used to go swimming together. Remember those hot summer days?" Sky swam toward him, taunting him all the way. Where had she learned to talk in such a silky, seductive tone?

It definitely wasn't swimming naked, Joe thought, remembering their half-clothed romps during what seemed like a lifetime ago. "That was before I knew what girls were."

"Oh, I think you always knew."

She was right. Orphaned and on his own at fifteen, he had been befriended by women everywhere he went. But Sky had always been just a pal—the freckle-faced little girl who trailed after him, studied with him, got him in trouble with her pa. She now wore her curly hair short instead of in long braids, and it was hard to believe that same little girl was swimming toward him, all grown up.

Suddenly Sky stood in the waist high water and Joe's breath hissed through his teeth. He snapped his eyes shut on a groan, but not before he got a tantalizing glimpse of creamy skin and luscious breasts, their crests peaked from the cool water. He had seen hunger in the dark look of her eyes, apparent even from this distance. He turned his back and heard the water splash behind him as she came up the bank.

Joe couldn't let himself think of her in any way other than his boss's daughter. If he did, he'd be kicked off the Double T faster than a rattler could strike.

"I'm heading back to the house, Sky. You get yourself dressed and get home. Bonita will skin you if you're late for supper." He reverted to the bullying tactics that had worked years before.

"You don't have to threaten me, Joe Dawson." Anger sparked in her voice and something else—hurt? "I'm not a little girl anymore."

"Honey, I had that one figured out all by myself," he muttered, vaulting onto Critter's back and running away as fast as he could.

Chapter Two

Sky dressed with care for supper that night. She told herself it was because her mother had always insisted they come to the table properly attired, and she and her father tried to carry on that tradition. She bit her lip to keep it from trembling, still missing her mother even after all this time.

She scrutinized her reflection in the mirror, forking her fingers through her short curly hair, suddenly wishing it was long and straight and that the freckles spotting her nose were not so prominent, and...she sighed. Nothing could change who she was at this late date.

She pinned a silver brooch at the throat of her white blouse, which snuggly outlined her breasts the way the navy skirt hugged the curve of her hips. Was the sash too girlish, or did it accent her hips like those bustles she had seen in a fashion magazine at McGuffy's Mercantile? Although she told herself she didn't want the latest fashions that could be ordered from back east, she still wondered if Joe would think her terribly backward and out of fashion. She didn't know where he had been or what he had seen, but figured it was more than the Double T offered.

She frowned. She shouldn't care what he thought, but realized she did. Her heart did a funny little flip-flop when she recalled how she had walked halfway out of the water before he had turned his back. The warmth of a blush now heated her cheeks at her bold behavior, but she had wanted him to realize she wasn't the little girl he had known.

Instead, he gave no reaction whatsoever. He simply turned and rode away. With a sigh, she pinched her cheeks to add color and turned from the mirror. What should she do now? Again she wished her mother was here. There were so many questions she needed answered, but they were not the kind she could ask her father. Most definitely not.

She left her room and hurried down the hallway, already thinking of the one person who could help her come up with a plan to capture Joe's attention. When she entered the study, she stopped short. Daddy sat in his big leather chair, but her gaze automatically slid to Joe, who leaned against the fireplace mantel.

He had washed the trail dust off and his hair was still wet, slicked back from a high forehead and brushing the collar of his shirt. The black he wore gave him a formidable hands-off appearance, but when she finished her slow survey from his boots to his face, she found silver eyes laughing at her.

"Good evening," she stated, swinging her gaze to her daddy to regain her composure. He rose and Joe straightened, their conversation immediately at an end. Sky then realized that whatever had brought Joe back to the Double T, her father knew about it already.

"Sky, you remember Joe Dawson?" he asked as she stepped forward. Apparently Joe hadn't said anything about seeing her at the pond earlier.

She put out her hand. Unexpectedly, Joe raised it, bowing ever so slightly. His twinkling eyes caught her gaze, and he smiled.

"Well, at least you haven't forgotten the manners Mama forced us to learn." Sky couldn't help but smile in return, remembering how Joe used to squirm when he took meals with them, and her mother tried to teach him social etiquette. His preference would have been to be outside with the cowboys because she had wanted the same thing.

He seemed reluctant to let go of her hand. "I'm still more comfortable with my horse than in a drawing room, but I do know how to behave."

"Have the past years required it?" Sky questioned, unbridled curiosity running away with her tongue. Her hand tingled from the calloused feel of his.

"Give the boy a chance," her daddy interrupted, handing her a glass of wine. "He got wounded working as a Ranger, protecting your pretty little Texas backside."

Sky's heart lurched as her gaze scanned him from head to toe. "Wounded?" Reports she had heard about the famous Texas Rangers rushed through her mind.

Then her brow furrowed in anger. "You weren't fighting Indians, were you? I don't understand everybody's frantic wish to eradicate the—"

"Whoa there, missy. Joe's a guest in this house and you won't get on your high-horse about Indian rights." Her father's tone brooked no argument.

"I thought you *hired* him," she returned before remembering it was an overheard conversation. "I mean, I assumed he was back for work." She noticed that Joe had realized her slip, for one eyebrow rose and his eyes crinkled at the edges in amusement.

"I did hire him, but still—" Her father didn't get to finish as Bonita announced supper.

As they walked into the dining room, Sky noticed for the first time that Joe walked with a limp. However he had been wounded, he was either not healed or the accident had left him permanently lame. Her heart hurt for him.

Over a meal of spicy beef, Mexican beans and fried corn, along with Bonita's delicious stone ground bread, Joe told them a little of what he had been doing as a Ranger. Sky watched him finish a third helping of apple crisp with cream before he picked up his coffee cup.

"You can't mean to say you agree with putting the Indians on reservations?" she asked.

"Sky," her father warned.

"It's okay, Coop. Sky always did say what she thought." The corner of Joe's mouth quirked, and she wondered which of the hundreds of times she had spouted off he was thinking about.

"The Indians have lost their hunting grounds," Joe started. "In fact, the buffalo in North Texas and Kansas are almost to the point of extinction."

"Only because the soldiers and buffalo hunters killed so many to feed the troops, along with what those easterners killed just for sport." Sky had little tolerance for waste, whether it was the land or the animals that roamed free across it.

"I realize it wasn't the Indians' fault," Joe agreed, "but that doesn't eliminate the problem. Without animals to hunt, they would have starved if the government hadn't stepped in."

Sky snorted. "Your government put them on barren land that they can't farm, even if they knew how."

"Some of the tribes migrated here on their own. Regardless, there's been numerous reports of renegades causing problems among the ranchers up around San Felipe Del Rio. Whether they hunt or farm—or don't farm—they don't have the right to destroy other people's property," Joe argued.

"That land shouldn't belong to settlers anyway," Sky retorted. "Besides the fact that San Felipe is far north of here, Black Thunder wouldn't allow his people to do that." Too late, she realized her admission.

"Black Thunder?" Joe raised a brow. "From the Kickapoo tribe?"

"Damn it, Sky. I've told you it would be better to stay away from the reservation," her father said at the same time.

"You give them beef."

"That's different," he replied.

Sky shook her head. It was his answer any time she disagreed with him.

"Your father's right, Sky. You shouldn't be seen anywhere near the reservations. Trouble is brewing and you don't want to be caught in the cross fire."

"You are." She stubbornly refused to give up.

Joe shook his head. "Not any more. When I took a bullet in the thigh, and not fighting Indians, they officially retired me."

"That's why you came back," she whispered, more to herself than to him.

"Partly." He shrugged. "And partly to decide what to do now."

"You can foreman the Double T, that's what you can do." Coop stepped into the conversation. "I can use some strong, young help around here."

Now was not the time to mention the conversation she had overheard. She would have to prove to her father that she was capable of running the Double T. Besides, she didn't mind that Joe was here. She would come up with a plan to make him realize he needed to stay here with her— to run the ranch with her. In the meantime, the less said about the Kickapoo Indians, the better. She didn't need her father forbidding her to see her friends.

* * *

The next day Joe curried the last of the horses. His thigh wasn't healed enough to help Coop break horses for roundup, but at least he could do some of the mundane chores. Every morning for the past four months he swam, squatted, stood and walked, trying to hurry the healing process. But some days, the pain almost doubled him over.

He groaned as he straightened from checking the horse's hooves. It was then he saw the sheriff ride into the yard. During most of his time with the Texas Rangers, he worked with the local law enforcement when necessary but never considered them more than professional acquaintances. Perhaps not all dealt the law with equal fairness, because when he was honest with himself, he realized his bitter experience with the sheriff and deputy of Camino most likely colored his thinking.

Sheriff Warren, the law at Eagle Pass, was not much different from the rest. Pin a badge on their chests and too many of them thought they owned the town instead of serving the town.

"Morning, Dawson," the sheriff said as he swung down from his horse next to the corral.

"Sheriff."

"Sort of a come down from rangering, ain't it?" The sheriff nodded towards the horses.

"Nothing wrong with honest work, far as I know," Joe replied. He hadn't liked the man's attitude when he introduced himself in Eagle Pass, but if he expected help locating his family, he had to hold his tongue.

"Got a telegram from one of your Ranger friends." Warren spit a stream of tobacco close enough to the horse's hoof to make the animal shy away. Joe caught the halter, speaking in a low, soothing tone. If he didn't need the sheriff's help....

Joe's silence got a scowl from the sheriff, but Joe didn't have to wait long for the man to continue. As he spoke he watched Joe closely, evidently expecting some kind of reaction.

"Joe Horner and his gang of outlaws have been seen around Del Rio and this friend of yours seems to think you might be particularly interested in some young kid riding with him."

Seth. Joe's heart slammed against his ribs, but he was careful to keep his face from revealing any emotion.

Before he got wounded, he had traced his brother to a dirt farm near Abilene. The farmer hadn't had anything good to say about Seth. Instead, he told Joe that he beat Seth often when the boy wouldn't work as long or hard as the man wanted. The farmer said he ran off weeks before and he'd beat him again if he came back. If another Ranger hadn't been there to hold Joe back, the man wouldn't have lived to see the sun set.

Now the sheriff was telling him Seth might be riding with outlaws. Joe only hoped his brother hadn't been directly involved with breaking the law so he could get him out before it was too late. The boy would only be about twelve or thirteen, too young to be turning to a life of crime.

"You ain't got nothing to say?" the sheriff asked.

"Thanks for the information." Joe knew the man was fishing and wasn't about to give him the satisfaction of thinking his information had value.

"I don't want no trouble around here, Dawson." He spit in the dirt again. "You got problems with Horner, you keep 'em out of my town, hear?"

"Sheriff, I'm no longer a Texas Ranger. What I do now is personal business and none of yours."

"Yeah, well, Cooper Tate is a powerful man 'round these parts. I'd sure as hell hate to have to shoot one of his men." His words were matched by his feral grin.

"I've got work to do." Joe took hold of the horse's bridle and walked off, leaving the sheriff standing alone at the corral.

* * *

Joe left town and headed back to the ranch late that afternoon. The sheriff's information hadn't led him to his brother, but some eavesdropping at the saloon in Eagle Pass yielded other useful information. Joe Horner's gang had robbed a bank in Comanche two weeks ago and they were heading this way. He also heard rumors about a possible hit on a bank in Carrizo Springs.

Even though he no longer wore a badge, he wouldn't allow Horner's gang to rob a bank. He hadn't told Sheriff Warren what he had learned because he wanted to make sure Seth wasn't involved. Although he shouldn't feel compelled to relay information to the sheriff, he'd make sure the authorities in Carrizo Springs were notified and hopefully a shootout could be avoided.

Joe turned to the south, deciding to take a circular route back to the ranch so he could check a group of cattle on the south range near the Rio Grande. As he sat at the edge of the grazing area, he watched the calves romping in the tall grass. Low mooing would quickly have them back at their mothers' sides. Coop still had plenty of pasture to feed them until roundup, but he wondered how hard the trip north to the railhead would be on the longhorns.

Checking the position of the sun in the western sky, he figured a couple of hours of daylight remained and had better head back to the house. He reined Critter around and kicked him into a canter, thinking about the Double T and its occupants. Coop and Tianna had taken him in and treated him like family, and it was the only home he cared to remember.

But he wasn't family, regardless of what Coop said about him taking over the ranch. His family remained scattered across the plains of Texas. He recalled his stepmother, Rebecca, with a certain fondness and his father with disgust, but his sisters and brothers remained constantly on his mind. No matter how much time had passed, he intended to find them and bring them all together under one roof. It was an oath he had sworn the night the sheriff forced him into running away, only to be caught.

For a brief moment, he let his mind drift back to that ill-fated day seven years before. By the time the sheriff had let him out of jail, Preacher Burke and his family were nowhere to be found. Joe tried to pick up a trail, but with no horse or money, he didn't get far.

He had resorted to stealing when Cooper Tate caught him. The older man made Joe understand that searching for his family would be easier with a stake. Then he gave him a job to earn what he needed.

Joe touched the silver concho he wore on a leather thong as he promised himself it was the last time he would let anyone down. It was the reason he had made sure Coop understood he would only work at the Double T if he could come and go as needed.

His head jerked when he heard a yelp. Scanning the horizon, he saw two riders, one behind the other, racing at breakneck speed across the plain, the one in back closing the distance. He kicked his own horse into a gallop when he heard the yelp again.

Indians.

What were they doing on this side of the river? The Kickapoo reservation was in Mexico, down below Ft. Duncan near Yacimoto. The war whoops grew louder and Joe rode faster, trying to make out the two riders. When he recognized the horse in front by its distinctive paint markings, he felt gut-punched. What the hell was Sky doing this far south of the ranch house?

"Go, Critter." He urged his horse to greater speed.

The Indian raised his spear in the air, wind whipping his angry yell across the flat plain, carrying with it the nightmares that haunted Joe from all the times he and other Rangers had come too late. Images of burning farms, overturned wagons and butchered cattle raced through his mind. It had never been the animals he worried about but rather the people. Now it was Sky.

He laid low over Critter's neck. He wasn't going to make it. He yelled a warning to Sky, hoping she would veer towards him, making it easier to intercept her. But she was looking back over her other shoulder at the brave.

Joe pulled his revolver and fired.

Chapter Three

Sky jerked upright at the sound of gunfire. She didn't immediately rein Stormy in but rapidly scanned the area. A cowboy was closing in from her right side, gun arm raised.

As Two Feathers whooped again behind her, she realized that whoever the cowboy was, he thought she was in danger.

She slowed Stormy down, turning in a tight circle, but keeping her eyes on the approaching cowboy. He appeared ready to shoot again, and she quickly put herself between him and her friend.

She and Two Feathers came to a stop, but she continued blocking him from the approaching man. It wasn't until the rider was much closer that she realized it was Joe.

"What in blazes are you trying to do?" she shouted as Joe's horse skidded to a stop, dust from the dry plains kicking up around them. She saw the hard flint of his eyes as he continued to hold his gun level with Two Feathers' chest.

She quickly reached over and placed a hand on Two Feathers' arm because she could see him tense under Joe's unrelenting gaze.

"Joe?" She tried to pull his attention away from Two Feathers.

"What are you doing here, Sky?" He lowered his gun, but didn't take his eyes off Two Feathers.

"It's Daddy's land. Why shouldn't I be here?"

"You know what I mean. I thought your father told you not—"

"I have lived here all my life," Sky interrupted, realizing what he meant to say and not wanting her friend to hear it. "I know where I should and should not be."

At that point Two Feathers spoke in Kickapoo for Sky's ears only. "Who is this stranger who tried to shoot us?"

She waved her hand, palm down in a short, hard movement. "It wasn't like that," she replied in his native tongue.

In English, she made the introductions, hoping to ease the tension she felt between the two men. "Joe, this is Two Feathers, son of the Kickapoo chief, Black Thunder." She turned to her friend. "Joe Dawson is a friend who works for my father."

"He speaks English?" Joe asked and Sky thought his eyes were a little more friendly.

"Two Feathers went to an English school, although that was before his people moved to the reservation."

"Sky, don't start," Joe warned. "You need to get your fanny home before your father sends some of his men after you who aren't as easy going as I am." He reached over and took the reins of her horse, turning her towards home.

Sky protested. "I am not a child."

"Then don't act like one by arguing."

Two Feathers laughed and Sky turned to glare at him.

"What's so funny?" she asked.

He answered in Kickapoo. "This is the one you are in love with? This man who treats you like a papoose?"

Sky's mouth dropped open, momentarily forgetting she had gone to Two Feathers in the first place to form a plan to capture Joe's heart. She should have known better. Men were men.

With as much dignity as she could muster, Sky turned her horse toward home. Thankfully, Joe released the reins, so she didn't have to ask.

"What did he say?" Joe asked when he caught up with her.

"Never mind," replied Sky, her cheeks warm under his scrutiny. "It really doesn't matter."

* * *

Sky didn't say a word the entire ride back to the ranch. Joe thought about finishing his lecture but from the stiff set of her shoulders figured his words would fall on deaf ears. By the time he came out of the barn after stabling Critter, he found her in a lively discussion with Patch, the chuck cook for the bunkhouse and trail drives. He leaned a shoulder against the fence and crossed his arms over his chest, content for the moment to observe.

When he had realized Sky wasn't in danger from the Indian brave racing her across the plains, a hot streak of jealousy had coursed through him. Though he hadn't been around for the past several years, he still considered Sky his friend. As he had caught up with the two riders, he was sure the brave had been looking at her with more than friendship on his mind. That had made Joe look at her again, frowning at what he saw.

Her short brown curls gleamed in the sun, the light sprinkling of freckles across her nose making her look half her age. But the curves beneath her tight shirt and trousers were the stuff of dreams—soft and rounded, just the right size for a man's hand. Even though he had seen her at the pond, how had he not realized she would grow up in his absence?

As she had spoken to her friend, her face had been animated, her hands punctuating her words. She talked to the brave in his language, sharing an intimacy that left Joe out. As if that weren't bad enough, when she laughed at what the Indian had said, the pure, sweet sound of it shot molten desire straight through Joe.

Her voice caught his attention now, and he straightened. Skyla Tate might have become a beautiful young woman, but Joe had no place for her in his heart. He snorted at the thought—what heart? His had been torn out by five pairs of haunted eyes, his sister crying his name in the night.

"Patch, is everything ready?" Sky questioned when Joe strolled up.

"You betcha, Miss Sky. We got the beef already roasting in the pit, and Bonita's been baking for nigh on to a week now."

"But what about the dance floor? You know we can't have a party without dancing?" Sky had hooked her arm in the old cowpoke's and was leading him off towards the house. Joe pursed his lips, knowing she was deliberately avoiding him. The two of them pointed this way and that, apparently discussing the right place for whatever the hell they were planning.

He stomped onto the back porch, stopping to wash up at the basin that was always ready on a table by the door.

Warm, fragrant air assaulted his nostrils when he walked into the kitchen. Bonita and two other young women scurried here and there, each with their hands full of plates and pie pans.

"Don't you go trying to sneak my pies today, Mister Joe." The short, round Mexican woman shook a finger at him before he even opened his mouth.

He looked at her in mock surprise. "Would I do that?" He pinched her cheek with one hand as he reached around her with the other, scooping a fruit tart off the counter.

Bonita waved a spoon at him. "You think you are too big for me to swat now?"

"No, ma'am." His grin belied his words. He licked the last drop of sugary juice from his fingers before grabbing a cup and pouring some coffee that was always hot and ready on the back of the huge stove.

"What kind of shindig is going on that everyone's making such a fuss?" He leaned against the counter, crossing his long legs at the ankles.

"Tomorrow is Miss Sky's birthday. You should remember that."

Joe nodded, now recollecting how in the past Coop would throw a huge party in the spring, inviting not only town folk but also his neighbors for miles around. It was always right before the spring branding, but he guessed he forgot it was really in honor of Sky's birthday.

"People will start arriving early and stay most of the day, some even camping out in wagons so they don't have to go home late at night," Bonita continued, but Joe only half listened.

He didn't know his own birthday and only had a fair idea of his real age. Nobody had ever thrown him a party, and he sure as hell never had cause to celebrate.

"After dark they'll light up the lanterns and dance. I think Mr. Tate would have a party even if it wasn't Miss Sky's birthday, but giving it in honor of her makes it more special."

Joe nodded, knowing Coop would do anything for his only daughter. That raised a question. "Why does Sky keep disobeying her father and riding into Indian Territory, or at the least, associating with them on Double T land?"

Bonita shot a look at the other girls in the kitchen before lowering her voice. "Mr. Tate doesn't like it much, and she knows better. But those two are about the only people around here who don't blame the Indians for all the raids. And she...." The woman broke off.

"What?" Joe asked.

"Never mind. Miss Sky will tell you what she wants you to know. It's not my business."

She moved to pass him and almost tripped over his boots. Joe grabbed her around her ample waist, giving her a hug as he scooted up straight.

When he set her back on her feet, she patted his cheek affectionately. "Now, if you can't wait for your supper, take another tart and then vamoose. We have work to do."

Joe knew he wouldn't get any more information out of Bonita, given her loyalty to Sky. He thought about confronting her directly but if cornered, she'd scratch like a wildcat. He didn't even contemplate talking to Coop about it because he didn't want to worry him. He would just have to find out on his own.

***

Bonita was right about one thing—people started arriving early in the day. Joe had never favored crowds, so he tried to remain hidden, currying horses in the barn and riding out to check livestock. Coop didn't pressure him to participate in the bronc busting and roping games organized to keep the ranch hands from drinking too early in the day, but towards sundown his boss's attitude changed.

"Joe, get yourself out of here and relax," Coop demanded, cornering Joe in the farthest reaches of the barn.

"I'm fine, Coop."

Coop crossed his arms on the top rail of the stall where Joe was finishing up a mare. "'Sides, all the ladies are asking about you. Seems word has spread that I got the best looking foreman in five counties." He snorted before adding, "Don't know about that. All's I can tell them is you're pretty handy with a curry comb."

Joe shook his head, figuring Coop had been drinking with some of the other ranchers and town folk long before they had brought out the whiskey-spiked punch.

"I'll be out directly." Joe gave Coop a steady stare until the older man shrugged and walked away.

"It's not an order, but I'll make it one if I have to." Coop waved a hand over his head without turning back around.

Joe sighed. "There's no help for it, girl." He patted the mare's rump as he exited the stall. Closing the barn doors, he edged around the back of the corral and entered the house through the kitchen. He couldn't go to the party smelling like horse, even as he realized it was just another delay tactic. As he washed up in his room and changed clothes, he could hear the fiddles and harmonica players, reminding him of past parties at the Double T. At that point in his life, he never understood how people could be so happy when he was so sad. Even now, if he let himself think about his family, his heart ached with the pain of not knowing where they were.

When he exited the house, he tried to circle the ladies sitting comfortably in the shade of the front porch. Even though Miss Tianna was no longer here to hostess this

33

annual event, the ladies of the area still came with their men folk if for no other reason than to celebrate the end of another long winter. Joe figured it was more the opportunity to catch up on the gossip. The ranches were far enough apart, and the towns even more so, that town folk stayed pretty close to home during the winter months, even if Texas had milder weather than most places.

His thigh hurt worse than usual and he hesitated at the porch steps. He hobbled down the first two when the words he heard behind him made him twist around.

"Joseph Forde Dawson, is that you?"

Pain shot down his leg as his boot heel skidded off the step. He grabbed the rail to keep from falling. Nobody knew his full name.

Nobody.

"Ma'am?" Joe turned to the woman who had risen from her seat and quickly approached him.

"Oh my god, is it really you?" She reached out to touch his cheek.

Joe automatically jerked back. The woman was older, small and slim, with black hair liberally streaked with gray.

Clearly flustered, she dropped her hand to her side. "Oh, I am sorry. You don't even know me."

"No, ma'am." Joe shook his head.

"I'm Karah Morgan."

Joe scrunched his eyebrows together. The name was no more familiar than her face.

Apparently the lady understood his facial expression because she jumped in. "Karah *Forde* Morgan. Your mother was my sister."

A fist slammed into Joe's chest. He had never known his family's history. His pa had moved the family from San Antonio to Camino when Joe was only two. His ma died when he was four. He didn't know of any family because even when he was old enough to ask, his pa would never talk about it.

"I don't understand."

She shook her head in sympathy. "We were never in favor of Martha marrying Carl, but she was in love. Your father said he was taking you and your ma to California and that was the last we heard. They left under less than favorable circumstances, but I thought your ma might write one day. She never did." She shook her head again and Joe read sorrow in her eyes.

"Three years ago, my husband was assigned to a patrol around Laredo. That was when I found out Carl and Martha were buried near Camino. I didn't even know they had stayed in Texas. I asked around about you but nobody seemed to know where you'd gone. Then my Nathan got transferred to Ft. Duncan." Her lower lip trembled. "I'm very sorry I didn't seek her out earlier."

Karah Morgan's story stunned Joe. He had family—an aunt. He suddenly wondered if there were more. "You said *we*. Is there more family still in San Antonio?"

The woman shook her head. "Our parents died some fifteen years ago, and I lost Nathan last year. I couldn't live at the fort anymore, so I'm running a boarding house in Eagle Pass now."

"Joe!" He heard his name yelled from across the yard. He turned slightly to see Coop waving him over. He turned back to Karah Morgan.

"I know you have people to visit," she said. "I don't mean to keep you. I just couldn't believe it when I saw you walk out the door." She lowered her voice. "Even though you weren't more than a baby when your parents left, you've grown up to look just like your mother. You have her beautiful eyes and hair. I would have known you anywhere." She let out a sigh. "I'm sorry I never found you all those years ago. I hope one day I can make it up to you."

Joe would have liked to talk to her longer but didn't think this was the time or place. He had found family, even if it wasn't his sisters and brothers. The ice on a little corner of his heart began to melt.

"Ma'am, I would really like to talk to you more, but…."

"I understand, really I do."

Joe didn't want to leave it at that. "Maybe I could stop in town and talk to you?"

She patted his arm. Her fingers were brown and calloused—a working woman's hands. "Anytime you want, Joseph."

"Call me Joe."

She smiled. "I still can't believe I found you…Joe."

"Joe!" Coop called his name again.

"Would you excuse me, Mrs. Morgan?" he asked.

"Joe, we're family, even if it's been far too long for you to remember." She glanced over at Coop before she continued. "Cooper Tate is a good man. But if you ever need family…." She left the sentence hang in the air and Joe felt his heart squeeze.

"Yes, ma'am," he nodded politely, turning to go.

"Call me Karah," he heard her say, followed by a soft sigh.

Joe didn't have time to think about what Karah Morgan had told him before Coop slapped a hand on his shoulder.

"You remember Charles Windstead and William Cazneau? Their ranches border the Double T."

Joe inclined his head at the two older men standing by Coop under the huge willow tree. "The Cross S ranch and the Circle C, right?"

Cazneau nodded. "Hear tell you spent time as a Ranger. We ever going to get rid of the damn Indians?" His dislike was readily apparent.

"Now, Bill," Coop admonished. "You know there's no talk of Indians or politics at this party. The women folk will have our hides."

Joe was happy Coop had interrupted a subject he'd prefer not discussing. Just then the music stopped and Sky swung off the dance platform, a tall, blonde man in tow. Coop and the others drifted off toward the back of a wagon where Joe was sure the more potent punch was being portioned out.

Joe watched as Sky took a moment to compose herself, breathless from the exertion of dancing. She had taken her party dress from her mother's Spanish heritage—full gathered skirt in multicolored bands of bright cotton and a

36

sheer white blouse with short sleeves and a gathered neckline. That's where his gaze stopped.

The sleeves were set off her shoulders, the neckline scooped, showing what Joe thought was an immodest amount of creamy smooth skin. His pulse quickened, matching the beat discernible right at the point where her neck met her shoulder. His gaze slid to the man who had partnered her in the dance. *His* gaze was riveted to Sky's heaving breasts and Joe felt the urge to hit him in the face.

"Joe, here you are. I thought maybe you weren't going to celebrate my birthday." Sky greeted him in breathless gaiety. "This is Mason Winstead from the Cross S. I don't think you met the last time you were here." She hugged the man's arm, her breast pressing against his side. Mason grinned down at her.

"Joe Dawson." He thrust out his hand so the other man was forced to untangle himself from Sky to face him. "You ranch with your father?"

"Actually, I just returned from Washington."

"Mason's a Senator, Joe. Can you believe it? And look what he brought me from the Capitol!" Sky touched the necklace circling her slim neck, the multicolored beads glittering in the lantern light.

"You know I'd never forget your birthday," Mason replied in a low voice that hinted of a certain intimacy.

Joe ground his teeth when a blush crept up Sky's neck and cheeks.

"Would you be a dear and get me some punch?" Sky patted Mason's arm and batted her eyelashes at him. Joe couldn't reconcile this grown up flirt with the Sky he had known.

The minute the man walked away, Joe opened his mouth without stopping to wonder why he cared. "So who is this fellow to you?"

Sky looked up at him, her eyes innocently wide. "A friend."

"I'd look out for him if I were you. He doesn't look like he'd be satisfied with just being friends." He didn't know Mason, but he well knew the male species and how they reacted to a pretty young woman.

"I've known Mason all my life. He thinks he wants to marry me." She shrugged. "You know, marry and create a cattle dynasty."

"And are you going to?" Joe didn't even know why he was asking. It didn't matter to him.

"Maybe," she drawled. "Would you care?"

That was not a question Joe had ever thought about and he didn't dare think about it now. "Just don't be taken in by him, Sky. All he wants is the land." He turned to go.

Sky put her hand on his arm to stop him. "Let's not argue, Joe. Dance with me."

He shook his head. "My leg...." He muttered the excuse, knowing it had nothing to do with his injury.

"But it's my birthday," she continued.

"Sorry. Maybe another time." He turned away from the party, unintentionally applying force to his bum leg, which nearly buckled. It took all his concentration to remain on his feet. *Damn,* but she had no right to affect him like she did.

Anger dogged his stride, but by the time he reached the barn he realized she was right. He had no reason to question who she associated with. He was left to wonder why it bothered him. Before he had returned to the Double T he had very clear-cut goals. Now, in less than a week, Sky had him thinking of her gentle curves more often than he thought of the chores he was supposed to be doing.

He grabbed his saddle and blanket, tossing it onto his horse as he muttered to himself, "Why the hell did she have to grow up?" More important, what the hell was he going to do about it? Not only was the Double T strategically located for his search, but he needed this job to earn the money that would eventually buy his family a ranch. But how was he supposed to work when every time he turned around, Sky was in sight?

"Why did you run off?" Her soft voice reached him as he exited the stall. He slammed the gate harder than intended, causing Critter to shy back and whinny.

"Damn, Sky, you should know better than to sneak up on a man like that." He chewed her out even as he soaked up the sunshine fresh sight of her. Her short curls framed a smiling face still alive with the exhilaration of dancing.

"If you won't dance with me, at least give me a birthday kiss," she spoke in a soft, seductive voice.

Where had she learned that? Joe thought maybe he should speak to Coop about his daughter, but while he was thinking, she stepped closer. With a sigh, Joe dutifully kissed her on the forehead.

Her full lips formed a pout. "A real kiss, Joe."

"Why would I do that?"

"Because it's my birthday, and that's the present I want."

"We don't always get what we want."

"I do."

"You're spoiled."

She narrowed her eyes at him. "That's right, and Daddy will get me whatever I want."

"I'm not for sale, sweetheart." Joe sent her a caustic look. Sky had never thrown her father's money in his face and he didn't care for the attitude now.

"I'll tell Daddy—" She never finished the sentence as Joe jerked her to him.

He skewered her with a glare that meant business and didn't relent until a flash of panic darted across her face. Better to have her scared.

"You don't want to make me that mad." Before he did something he would regret, like actually give her the kiss she desired and he dreamed about, he pushed her away and led Critter out of the barn.

Swinging into the saddle, he kicked the horse into a canter and left the out buildings of the Double T behind him, reining his horse toward the Anacacho Mountains north of the ranch. He let his senses soak up the night sounds while his mind mulled over the events of the evening. His brain waged a war between thinking about Sky's impossible behavior, and the discovery of his aunt, Karah Morgan.

Sky won. His mind was consumed with her and his body ached for her. Even with the night breezes blowing against his skin, he still felt her heat and smelled the scent of sunshine that always seemed to surround her.

Sky acted like a spoiled brat, yet there was something about her—some quality she didn't want him to see—that led Joe to believe it was all an act. He had watched her during his time at the ranch. She had a gentleness with animals and never ignored the youngsters of some of the ranch hands. She was the boss's daughter, but never talked down to the cowboys and treated everyone with respect.

Joe sighed. It was that gentleness that pulled at him; that he longed to claim. But what he had told her was true—he wasn't for sale. He would have freely given her what she wanted had she not been Coop's daughter. He owed the man more than that. And Sky deserved more than a romp in the hay with a man who had no future.

He allowed Critter to pick his way along the narrow trail that ran beside a strip of woods at the base of the mountain. To his right was a vast pasture of tall grass where late in the summer the cattle grazed. He, along with other cowboys, would stay out here for a week at a time, checking cattle, mending fence, and making sure that rustlers stayed on the other side of the Rio. It was the life he wanted.

As his horse meandered, he forced himself not to think about Sky, which opened his mind to his conversation with his aunt. For all his bravado about not needing anyone, part of his reason for originally joining the Texas Rangers was to have a sense of belonging. Yet he wasn't sure how he felt about having an aunt. He was a grown man—he didn't need some woman hovering over him to make him wipe his feet before entering her kitchen or making sure he didn't slurp his coffee. Still, it was incredible to think he actually had family besides his brothers and sisters.

His thoughts diverted when his senses detected smoke. Instantly alert, he scanned the area for any signs of a fire as he tested the wind direction. He couldn't see anything in the dark, but the smoke was coming from west of the trail he rode. He knew better than to take Critter through the woods, so he climbed down, ground tied him, and began silently moving toward the source of the smoke. As he inched forward, he heard voices. Luckily there were enough trees and scrubs on the side hill to offer him cover. When he could see the small clearing, he crouched, took a few more steps, then crawled forward on his belly.

A small fire cast shadows across the forms of five men. Springtime in Texas meant the temperatures dropped at night, especially in the foothills and mountains, so he figured all the men were scattered within a few feet of the flames. He carefully surveyed the surrounding area, taking in the picket line where the horses where tied. Apparently this particular group of men thought they were safe and had not posted a lookout.

He couldn't distinguish the men's faces from this distance, and their voices were pitched too low to make out their conversation. He inched closer.

"I say we hit it tomorrow," a gruff voice said.

"Goddamnit, I said we go Saturday. Frank's been down there. The sheriff always goes over to the whorehouse on Saturday and that dumb deputy can't find his butt with both hands."

"Yeah, but what if word gets out we're in the area? I heared tell there's a Ranger in Eagle Pass."

The horses whinnied and shuffled in the still night. Joe held his breath as all the men stood simultaneously and pulled their guns, turning away from the fire and staring towards the picket line.

"Seth! Where the hell you at, boy?" One of the men growled in a low voice.

"Ain't nothing wrong here, Horner," came a voice in the dark.

Joe's breath hissed out. He swung his gaze from the group of men to the horses. Only then did he notice a pair of legs among the horses that he had overlooked before. Or maybe he had been hiding behind a tree. It didn't matter. He cautiously waited to see what would transpire.

"Keep them damn horses quiet," the man growled.

41

Joe's heart beat rapidly against his chest as he forced himself to remain still in his hiding place. He exhaled, and then slowly inhaled. There wasn't a breath of a breeze to cool him as sweat popped out on his forehead and trickled into his eyes.

Was it his brother? The brother he hadn't seen in seven years? He needed to talk to him and find out. But first he had to get him away from Joe Horner's gang. He could only think they were discussing a bank job when he had first come to the edge of the clearing and he wanted his brother away from any trouble.

He couldn't do anything until the other men were asleep. He set his hat to the side in the dirt and rested his forehead against one arm. There was no moon, so he didn't worry about being discovered. He settled in to wait.

Joe never slept in the two hours it took the men to drink enough to pass out or fall asleep. Even then, he waited another hour before he moved quietly to the side, edging his way towards where he had last seen Seth. He gave the horses a wide berth, hoping they wouldn't catch his scent. He paused behind a group of trees, determining the best way to approach Seth. He could see the boy sleeping, his back against a tree.

Joe circled around and approached him from behind, cautious to keep the men by the fire in his sights. In one smooth motion, he clamped a hand on Seth's mouth and pulled the boy to his feet, locking his other arm tight around the boy's midsection, anchoring his arms to the side. He edged back into the trees.

Joe immediately got kicked in the shin. "Seth, it's Joe," he hissed close to the boy's ear. Another boot heel hit his shin again. "Your brother Joe."

Joe kept backing away from the circle of men, but it was hard to maintain his hold on his brother. He had always thought of Seth as being the same size he had been when he'd last seen him seven years ago. The kid was still small but Joe felt muscles in his arms, and his legs definitely packed a wallop.

When he had dragged him far enough away to be safe, he slowly set him on his feet, still keeping a tight hold on him.

"I'm going to let you go, but first you listen to me, okay?" Joe waited to feel a nod. "Your name is Seth Dawson and you have sisters named Mary Elizabeth and Jessica." Seth went utterly still beneath Joe's grip. He removed his hand and Seth spun around and stared at him.

"You that Ranger what Horner was talking 'bout?" Joe could hear the fear in his voice, see it in his eyes.

"You got reason to be afraid of a Ranger?" Joe had to know.

The boy shook his head. "I ain't done nothing."

"You're running with outlaws," Joe countered.

"Yeah, well, they don't let me do nothing. If I even go with 'em, all I got to do is hold the horses." He almost sounded disappointed, and Joe could only be thankful he had found his brother when he did. "Who'd you say you was?"

"Joe Dawson, your brother." Joe tried to ignore the hurt he felt that his brother didn't recognize him. He wouldn't have mistaken Seth for anything. He had the same sandy colored hair and blue eyes that Rebecca had. Joe figured he was twelve, maybe thirteen years old by now, but he had yet to fill out.

"Shit, I ain't got no brother. I'm orphaned." The kid had an attitude, and Joe didn't like his language. As he reached into the opening at the front of his shirt, he wondered briefly if he would have grown up with a chip on his shoulder like Seth if it hadn't been for Cooper and Tianna Tate.

Jerking the leather thong out from beneath his shirt, he swung the concho in front of his brother's face. "Recognize this?"

Seth's mouth dropped open. His hand flattened against his chest, then he too reached beneath his shirt to pull out a similar silver button, tied around his neck with a filthy piece of sinew.

"The preacher said you was dead. That you—"

Joe clapped a hand to Seth's mouth, putting a finger to his lips. They both turned back toward the camp. The fire had died down enough that it offered no light. They listened in silence as one of the outlaws relieved himself in the trees. A loud belch followed and then they heard twigs break as the man found his way back to the safety of the circle.

"We've got to get out of here," Joe whispered once quiet descended again. "Can you ride bareback?" At the boy's nod, Joe continued, "I want you to wait by the picket line and count to fifty. I'm going to circle round and create a distraction from the other side. When I do, get on a horse quick, cut the line and scatter the rest. Ride east but be careful of the trees. My horse is at the edge of the trail. I'll meet you there. You have a knife?"

"Yeah, but...." Seth didn't move.

"What?" Joe asked.

The kid shrugged, then hung his head. "I cain't count to fifty."

Damn, Joe swore to himself. The Sheriff of Camino was going to pay for what happened to his family.

"Okay, get to the horses and wait until you hear me. You'll know when to make a break for it."

In less than five minutes all hell broke loose. Joe started yelling from one side of the camp, calling out Horner's name and telling him he was a Texas Ranger. He kept moving and changing his voice to make it sound like there were more men surrounding them.

At the same time, Seth yelped and hollered and the horses scattered in every direction. Joe continued his subterfuge until he felt sure Seth was well out of harm's way. He then took careful aim and fired two shots, wounding two of the five men in the legs. That would at least slow them down and perhaps prevent a bank robbery.

He reached the trail and vaulted onto Critter's back. The horse took off, trained to react to Joe's every touch. "This way," he hollered at Seth who was waiting at the other side of the path.

44

One behind the other, they rode like hell down the mountain path. They entered the flatland where Joe could barely make out the landmarks and terrain. He slowed, waiting for Seth to come abreast of him.

"We're going to head southwest to Indio Creek and cross, then double back. We're on Tate land, but I doubt that will stop Horner if they manage to round up their horses."

Seth's eyes were wide and Joe couldn't mistake the awe in his voice. "Did you kill them?"

"No. I was creating a distraction."

"Yeah, but they're outlaws."

"I'll inform the sheriff. Let him worry about them. I was only trying to get you out of there. Besides, I'm not a Ranger anymore."

"Shit, you really was a Texas Ranger?"

Joe heaved a sigh, slowing his horse to a stop.

"Seth Dawson, if I hear that word from your mouth once more, I'm going to blister your butt like I used to."

Seth glowered at him. "You ain't my pa."

"Well, I was the closest thing you had at one time and you're going to listen to me now."

Before Seth could mouth off yet again, a shot rang out. His brother yelped, going down with his horse.

Chapter Four

Another shot whistled past Joe's shoulder; the outlaws were shooting blindly in the dark. He pulled his rifle from the sheath as Critter automatically obeyed his knee signals, turning in a tight circle. Seth scrambled to his feet.

"Get up behind me," he yelled, kicking a foot free from the stirrup while firing several quick shots in the direction they had come. The minute Seth swung up behind him and grabbed his waist, he whistled and Critter turned again and broke into a run. Joe kept his rifle in one hand and grabbed the reins with the other, urging the horse faster as they raced for cover in a grove of trees on the far side of the creek.

When he felt safe enough, he slowed to a stop and gave Seth a hand down, following him to the ground. They cautiously scanned behind them and Joe listened carefully for sounds of approaching riders. When he heard nothing for several minutes, he hoped they had returned for their wounded friends. Now he didn't have a choice but to ride into Eagle Pass and inform the sheriff. Someone might come looking for a doctor, but more important, they were planning a robbery. He was happy he had gotten Seth away from them before there was worse trouble.

He turned to his brother. "You okay?"

"Sh...yeah. Take more than a fall from a horse to get rid of me."

"Sorry about your horse." Joe knew how much a man depended on his horse, but Seth just shrugged at his comment.

"Hell, it was stolen anyhow."

Joe paced the area around his horse, trying to decide what to do with Seth. Coop wouldn't mind bringing him back to the ranch, but it wouldn't be fair to show up with

46

no warning. And he sure didn't need the unwanted questions he would get from Sky. He pressed a fist against his throbbing thigh, the running and riding of the past hours getting to him. Damn, he hurt.

He pulled the saddle off Critter, dropping the reins to ground tie him but allowing him to graze. He dropped his saddle by a tree, tugged the lacings and removed his trail gear. He tossed his brother a blanket.

"We'll stay put as long as it's dark. I want to see behind me before we go any further." He groaned as he lowered himself to the ground. "No fire. They may still be looking for us, and regardless of being on Double T land, if they want us, that wouldn't stop them."

Seth shrugged. "Ain't no big deal. I'm used to sleeping out." He wrapped the blanket around his shoulders and dropped to the ground, cross-legged.

Joe took a closer look at the brother he hadn't seen for seven years. The boy kept his distance, back against a tree, his gaze constantly darting between Joe and the dark surrounding them. He looked like a spring wound tight, ready to jump at the first sign of trouble. What had happened to him? He had a rough edge, but from the quiver in his voice just now, Joe felt the tough exterior was all an act.

He wasn't at all sure how to approach him because Seth either didn't remember—or refused to remember—his family. Maybe at five years old, it had been too traumatic. Joe hadn't prepared to be out overnight, so he didn't have much in his saddlebags to make a peace offering. He tossed Seth a strip of jerky and his canteen. He spent long minutes massaging his leg, not saying anything, hoping Seth would start chattering as he had as a kid. When the silence stretched long and dark, like the night, he looked up to see the boy staring.

"Where are Mary Elizabeth and Jessica?" Joe asked, thinking perhaps mention of their sisters would open him up. The thought of finally finding his family renewed his hope.

"Who're they?" Seth gave a shrug as he gnawed on the jerky.

Joe's brows lowered. "What do you mean? They're your sisters."

"Told you. I don't got no family."

"Maybe you just don't remember," Joe suggested. "You remembered me."

"You got a silver button like mine." Another shrug. "I figure we must be connected somehow."

Joe looked at his brother in amazement. "How could you forget your family?"

Seth shot to his feet, ramrod straight, hands fisted at his sides. Anger distorted his features. "Yeah, like you should talk. You say you're my brother? How the hell did you forget about me? Where you been the last years?"

Joe opened his mouth to remind him about swearing, but realized that wasn't what he needed. And he was right. Although he had searched for years, the boy didn't know that, probably wouldn't believe him if he said so. And for a five-year old, the whole thing must have been a nightmare.

"What happened, Seth?"

Another elaborate, *I-can-take-care-of-myself* shrug. "Preacher sold me to the first farm he come to."

"Sold you?" Joe choked.

"For two whole silver dollars. So I don't know nothing about no sissy girls."

Joe's heart ached. "Did you go to school; church? Did you have a ma?"

Seth's eyes narrowed. "Sh…it," he said, and Joe forced himself not to react because he knew the boy was just trying to trigger his anger.

"Tell me."

"I got to work my butt off from morning to night. I got to sleep in the barn with some old horse blanket for cover, and most days I got fed, if I could talk him into letting me slop the hogs."

Joe bit the inside of his cheek until the pain replaced the threat of tears. He never cried, damn it. But the pain and anger in Seth's voice cut right to his heart.

Even their own pa hadn't treated them so mean.

"You stayed there for seven years?" he asked incredulously, wondering if he could have endured that.

"Hell no. First chance I got, I clunked the old man over the head, stole his money and some food and lit out of there. Week or so later, I met up with Horner and he's been taking care of me since."

"He's an outlaw."

"Yeah, well, at least he was there." The boy dropped back beside the tree, tugged the blanket around him and rolled over, his back to Joe.

Joe knew it would take more than rescuing Seth from outlaws to gain his trust. And now he wondered about the rest of his family. Was he too late to save them?

* * *

"Don't know," Patch answered when Sky asked about Joe.

"Come on, Patch, you know everything that goes on at this ranch." Sky tried to weasel the information out of him.

"If'n I did, I'd know why you were so dang interested, missy," the old range cook returned, stacking another mess of tin plates on the ground by the chuck wagon.

Sky sighed. She hadn't meant to chase Joe off into the night. The party hadn't been quite as much fun after he left, even though Mason had been unusually attentive. He was handsome, a wonderful dancer, and entertained plans to be a powerful politician someday. They grew up on neighboring ranches and knew each other all their lives. But where he had always been willing to acknowledge her accomplishments when it came to riding and roping, lately he acted as though he had propriety right to her.

He even kissed her last night in the shadows of the huge oak tree, right before he told her she needed to spend more time in the kitchen and less on the back of a horse. She would have gotten mad, but Mason's opinion didn't really matter, and it wasn't his kiss she wanted. She sighed, wondering again about Joe's refusal to give her what she wanted. She usually didn't act like a spoiled brat, as he had called her, and he recognized her empty threat as such.

What was one little kiss, anyway? But she knew as she walked back into the house that if he had kissed her, it would have been an acknowledgement that she was a grown woman. She wondered if he was afraid of that knowledge or if he just didn't care for her in that way. Why did she act so crazy where he was concerned?

"Bonita, is everything ready?"

"Yes, but I still say you need to take someone with you."

"We discuss this every time, Bonita. There is no one on the ranch who cares what happens to the Indians. Well, except Daddy and maybe Patch, but they're both too busy getting ready for roundup. I can't bother them. Besides, I promised Mr. Winstead I would stop and see Dorothy. She wasn't at the party because she's feeling poorly and I want to take her some food."

Bonita shook her head. "It's not just the Indians and you know it. My Paul heard something about outlaws in the area."

"Well, they certainly wouldn't be on Double T land." Her father had men patrolling at random along the borders of Double T land north and east. The Rio Grande lay to the west, and the Cross S and Circle C ranches bordered them to the south. She doubted anyone could access the ranch without someone knowing. In fact, now that she thought on it, she wondered if Joe hadn't gone on patrol.

"I'm getting a late start, so I won't return until tomorrow." At the housekeeper's stern look, Sky added, "Daddy won't even miss me. He's too busy."

Before Bonita said anything more to make Sky feel guilty, she climbed onto the wagon seat, set her rifle in the nook beside her and gathered the reins to set the horse in motion. There was talk last night about more Indian raids down around Carizzo Springs, but Sky couldn't make herself believe it was anyone from the Kickapoo reservation.

She thought about all the food and supplies in the back of the wagon. There had been so much food left over from her party, she told Bonita to wrap it up in oil cloth and she would "get rid of it." In addition, baskets in the wagon bed held lengths of material, buttons, hair ribbons, sketch paper and watercolors, even a copy of that new magazine, *Ladies' Home Journal*. She was helping several tribal children learn to read and the young girls would love looking at the fashion patterns in the magazine.

She touched the string of beads around her neck that Mason had given her. Friends and neighbors had been most generous, but she didn't need any of it. The only gift she kept was the leather bound copy of Mr. Twain's *The Adventures of Tom Sawyer* that her daddy gave her. Even that would have to wait until next winter to be read as there was too much going on at the ranch in spring and summer.

She certainly didn't have time for the womanly pursuit of watercolors, even though Mrs. Mayfield, the mayor's wife, had intoned that was how any *lady of quality* should spend her time. It didn't seem to matter that they were out in the west edges of Texas. Many of the women in Eagle Pass, transplanted to Texas after the war, preferred to retain the decorum of their southern plantations. Sky personally thought it ridiculous to wear three or four petticoats when it was hotter than blue blazes.

She put her booted foot on the front rail of the wagon and stared down at it. She would much rather wear pants and boots and ride a horse. It wasn't that she didn't appreciate all the wonderful gifts she had gotten. She just felt they could be put to better use by Black Thunder's tribe. The fact that her father was busy and Joe had disappeared made it that much easier for her to deliver her bounty to her friends. She would stop at Eagle Pass and use her allowance to buy staples such as flour, sugar and canned goods. If it got too late to return to the ranch tonight, she could always spend the night at her friend's, Susan Morgan, whose mother ran a boarding house.

After visiting with Dorothy, she crossed the Rio west of their ranch, steering the wagon along a well-worn path to the reservation in Mexico. She knew the way by heart and soon pulled the wagon to a stop as many of the children gathered around her.

"You know what we must do first," she quietly chided as some of the boys climbed eagerly into the wagon to see what she had brought.

They immediately quieted. Sky took the beads from around her neck, found the brightest piece of fabric and called politely at the front of Black Thunder's lodge. The chief came out, towering over her. She was always in awe of the Kickapoo warrior. Even though they were resigned to the reservation, he maintained the regal haughtiness of a once fierce tribe. He stood straight before her, his long grey hair a symbol of the years he had lived, his face lined with all he had seen. Yet his eyes held a gentle light as he faced her.

"Welcome, my daughter," he spoke English as an honor to Sky.

She returned the honor by addressing him in his native tongue. "Greetings honored Black Thunder. I have brought you gifts." She held out her hands.

The chief took the gifts with a nod, for he knew Sky wasn't acting out of charity but out of the goodness of her heart. Just as she had from the first time she came with her father when he delivered beef.

"Why do you give away your birth presents, Oota Dabun?"

Sky smiled at the name, which meant *day star*, and for the fact that he remembered her birthday.

"You and my father have taught me the gift of sharing," she replied. "And I knew the children would like the sweet taste of the cake Bonita baked."

He laughed. "You know the way to their hearts. I will leave you to share your bounty."

By the time Sky returned to the wagon, several women had gathered with the children. Together, they divided the food and presents so each family would have something. She took the cake and a book and walked to the huge tree that shaded the edge of the circle of lodges. She felt like the

Pied Piper as the children excitedly followed her, chattering in a mixture of Kickapoo and English.

She was trying to teach the children English. Regardless of how some of the warriors disregarded the government regulations, the times were changing, and it was important that the children adapt.

As she read the children a story, they devoured the cake. When she closed the book and looked up, all the children sat quietly, eyes open in rapt attention, remnants of sugar frosting on their faces.

"Little Fox, I didn't see you earlier." She spoke to the young boy who sat near the back of the group.

"I was with the shaman," he quietly replied.

"Is your brother not here?" Sky looked around for the other child, one who looked just like Little Fox.

"He is with the others," Little Fox replied.

She knew Little Fox and Angry Dog weren't of Indian origin. They both had dark hair, but more brown than black, and blue eyes, but they had been with the tribe as long as she could remember. The Kickapoo didn't raid, so the boys must have been found alone somewhere along the trails the Indians traveled. The Kickapoo would never leave a child helpless, and so they had become part of the tribe. Even though they looked alike, they acted opposite with one wanting to become a warrior while the other seemed more inclined to study with the shaman.

She sometimes thought to ask Black Thunder about them, but she was an outsider, even if the chief treated her as a daughter.

She took supper with Black Thunder's family and slept on a pallet next to his daughter before starting back to the ranch the next morning.

Chapter Five

Joe groaned as he rolled over. The ground beneath him was hard and rocky and he had never gotten comfortable enough to sleep. He slowly got to his feet, his thigh killing him, pain shooting clear down his leg so that even his toes hurt. The morning sun hadn't crept above the hills yet, and the gully where they slept was bathed in deep shadows and flickering gray light as a breeze kicked up.

He looked over to where Seth lay curled in a tight ball under the small trail blanket. He half expected him to be gone this morning. The boy had no reason to trust Joe and seemed to think Horner took care of him pretty good.

"Time to hit the trail." Joe nudged Seth with the toe of his boot.

The boy shot up and scurried backward, eyes wide and frightened. "I didn't fall asleep, honest I didn't." He repeatedly shook his head, his narrow shoulders hunched as if he expected a blow.

Joe's stomach clenched at the fear he saw on his brother's face. What he wouldn't give to take back the last seven years. Knowing that was impossible, he squatted, bringing himself to Seth's level. He realized he couldn't just tell the youngster not to be afraid. First off, boys didn't admit they were afraid of anything. Second, as much as Joe wished otherwise, at this point there wasn't much difference in Seth's eyes between himself and Horner.

"It was my turn to stand guard. You were supposed to sleep." He wanted to eliminate the guilt he saw on Seth's face but at the same time he knew the boy wouldn't want to be coddled.

"Time to move." He stood, groaning, and hobbled over to his saddle as he whistled for Critter. The horse nosed its way around the mesquite and scrub, about all there was for cover in these parts. By the time Joe had his saddle cinched down, Seth silently handed him the blanket, already rolled tight. Joe nodded and tied it behind his saddle.

"We have to go back to Eagle Pass, but we'll take a roundabout way so as not to run into Horner. You know where they were headed?" The question was asked casually as Joe swung into the saddle. He knew sure as shooting Seth wouldn't talk if he interrogated him. He kicked his foot free of the stirrup and put his hand out.

Seth hesitated and Joe patiently waited. At twelve, Joe had thought himself a man and ready to take on the world. He didn't reckon Seth was any different, and having to ride behind him like a girl wouldn't sit well. Joe looked around at the near desolate landscape. Scrub brush dotted the hillside and mesquite poked up here and there in the gully where they stood. In any normal year, this would have been a fast flowing creek, but there was no running water for miles. Nothing to sustain a man if he was left out here alone without a horse or provisions.

"You want to stay, take your chances with Horner?" He cast his gaze back to Seth, giving the kid a choice although couching it so there really wasn't one.

Seth scowled but reluctantly grabbed Joe's hand.

"Don't make no difference," he muttered as Joe swung him up behind. Joe swore he would change the kid's mind before all was said and done.

Not wanting to tire the horse with the extra weight, but not willing to be caught out in the open if the Horner gang was still in the area, Joe kept Critter at a fast walk. They reached Eagle Pass by late morning. The first thing Joe did was stop at the sheriff's office. Regardless of his feelings for the man, he still felt obligated to inform him of any possible threat. He did caution Seth to stay with the horse, which he had tethered across the street from the sheriff's office. He didn't want Sheriff Warren taking it into his head that Seth might be part of the gang.

Their conversation didn't take long. The sheriff was condescending and Joe had just enough patience to spit out the news that the Horner gang was in the area. Because Joe had spotted them on Double T land, the sheriff didn't appear to think it was his problem. When Joe informed him he had heard talk of a bank robbery, the sheriff reluctantly agreed to look into it.

He stormed out of the building and across the dirt street to where Seth waited. One look at the boy's face and Joe silently cursed himself. "I'm not mad at you, Seth." He wondered how long it would take before Seth could look at the world with any kind of acceptance or tolerance?

"The sheriff looking for me?" He had Critter between himself and the office and cautiously peeked from beneath the horse's neck.

"He doesn't know your name, or that you were with the gang. There shouldn't be a problem if you keep your nose clean in town."

"You live in town?"

Joe had had plenty of time last night to figure out what to do with Seth, although the boy might not like it. "No. I work on a ranch. But I found out we have an aunt here in town and I'm sure you can stay with her."

"I ain't gonna stay with no stranger. Done 'nough of that." He glared at Joe.

"It's just until I see if my boss would mind you being out at the ranch. I can't just show up with a kid."

"Ain't no kid." Still scowling, Seth straightened his spine.

Joe sighed. "Okay, fine. But until you're old enough to earn yourself a living, I'd appreciate it if you'd go along with my suggestions.

"Aunt Karah runs a boarding house here in town and I'm sure she will give you a place to stay and feed you in exchange for you doing some chores for her. Do you think that's asking too much for a roof over your head and nobody beating you?" Joe had been impatient all his life, wanting things to happen quicker than they did. Now he realized some things were just going to take time.

Seth didn't disagree—or agree for that matter—as Joe led his horse down the dirt street. But he did follow along, so Joe thought that a good sign. Though he hadn't been to the boarding house before, Eagle Pass was small enough he had no trouble finding it.

Karah Morgan greeted him with a wide smile and open arms. Joe still had a little trouble thinking of her as his aunt, but she was so quietly welcoming that even Seth relaxed. Though she looked at Seth with questioning eyes, she said nothing as they followed her to the big open kitchen.

"Sit, sit," she insisted, waving them to chairs around a large table covered in a checked cloth. The place was homey and bright, something neither Joe nor Seth had experienced in their younger years. Without asking, she poured Seth a large glass of milk and Joe a cup of coffee.

"I drink coffee," Seth said, frowning at the milk.

Aunt Karah nodded. "That may be, but growing boys need milk." She turned back to the counter.

Joe punched Seth lightly on the arm when he opened his mouth, most likely to refute her calling him a boy. His brother needed some manners, but his mouth turned into a toothy grin when she set a chunk of chocolate cake in front of him. Joe was sure his own face reflected the pleasure of such a treat when she put a similar plate before him.

"Now, you two boys eat up, then tell me what's going on." She took a sip of her own cup of coffee and looked from one to the other. Seth was too busy devouring his cake to notice her reference to them both as boys.

Joe had thought about it some on the way into town and decided that his brother needed to stay with his aunt until Joe could find a place for his whole family, not just until he could ask Coop about bringing him to the ranch. The kid needed to get some learning and needed a woman's influence. Besides that, Joe would be going on roundup before long. It didn't seem prudent to tell Seth that, seeing as how the kid didn't want to stay in town.

When he explained to his aunt that Seth was related, she was so happy she cried, a contradiction in Joe's mind, but that appeared to be the way of women. She lifted a corner of the apron she wore and dabbed at her eyes.

"Martha's child?" she asked.

"No," Joe answered. "Ma died when I was just a little 'un, and Pa married again. Rebecca was good to us, but then she died too, after birthing five young'uns. Seth here's the oldest of the boys."

"Five? But where are they?" Aunt Karah looked at him in disbelief.

Joe shook his head. "That's the mystery. When Pa died, the sheriff rounded us up like so many cattle to the slaughter. If Pa hadn't drunk the farm away, I could have kept us there, but we got separated and I've spent the last seven years trying to track them down."

Seth snorted in disbelief and Joe shot him a look.

"Why, you would have only been a boy yourself, Joseph." His aunt came to his defense.

"Yes, ma'am, but I told them when the sheriff came that I would find them, get us back together. Seth is the first one I've been able to track down."

"Didn't ask you to," Seth piped up, as though it had been a distasteful chore.

"You're family," Joe replied. "Family belongs together."

"Sometimes doing what people think is right, like parceling you all off to different families, just isn't what a body needs." Aunt Karah reached across the table but Seth jerked his hand out of reach.

"Well, you have more family now." His aunt ignored Seth's rejection and nodded her head. "Seth can stay here, go to school, and get to know other boys his age."

Joe sensed Seth getting fidgety. "I was hoping that would be the case. Just 'til I can get things settled out at the ranch." It was a little lie, but he felt it necessary.

Aunt Karah propped her elbow on the table and put her chin in her hand, looking thoughtful. "You know, some of my boarders come and go, traveling the countryside. There may be a possibility that I could find out some news of your other sisters and brothers from someone passing through."

Joe nodded. "That would be welcome." He lifted his cup and finished his coffee. He really should head out to the ranch if he hoped to get there before dark, but he was hesitant to leave Seth as he had just found him. Maybe he should just take him out to the Double T. Coop would no doubt understand.

He glanced over when his brother slurped his milk. Before Joe could correct him, he was scraping his plate with his fork to get the last cake crumb into his mouth. Well, at least he used his fork, Joe thought, but it helped decide that Seth would be better off in town. He just had to convince the boy.

"Afternoon, Mama." The musical voice announced a female, causing both Seth and Joe to jerk around. A young woman about Sky's age floated into the room, swept around the table and bent to kiss Karah's cheek.

Joe quickly stood and glanced at his brother. Seth was openly staring at the woman, his mouth agape in awe. Joe pulled him up by the arm.

"Why, hello." The woman smiled at them as though just now realizing they were in the room.

"Ma'am." Joe nodded. Seth said nothing, his jaw still hanging.

"Oh, please." She laughed as she draped an arm around her mother's shoulders. "You can call my mama, ma'am. I'm Susan."

"This is my daughter." Karah smiled and Joe noticed a resemblance. "Susan, remember me telling you about my nephew, Joe Dawson?" At the girl's nod, she continued. "Well, I just now found out I have another—Seth."

"Oh, how wonderful. As much as I love Sky Tate and consider her a sister of my heart, I love knowing that I have cousins." She grinned mischievously. "Even if you are *boy* cousins."

"You know Sky?" Joe asked. Although Aunt Karah had been at the party, Coop always invited the whole county, so that hadn't been unusual.

"Women were in short supply not that many years ago," Karah said, "so it was easy to make friends. Our girls enjoyed playing together when they could. Tianna Tate was an exceptionally gracious woman during my early years here at Eagle Pass, even if she didn't get into town as often as we both would have liked after they built the ranch house. I miss her to this day."

"Well, welcome to Eagle Pass," Susan said, giving him a sweet, somewhat flirtatious smile.

"I won't be staying," Joe was fast to reply. "In fact, I was about to make my excuses so I can get back to the ranch by nightfall."

"Now that's a shame." This time, Susan's gaze showed clear interest.

"I'll be staying," Seth piped up for the first time.

Joe looked sideways at his younger brother and very nearly burst out laughing. If he wasn't mistaken, Seth was smitten. Such were the ways of boys and men when it came to a pretty woman. While that might make it easier for Joe to leave, he felt a bit of sympathy for Seth and hoped that Susan would be gentle when she let him know he was much too young for her.

As he said his good-byes and dragged Seth away, he thought about Sky, his first crush. Although he told himself he didn't have time for anything but work and searching for his family, he wondered if he didn't still have feelings for her now that they were both grown up.

"What you need me out here for? You said I had to stay." Seth looked longingly back through the open door.

"You are staying. I just want to make sure you know the rules."

"You ain't my pa," he started but Joe cut him off.

"You keep saying that but I'm the one who found you and I'm the oldest, so until you can fend for yourself without getting in trouble with the law, you'd better listen." He waited a moment until he was sure he had Seth's attention. "You mind Aunt Karah and you help out around the house. You go to school and learn to read and do your numbers so you can be something when you grow up."

"I know how to shoot and ride. I can be a Ranger like you was."

Joe shook his head. "It takes more than that to be a Ranger. You aren't old enough, anyway. So in the

60

meantime, take advantage of having a roof over your head and food in your belly."

"And you just go riding off? Thought you were all about family?"

Joe heaved a sigh, knowing Seth was at least partly right. "Look. I've been searching for all of you for a long time. Now, in order to take care of you—us—to put a roof over our heads on land better than that dirt farm Pa had, I've got to work. I'm not just riding off. I'll be back into town as often as I can to check on you."

"Yeah, sure you will." Seth's shoulders slumped in defeat.

Joe took a chance. He grabbed his brother in a fierce hug, feeling his thin shoulders in a body too frail to act so tough. "I'm sorry I haven't been there for you and I swear to make it up to you."

For just a moment, Seth leaned against him, then he stiffened. But it was enough for Joe. He gave a slight smile when Seth said a gruff *bye* and turned to go into the house.

* * *

Joe made good time getting back to the ranch, but even so, the sun had sunk low in the west as he came upon the pond down the trail away from the ranch house. Deciding it was a good opportunity to wash away the trail dust, he dismounted and ground tied Critter. Even though the water would be cold, it would be better than the old slipper tub, which wasn't exactly big enough for Joe's tall frame.

As he stripped down and waded into the water, he watched the sky change colors. There was nothing like a West Texas sunset, he thought as he dipped under the water and came up gasping. Droplets clinging to his eyelashes fractured the light into diamonds of red, yellow and brilliant orange. He shook his head, then tipped back and floated. Above the bands of color, the thin threads of clouds were the palest pink and farther up, the sky darkened to indigo that would soon become black.

For a moment or two, Joe felt content. He had found Seth. Though wild as the mustangs roaming the plains, Seth would settle down once he realized he had people to care for him; he had family. As quickly as it had come, the contentment flew in the face of anger. How could someone sell a child? Had the preacher done the same with the rest of his siblings? Where had they scattered to and how would he ever find them all?

Frustrated and antsy for action, Joe strolled from the water and quickly dried himself with his worn shirt. He jerked on his pants.

The snap of a twig, barely discernible over the other night sounds, had him swiveling with pistol in hand.

"Damnit, Sky!" He sucked in a breath as he slid the Colt back into his holster. "You could get yourself shot sneaking up on a man."

She didn't say anything, just stood there staring at him, her eyes catching the last of the light and making them twinkle.

Twinkle? Had he actually thought that? He was certainly feeling fanciful tonight. He tried to get his brain to function.

"Does Coop know you're out gallivanting around in the middle of the night?" It was barely sunset, but he hoped to put the fear of God into her. He should have known better.

She smiled, shaking her head. He watched as she swallowed, his eyes sliding over the creamy skin of her throat, clear down to where the buttons of her shirt began. Coop may spoil his daughter rotten and let her run wild, but sometime when he had been gone, she had become a beautiful woman, and Joe felt his body respond to the lushness of her curves. Her breasts rose and fell with her rapid breath; her hips flared gently from her tiny waist and trailed into long slim legs. But she was Cooper Tate's daughter, and that put her off limits in so many ways he couldn't count.

If he knew what was good for him, he'd get the hell back to the ranch. He reached for the clean shirt he had thrown over a bush.

Her warm hand on his bare back stopped him cold. He jerked upward and tried to move away from her touch. For every step he took, she took two.

"Skyla Tate." His voice rumbled in warning.

"Joe Dawson," she mimicked him before adding, "Look at me." Her breath whispered across his back. His muscles tensed.

"You don't know what you're asking." Joe squeezed his eyes shut but couldn't block out her touch. And then it was gone.

He quickly opened his eyes to find her directly in front of him. Catching him unaware, she pushed against his chest with her open palms, hard enough to have him stumbling backward.

"Hey. What was that for?"

"You know what for."

"Hell, if I knew, I sure wouldn't be asking." He skewered her with a fierce look, something that had always worked when she was younger. She took a step back and Joe breathed easier without her hands on him. Easier, but still with some pain in his lower regions.

Then she had to go and toss her head, causing glossy strands of curly hair to swirl around her face. He was sure he groaned.

She slapped her hands on narrow hips and threw her shoulders back. Joe knew he groaned then.

"Look at me. What do you see?"

"What?" His voice cracked.

"You heard me. I am not a little girl anymore. I'm a woman grown and you've never even noticed."

Oh, he noticed all right, and that was exactly why he was staying away from her. Her lush mouth made a man want to drink from her pouting lips and her womanly curves where meant to keep a man warm at night. But she was not for him.

63

Joe had known his fair share of women, good and bad, young and old. One thing he never learned was how to understand them. What he did know, was that no matter what he said, it would be wrong.

"I work for your father, Sky—"

"That's neither here nor there," she interrupted with a wave of her hand.

"You're wrong. Now go on back to the house before it gets any darker and you lose your way."

Her mouth dropped open at his unintentional command, as though she were a small child.

"I am not twelve anymore," she shouted at him. For an instant, he thought he saw tears in her eyes, then she spun around and raced for her horse as though the devil himself was after her.

Joe cursed, knowing the devil stood right there in his boots, making him want what he couldn't have.

Chapter Six

Roundup was one of Sky's favorite times of year. Where weeks ago they'd had a heat wave, this morning was crisp enough for her fleece vest but with freshness promising spring. The sky was bright blue, and though the sun was a huge yellow disk creeping over the horizon, it wouldn't be as hot as later in the summer. If they were lucky, rain would soon turn the pastures lush green, enough to fatten the cattle through the summer. Her father would keep the herds close to the ranch for a bit yet, until he was sure all the calves were hardy and able enough to make the trek to higher pastures. And while they needed rain, she hoped it would hold off until they had the new calves branded.

She never went on the long cattle drives to the railheads in Kansas, but her father did let her help during spring round up and when the cattle were moved throughout the summer as the lower pastures dried up and water became scarce. There was something about being out in the open, under God's canopy that she would never give up.

She let Stormy pick her own way through the grassland as she glanced casually across the open land at the numerous cowboys trailing behind the ambling cattle. As there were few fences, cattle from the Circle C and the Cross S, both bordering the Double T, intermixed as the cattle ranged where the grass was green. After spring calving the cows were led in the valley where the cowboys would sort them by brand. The new calves would stick close enough to their mamas for the men to know which belonged to what ranch.

She glanced over at Mason, who rode beside her even though most of his crew were farther ahead, wondering if he was home to stay this time, or if Washington would lure him back. Personally, she didn't understand how he could bear being cooped up inside all day, talking politics. In Washington, he didn't even have his own horse to ride and instead was hauled around by a driver in a carriage.

With an unladylike snort, she shook her head. She'd have to be near dead before she would give up her horse and her freedom.

Mason turned to give her a look but never stopped his dialogue about life in the big city. Sky only half listened, studying his profile instead. His blonde hair glistened in the early morning light as he lifted his hat and rubbed a forearm across his brow. He was a handsome man and clearly had intentions toward her. So why did she toss and turn all last night thinking about a rude, insufferable, dark haired man with piercing eyes the color of liquid silver and a smile that would melt ice in January?

Her gaze shot past Mason to the object of her thoughts, riding on the fringe of the herd. As always, he was entirely in black save for the bright blue bandana around his neck. Even from this distance, she could see his erect posture, his total focus on the herd. The fact that he appeared not to care, one way or the other, whether she was here had her wanting to chase him down and knock him right off his horse.

"You okay?" Mason asked, one brow raised, and she realized she had grumbled out loud.

"Of course. Why wouldn't I be?" She glanced again at the distant silhouette, deciding it made no sense holding a grudge on such a fine day. She gave Mason a brilliant smile and all her attention.

* * *

Patch had set up the chuck wagon in the valley between the Double T and the Circle C and Joe smelled coffee brewing even before he dragged himself wearily from his horse at dusk. The valley provided a natural corral for the cattle; water ran nearby, and the surrounding hills meant shelter in the event of an unpredictable storm. The various crews from the other two ranches would be close by, everyone helping in the roundup.

The longhorns seemed to know the routine, and there were few strays to be gathered along the way, so the day had been less than exciting. Even so, his thigh ached as he lowered himself to the ground, holding tight to the saddle for the time it took his leg to regain its feeling. The real work would begin tomorrow as the calves were separated from the cows into individual holding areas and each ranch's crew would brand the newborns. Coop had encouraged him to stay at the ranch, but Joe wasn't about to let a roundup happen without him. It had been a long time and if he was to show he had what it took to be foreman that meant participating in all facets of the work.

"Too old for this, cowboy?" The musical voice taunted him as he dragged the saddle off Critter with a grunt. He turned to see Sky unsaddling her mare.

He couldn't forget their conversation at the pond the other day, and yet she had ridden close to Mason Winstead all day. He told himself it made no difference, but then he couldn't figure why that now made him angry.

"The days are longer than I remember." His voice came out just short of a growl.

Sky laughed. "And the rest of the week will be even longer." She put a feed bag over the mare's muzzle, then turned toward the campfire. "Hey, Patch," she called. "Got something good for supper?"

Joe stayed in the shadows a while longer. Sky's contradictory behavior had his head spinning. She had been mad as a hornet yesterday, but now she acted as content as a bear with a honey jar. He had too many problems of his own to figure her out, yet her very presence put him on edge and made him yearn for the unreachable. "What is it about her that sets me to thinking the impossible?" he spoke quietly to Critter. The horse snorted and blew, then shook his big head. "Yeah, you can't figure her out either." Joe rubbed his forelock and Critter pushed his nose gently into his chest.

Joe finished currying his horse before heading over to the water bucket Patch had set on an old tree stump. The cool water felt refreshing against his face. Though the temperature had remained comfortable all day, the sun had been a constant reminder that summer wasn't far off. As he used his bandana to dry off, he couldn't help but smile as Sky made a comment about doing the cooking and Patch let out a loud *guffaw*.

"Honey, way back when you was a young'un, you was riding your pony and roping steers when you shoulda been in the kitchen cooking. Now it's too late for you to be telling me how to make my famous Patch stew."

Nearby cowboys laughed, then fell to talking quietly until Patch was ready to call them to supper. The evening kicked up a slight breeze, stars winking in the darkening sky, and Joe relaxed, content in knowing this was where he belonged. He had enjoyed his work as a Ranger, but his heart hadn't been in it because he was always looking for his kin wherever the captain sent him. Although he still had family out there somewhere, at least he had Seth now, and could begin to think of a future. Maybe one day he'd have a spread like Coop, and his sisters and brothers could help run it.

Pouring himself a cup of thick hot coffee, he groaned as he lowered himself to the ground and leaned against his saddle. Surprisingly, Sky appeared and gracefully folded herself cross legged beside him. He glanced her way out of the corner of his eye, but she seemed content to sit, gazing into the campfire.

His attention was diverted when Culpepper, one of the newer ranch hands piped up. "Hey, Patch. How'd you get a name like that, anyway?"

"Well, now, I'll tell you," Patch began and Joe groaned. He'd heard this story a hundred times if he'd heard it once, and each time it got bigger in the telling.

"My paw said Maw used to spend all her time patching me up seeing as I kept falling in the creek and tumbling out of trees. If it 'tweren't me, it was my clothes that had more patches than not. Then there was the time an old grizzly took off after me and tore a hunk right outa my...." He looked at Sky, coughed, then finished, "...backside. My maw couldn't patch up a hole the size of Texas in my britches that time."

The cowboys laughed at the story as Patch puffed up his chest and banged a spoon on the dinner triangle hooked to the back of the chuck wagon. "Come and get it!" he hollered loud enough that some of the cattle lowed off in the night.

"It's funny," Sky said quietly while the others scrambled up to get in line for food. "I never really think of Patch as being a little boy, having a mother and father." She shrugged. "He's always just been *Patch*—old and wizen and a shelter for all the times I got hurt. Especially after mama died."

Joe rolled to his feet, then for some mysterious reason turned and stretched out a hand to Sky. "Everybody's got history. Sometimes we know it, and sometimes we're better off not knowing." She grabbed his hand and he tugged her to her feet. When she didn't immediately let go, he glanced down into her wide eyes; eyes he could drown in.

"But what if you *want* your history tangled up with someone else's?" she whispered. "Then there shouldn't be any secrets, should there?"

He had no answer and didn't even want to think about what she might mean. When he said nothing, she sighed and let go of his hand, striding over to get the plate of food Patch held out. He watched as she settled onto an upturned barrel and dug into her supper. Joe's stomach twisted. Instead of eating, he turned and went to check on the horses.

* * *

Joe ate supper late and after downing one last cup of coffee, took his turn on watch, heading out to relieve one of the cowboys who had yet to eat. One thing about roundups, the stew and coffee pots were always hanging over the fire pit.

69

Because they were in a protected valley and the cattle fairly close, he saddled Critter but walked him into the night. His thigh ached at the thought of hefting himself into the saddle again, so unless there was a need, he'd do his time on the ground.

He tossed out his bedroll and stretched, alert but relaxed. The cattle settled for the night and the only sounds were the occasional bawl of a calf trying to find his maw. There was little moonlight, so the herd was mere shadow. He looked up at the pinholes of light sprinkling the black sky.

Joe heard steps approaching. A part of him feared it was Sky; a bigger part hoped he was right.

"There must be thousands of stars out tonight." Her soft voice barely carried in the dark.

"Millions." He upped the ante as she sat down beside him on the blanket.

"Billions," she replied, laughing, gently bumping his shoulder with her own.

"Trillions," he finished, recalling the times they had done arithmetic together and Sky always thought she could count farther than he.

Her laughter died when he turned toward her. She stared at him with an intensity that made his breath catch and his heart beat faster. Starlight flickered in her eyes and even without the moon he could see the soft planes of her face. She had looked at him in such a way when he was at the ranch the first time, but they were kids and he didn't understand what the snakes in his belly meant.

Now, he wanted to kiss her. She was no longer the little girl who tried to outdo him in everything from arithmetic to calf roping. She was a woman full grown and beautiful, and he was drawn to her by some invisible rope. He watched as her tongue peeked out to lick her upper lip. Her lips parted as if she were going to say something.

He didn't give her a chance. Reaching his hand to the back of her neck, he gently pulled her toward him, brushing his lips across her forehead, her cheeks. When she didn't pull back, he settled his lips across hers, tongue teasing

70

until she opened for him and he delved deeper, forgetting the cattle, the night, even forgetting to breathe.

Sweet, like the chocolate he loved. But in this, he couldn't get enough. How long had it been since he felt a woman's touch?

Joe didn't know if the sound she made was protest or surrender, but in the next moment, her arms wrapped around his neck. He lowered her to the ground, peppering kisses across her eyelids, down her nose, sucking gently on the lobe of her ear.

"Joe." Her hands moved restlessly across his back, igniting fires that shot straight to his groin. Her chest rose and fell erratically. He slid a hand up her arm, over the soft skin of her collarbone before gently trailing his fingers over her shirt. Her heart beat a rapid tattoo against his palm. Her eyes flickered, then closed on a sigh as he cupped her breast in his large hand.

He heard a moan, not knowing whether it was her or him. All he felt was her exquisite softness and her surrender when he nudged her legs apart with his knee. And it was that yielding, that total trust in him, that made him jerk back and stumble to his feet.

"Son of a bitch," he swore, running a hand through his hair as he paced back and forth.

Sky curled upward, hugging her arms around her knees as she rocked to and fro. "Please, Joe."

"Don't." He couldn't handle her quiet plea. He needed to stop before it was too late for both of them. "I can't give you what you want, Sky, what you deserve. I can't give it to anybody."

Unable to endure the wretched pain that crossed her face, he turned and stalked off into the night. When he returned long minutes later, she was gone.

71

Chapter Seven

As much as she loved being outside and the headiness of being part of the ranch workings, a week on the range and Sky was more than ready for her feather bed. When she saw the peaked roof of the ranch house, a curl of smoke pluming up from the chimney, she kicked Stormy into a canter and left her father, Joe, and the rest of the cowboys behind.

"Bet she's in a bubble bath before we get our horses unsaddled," she heard her father say as she raced ahead.

He wouldn't be wrong. In record time, she had Stormy unsaddled, curried and fed. By the time she came into the house via the kitchen, Bonita had a blueberry tart on a plate for her.

"Is it ready?" Sky asked.

Bonita gave a *tsking* sound. "Do you think I would not look after my *'mija* when she work so hard trying to prove something to her papa?"

Sky didn't waste time arguing. She grabbed the plate and headed for her bedroom, munching the warm, crusty tart on the way.

"Ah," she sighed, seeing the oversized tub in the corner, full almost to overflowing with steamy water. Within minutes, she was stripped and soaking, swearing she wouldn't get out of the hot, sweet-scented water until her skin shriveled, and maybe not even then. She closed her eyes and settled her thoughts on just one thing. Joe had kissed her. She still felt the pressure of his lips, his hot breath mingling with hers. Her stomach tightened and her breasts tingled as she daydreamed of him taking her far beyond that first kiss.

It could have been an hour or just minutes when Sky heard the musical chimes of the bell Bonita used to inform them supper was half an hour away. Reluctantly, she levered herself out of the water, which had cooled anyway, toweled off and began to dress. As she reached into the wardrobe for a clean pair of Levi's, she paused.

The kiss she and Joe had shared was everything she had thought it would be. But when she wanted more, he quit, leaving her aching for something she couldn't identify. Maybe he didn't see her as a lady. She shuffled clothes back and forth. Maybe she needed to prove she was feminine enough, pretty enough, to be worthy of his attention.

She grabbed a dark blue skirt and tugged it on, the sleek sweeping lines accenting her narrow waist. She brushed her hair until it gleamed, then ran her fingers haphazardly through it to make curls pop up. She plucked at ones around her face, debating whether to let them curl or to pin them back.

"Damn," she swore softly, then bit her lip. She turned her head from side to side. "Is he worth all this bother?" Yet she couldn't deny the heat in their kiss or the ache that hadn't gone away.

She gave her reflection one last look. The creamy silk of her blouse set off her complexion which had turned golden from days on the trail. "Just you look out, Joe Dawson."

* * *

Joe strode into the study in the midst of an argument between Coop and Sky. At least it sounded like an argument to him, but then he was preoccupied. He poured himself a drink as he thought on the message that had awaited him when the crew returned to the ranch. Aunt Karah had written that there was trouble between Seth and other boys in school, something about his brother telling whoppers about riding with outlaws. Of course the other boys didn't believe him, so fights had broken out.

Joe figured he could be to blame for that, seeing as how he hadn't told his aunt where he had found Seth; so

73

she might have figured Seth was lying. Seth should have kept his mouth shut, except being the new kid in town, he would probably try to fit in by boasting. Regardless, it meant another trip to town, taking time away from the ranch and his responsibilities to Coop.

"But Daddy, we have the money. Why can't I have just a bit more?" Sky's voice broke through Joe's thoughts. He took a sip of whiskey, feeling sorry enough for himself to make a comment that should have been left unsaid.

"Still the spoiled brat?" He lifted a brow as he turned to look at her and immediately regretted his comment. She wore a skirt and ruffled blouse that exposed her slender neck and creamy shoulders; silky skin he had wanted desperately to kiss the other night. At his comment, her cheeks flushed and her eyes narrowed to dangerous slits. If he had wanted her to forget about him, his big mouth had certainly done the job.

"You always were a big bully. Daddy, make him leave."

"Now you two—" Coop started.

"Dinner is ready," Bonita said at the same time from the doorway.

Sky didn't wait for either of them but turned with a huff and left the room. Joe looked over at Cooper, hoping he hadn't insulted his friend and mentor.

Coop shook his head. "You two always did go after each other, but lately, I don't know what's gotten into her."

"She grew up," Joe said, grumbling just as much as Coop. Why couldn't things remain simple?

"Ever since her mother died…well, it hasn't been easy. I probably let her get by with more than I should, but damn, girls are sure different."

Joe didn't know what to say, so instead took another sip of his drink and poured one for Coop. When they went in to supper, Joe hoped Bonita was serving something that would set well on his twisting stomach.

One thing about working a cattle ranch, the beef was always prime and cooked to perfection. Bonita set a huge

74

roast in front of them, along with bowls of spring peas, mashed potatoes, and plenty of dark, thick beef gravy.

"You save room for dessert," she admonished as Joe dug in.

"You spoil me, Bonita." Joe gave her a wink. "I may just run off with you one of these days."

"You forget my Paul," she replied. "He can be fierce."

Joe sighed dramatically. "You're right. I wouldn't want him to hurt me."

She laughed as she left the room and they settled down to eat. While Patch's trail food was good, there was nothing like a roast and potatoes deep in gravy.

The fact that Sky was quiet didn't miss his attention, but if she wanted to pout, Joe shrugged it aside as he dug into another helping of potatoes and gravy. After a dessert of blueberry tarts and heavy cream, Sky excused herself, stating she was tired from the week and was going to bed. Joe accepted Coop's offer for another drink and they settled themselves next to the low burning fire with a decanter of fine whiskey between them.

Joe briefly told Coop about Seth's troubles in town, and by the third whiskey, was lamenting about the man's own daughter.

"I lost everything I loved at one time. I can't go through that again."

Coop gave a drunken smile, or at least Joe thought he was the drunken one, until he spoke.

"The way you pick on each other must mean you care." The man spoke the gospel.

"Hell, she makes me so mad some days, and others she's as mad as a hornet at me. Even so, I just want to take her and…." He realized who he was talking to when the man raised an eyebrow.

"I won't have her hurt, Joe," Coop spoke softly but with an edge of steel, and even through his somewhat drunken stupor, Joe clearly understood his meaning.

"Believe me, sir, that's the last thing I want. I gotta go into town. Maybe it would be better all-around if I just kept on going."

75

Coop shook his head. "You came back here to settle things. Now, you go into town and bring that boy back out here where we can keep an eye on him. Just think about the rest for a while. Nobody's going anywhere around here anytime soon." He reached over and slapped Joe's knee, then got to his feet. "This old body sure isn't used to the hard ground anymore. I'm heading to bed."

Joe sat awhile longer, staring at the fire and contemplating all that Coop had said, and what he hadn't said. The yearning to settle down and make a life for himself was so great it consumed him. But overriding that was the promise he had made seven years ago. A promise he was a long way from keeping if he didn't give up his own dreams, at least for the time being.

* * *

Sky heard enough of their conversation to know Joe was heading for Eagle Pass in the morning. She sensed that something nagged at Joe, something that drove him, but he certainly wasn't telling her. So, she would follow him and see what it was that he had to do. Perhaps if she could help him in this, he could finally settle down at the ranch with her.

And while she was in town, she could get the school supplies she needed for the reservation. Last night her father had fumed at her wanting more money to buy supplies, but he never refused to pay the bill from the mercantile. Like her, he had a soft spot for the Kickapoo and felt the government had given them a raw deal.

She trailed far enough behind Joe that he wouldn't notice her, but once or twice she lost sight of him. Then suddenly, he came up behind her.

"If I'd been an outlaw, you'd be dead." His soft voice shot across the distance and caused a shiver down her spine.

She had heard a noise and unsheathed her rifle, but he was right; she wouldn't have been fast enough. She silently put her rifle back in its sleeve as she looked over at Joe. His face was drawn. Stubble shadowed his jaw and dark circles hollowed his eyes. His mouth was set in a grim line. For once he looked less than comfortable in the saddle.

"You don't look like you could shoot a rock, much less a person." She thought to tease him, but he scowled.

"Yeah, well, you're stubborn as a rock, so it would be the same difference."

Sky's mouth dropped in protest, but just as quickly she snapped it shut. She knew from experience he was picking a fight, so she would leave him alone. This time, it wasn't going to happen.

"I was riding into town before you came back to the Double T, Joe. I can still get around my daddy's land without protection." She could see him working up to an argument, so hurriedly continued. "Besides, I need to get some supplies for the Kickapoo."

He gave her a look of surprise. "Does your daddy know you spend all your money on them?"

She shrugged. "He gives me a fair amount of pin money, and more when I ask, and I certainly don't spend it all on useless, frivolous clothes."

"That doesn't answer my question."

"He doesn't care...." she started but Joe had lost interest.

He looked off to the west, chin raised and nose twitching as though scenting something. The horse he was leading fidgeted. Sky recognized it as Two Bits, one from her daddy's stock.

"You stealing a horse?" she asked, knowing better but wanting to get a rise out of him.

He shook his head like he used to when she followed him around asking a hundred questions. "You should put off your trip a bit. There's a rain coming. This time of year you never know if it'll be a gully washer or not. Seeing as we have to cross Indio Creek getting back to the ranch...."

His expression told her that, while he had used the word *we,* he didn't want to be there with her but wasn't about to leave her. "Don't worry, Dawson, I can get to town and back by myself."

"I can't leave you out here. Let's ride." And just like he always did, he took off at a canter, expecting her to follow.

Sky did, but only because she was going to town anyway and wanted to see what he was up to.

Unfortunately, while she was picking out pencils and tablets, Joe snuck out of McGuffey's and disappeared. When Sky emerged from the store looking for him, she saw instead that the sun was hidden by dark gray clouds heavy with rain. She looked east, the direction of the ranch where the horizon was lighter. She decided to take a chance on getting back. While thunderstorms often came across the mountains, this looked as if it would only give them a nice steady rain, which was sorely needed.

Even so, she popped back into the mercantile, dropping her bundle. "Rain's coming. I'll be back for these another day. No sense in everything getting wet."

"You take care, Miss Sky." Thom McGuffey sounded concerned.

"You know a little water won't hurt me any." She gave him a wave and left, hurrying to where Stormy pranced nervously. "Won't hurt you either," she told the horse as she climbed into the saddle.

She might have known she wouldn't get far without Joe catching up to her.

"Are you crazy, heading back in this weather?" It wasn't a question so much as a comment, and likely he was thinking she was stupid, not crazy. He shoved his hat down as the wind picked up.

"It's clear over east. We can make it." She spoke to Joe but was busy studying the young boy who rode Two Bits. He wore a scowl that reminded her of Joe, but with sandy hair and blue eyes, the two looked nothing alike.

"Don't ask," Joe told her before she could form a question. "Let's go."

He and the boy took off and Sky sat for a moment holding Stormy on a tight rein. Why did he think he could keep giving her orders? She had already been heading back to the ranch, so why did he think he had to *tell* her to go?

He had no business…. Thunder rumbled in the distance and Sky shook off her contrary thoughts, riding fast to catch up.

The rain started just before they reached Indio Creek. Without stopping, she reached back and pulled a slicker from her saddle bag. More thunder rolled across the sky and Stormy shied, but Sky kept her seat. She watched Joe pull up at the creek bank.

"Damn," his voice carried across the wind.

Water in the usually slow running creek was rushing downstream, splashing over rocks.

"This storm must have hit the Anacacho first," Joe hollered, referring to the mountains to the north. Any runoff from there would gain momentum as it traveled south.

"This creek isn't deep," Sky replied. "We can cross it, then get to the line shack just to the other side."

Joe tipped his hat forward, trying as she was to keep the water out of his eyes. The boy, without a slicker, was rapidly getting drenched. She watched as Joe looked from her to him, then back to the water. Her horse was skittish, but she clamped her knees and kept her on a tight rein. She was well trained and would follow Sky's command, even if she didn't like it. However, Two Bits snorted at the rough treatment when Joe grabbed the reins.

"Can you swim?" he shouted to the youngster, whose eyes were wide and frightened. The boy shook his head. Looking back at the river, there was no debris, which would make the crossing less hazardous. Still….

"Hold on!" Joe kept the reins as the boy clutched the saddle horn and they started forward.

Sky did the same, loosening her hold on the reins and grabbing the saddle horn, knowing her mare would have the good sense to pick her own way across the swollen creek without Sky's help. She ignored Joe and kept her gaze between her horse's ears. The water wasn't as deep as it was fast moving, but even so, Stormy kept her footing and soon clambered up the other bank. It was only when they were away from the water that Sky realized she was holding her breath. Sucking in air she turned to find Joe.

"Joe!" She cried his name as his horse came galloping up the embankment without him.

Jumping down, she grabbed the rope from her saddle and ran downstream along the bank, her gaze scanning the churning water. Just as she reached a fallen tree, Joe surfaced, tugging the youngster by the collar. Sky threw the rope aside and instead reached out a hand for Joe's arm. Together they stumbled upward before collapsing high on the bank.

"Seth, you okay?" Joe coughed out water as he shook the boy.

He gave no response. He lay, face ashen, eyes closed.

"Seth!" Joe grabbed him and rolled him over on his side, pounding his back with a hard hand.

Sky watched, horrified, as Joe muttered under his breath.

"God damn it. I didn't come this far to find you, only to lose you again." The pain in his voice shook Sky deeper than the cold now shaking her bones. Whoever this boy was, he meant a great deal to Joe. She sent up a prayer that he would be all right.

Her eyes popped open at the sounds of a ragged cough, gag, then more coughing. Joe had the boy hanging over one arm, still pounding his back, as the youngster emptied the contents of his stomach.

"Leave off, will you? You trying to kill me?" The hoarse voice was weak but caused Joe to laugh as he let go and sat back on his haunches.

The rain had let up slightly but the three of them were still wet, Sky perhaps less so because she hadn't taken a swim in the creek.

"We need to get to the line shack." She stood. "I'll get the horses." She looked around, knowing Stormy and Joe's horse were well enough trained they wouldn't have gone far, even in a storm. "I don't see Two Bits." She turned back to Joe.

He pointed to the creek and when she looked, she saw the horse racing up and down along the opposite side of the creek. Without a rider to guide him, he wouldn't ford the creek by himself.

"You sure are hard on horses," Joe told the youngster he had called Seth.

"Yeah, well, I just hope you didn't steal this one."

Joe chuckled, but of course she didn't understand the joke. As Joe rolled to his feet with a groan, then reached a hand out for Seth, she realized they had a history she knew nothing about. Swinging up on Stormy, she decided that was going to change, real soon.

The line shack was used by cowboys from all of the ranches as they checked on cattle throughout the year. It was a small one room building with a lean-to for the horses. As soon as they reached it, Sky leaned over for Critter's reins.

"I'll see to the horses. You and Seth are drenched to the bone and need to get dry. There should be wood inside for a fire."

Joe started to protest, but finally sighed, reaching a hand back for Seth, who slid from the horse without a word. Joe followed, holding onto the saddle for long moments before releasing it to hobble up the step to the small porch.

Most days he went about his work as usual and Sky had forgotten he had come back to the ranch hurt. She didn't know the extent of his injury because Joe refused to talk about himself or his troubles. A fine characteristic in a man, she supposed, but there were times when she wished he would just confide in her a little.

By the time she had the horses unsaddled and fed, the smell of wood smoke rose in the air. It was Patch's and her job to see that the line shack was stocked with necessary supplies, whether for a brief stay or if someone was hurt, but she didn't suppose Joe had started supper. Thinking coffee would be a good start, she opened the door and stopped short just over the threshold.

Both Joe and Seth stood barefoot and shirtless in front of the fire, but it was only Joe who captured her attention. The flames reflected off his wet skin and made it glow.

Muscles rippled across his chest and down his arms as he scrubbed his hair with a towel.

"Hey!" Seth cried, hugging the towel to his chest. Sky would have laughed if he hadn't looked so sincere in his modesty. He was short and gangly, his frame yet to fill out. It wasn't as though she hadn't seen a naked male chest before, but when she looked closer, she noticed yellowing bruises along Seth's ribs.

"You're hurt." She stepped toward him but Joe put a hand on her arm.

"He's okay." His answer was short and not unkind but had Sky's attention drawn to him.

Her eye caught the glint of the small, silver medallion, or button, hanging from a leather thong around his neck. She had seen it before, but now she quickly turned and saw that Seth wore a similar talisman.

"Joe?" The single word held a wealth of questions. "So help me, I'll lock you in this shack if you don't tell me what's going on." It was a ridiculous threat, and the look Joe sent her told her he knew it.

He took the time to wring out his shirt and hang it over the back of a chair before he answered. "Seth's my brother."

Sky knew her face registered surprise. In all the years Joe had been at her daddy's ranch, she never knew what drove him, what caused the sullen and withdrawn mood swings. "How? What?" The questions popped out as she tried to take it in.

"We got separated years ago," Seth spoke up when Joe remained silent. "He left us." The youngster glared at Joe.

"I didn't leave on purpose. I told you that. In any case, it doesn't matter now that you're back." He turned and started rummaging along the single shelf that held canned goods, a coffee pot and a few plates and utensils.

Sky stood in the middle of the shack, staring from one brother to the other. They looked nothing alike, for Seth was as fair as Joe was dark. He was also considerably smaller and younger than Joe, as it didn't look as though he even shaved. Still, there was something in the boy's voice that reminded her of Joe years ago—the same anger and frustration—but for what reason, or at whom?

She watched the taut muscles on Joe's back as he grabbed the coffee pot. Judging from his stance, he was holding in anger, but at his brother, or her?

She turned to Seth, wondering if she could get him to talk. He continued to scowl as he wrung out his shirt and hung it in front of the fire as Joe had done. The firelight winked off the silver hanging by a slender thread of sinew and a new question formed.

Seth and Joe both wore the same talisman, but where had she seen it even before either of them?

Chapter Eight

Joe's head pounded to the rhythm of rain hitting the tin roof of the line shack. He supposed it wouldn't hurt for Sky to know Seth was his kin, seeing as how the kid would be living at the ranch. But he shot a glance at Seth, hoping he wouldn't say anything else. There was no need in spilling it all, as Sky couldn't help and he didn't want her feeling sorry for him.

There were a multitude of other feelings he would rather she have, he thought, as he watched her open some cans and dump their contents in a pot to hang over the fire. He instantly recalled the kiss they had shared out on the round up. He had wanted more, even as he told himself he didn't deserve it. Now, her persistence in following him made it hard to ignore her allure.

Sky, wet or dry, was a picture to behold. Her pants clung to her fanny as she bent over and her shirt was like a second skin. Her short curls still glittered with raindrops and caught the firelight, bringing out the auburn highlights. He stared at the ceiling, hoping for patience and the ability to control his lustful thoughts.

His brother sighed, and he looked to see him staring at Sky. Joe was at once annoyed and thankful for his presence. Still, he gave him a smack on the shoulder.

"What?" Seth asked with a shrug and when Joe flicked his gaze to Sky and back, Seth had the audacity to grin and nod. The kid was certainly feeling his oats, and Joe couldn't blame him. Sky would appeal to any man, regardless of age.

"There's some hard tack, too," Sky interrupted his thoughts, "so I suppose this will have to do for now." She plunked the pan on the table, and Joe grabbed bowls and spoons from the shelf.

"I'm sorry it's not more of a meal," she spoke to Seth. "A growing boy needs to eat."

"It'll do just fine...ma'am." Seth added the last in a bare whisper.

Joe looked at his brother in surprise. He hadn't been at Aunt Karah's long enough to learn anything but where to find trouble, but somewhere in the past he'd picked up some manners.

Sky laughed as she spooned up the stew. "Did you just call me ma'am? I'm not near old enough to be your mama, and especially not your granny, so you can't call me anything but my given name—"

"Miss Tate," Joe interrupted.

Sky rolled her eyes. "Don't listen to him on this." She looked right at Seth and Joe could see his young brother lapping up the attention. "My friends call me Sky." She paused. "I hope we can be friends."

Seth grinned at Joe, pleased as punch.

"Eat your supper," Joe growled.

* * *

By the time they had eaten, the rain stopped. Joe walked outside and studied the sky. The darker clouds had blown eastward, and the air smelled fresh and clean. Judging from the position of the sun, there was enough daylight to get back to the ranch.

"We're heading in," he said as he poked his head inside where Sky had his brother scrubbing the pot and bowls. The kid was smitten, that's for sure.

"I do wish you'd quit telling me what to do," Sky stood, hands on hips, eyes flashing.

"Make sure that fire is out," he added with a grin, just to get a rise out of her. When she pursed her lips, he left, for he was sure he'd do something he'd regret. Like kiss those pouting lips, even if his brother was there. Something about her kept chipping away at his resistance.

He paused outside the window when he heard Seth.

"Ain't you afraid to sass him like that?" His brother's voice held just a bit of worry.

"Who, Joe?" Surprise laced Sky's voice.

"Ain't you afraid he'll do…bad things to you if you don't do what he says?"

Joe's heart ached again for all the lost years and for the bleak days and nights his brother had endured.

"Joe and I are friends, Seth," Sky stated firmly, and although Joe knew he shouldn't be listening, he couldn't make his feet move. "I can't know what's between you two, but maybe someday you'll tell me as I'd like to be your friend, too. In the meantime, remember this. Your brother is the most loyal, loving man I know, and he would never hurt anyone."

How could she have such faith in him? Joe wondered as he forced himself to move. She was too trusting, too naïve, he concluded. And yet part of him longed to believe her words, to believe in himself as much as she did.

* * *

As foreman, Joe assigned jobs to the cowboys at will, but he rarely changed the routine that had been established when he arrived at the Double T. The exception came the evening they returned.

Two Bits had managed to ford the creek and ended up trotting into the yard about the same time as they did. When Tyler, one of the ranch hands, grabbed the trailing reins to lead the horse to the barn, Joe called out.

"Seth will take care of it. The horse got spooked crossing the Indio." He swung Seth down as he talked, then dismounted. Before he walked Critter toward the barn, he turned to his brother, who stood grumbling.

"If you're going to stay here, you'll earn your keep. If you stay, you need a horse and you'll take care of that animal—brush him before you get a bath, feed him before you eat."

Seth chewed his bottom lip as though considering.

"There's no one here to pick a fight with," Joe continued, "and if you're wanting to brag about riding with the Horner gang, go ahead. Probably be some of these cowboys who've done worse at one time or another." Seth's eyes grew round. "But everyone here now works hard and takes orders, and they get paid."

"Real money?" Seth asked.

"A bed, hot meals, and real money," Joe confirmed. "But they do what they're told," he added with a firm grip on Seth's shoulder.

Seth walked away to take the reins of Two Bits and lead him into the stable.

Well, that was that. Joe was sure Coop wouldn't mind Seth being there as there was room in the bunkhouse and Joe would pay him out of his own wages.

By the time he got Critter settled, Sky had already gone to the house. She had talked to Seth on the ride in, telling him about the Double T, but she hadn't had much to say to Joe. Just as well, he thought, as he needed time to contemplate what he had learned.

* * *

As summer swept into West Texas, life once again became routine for Sky. There were a few patches of Buttercups and Blue Bonnets bordering the front porch, only because they took little care and came back year after year. No one spent much time or precious water keeping non-useable plants alive.

Instead, she helped Bonita with the garden they had planted back of the main house. The vegetables and herbs they grew would supplement the beef they butchered and ate as a steady diet. There were also chickens to feed, so they had a good supply of eggs and once in a while, a nice stewed chicken with fat noodles or dumplings.

Her favorite time was spent with the colts that had been born that spring. She often had Seth help her because he seemed to have an affinity for animals. He learned quickly and soon he was the one breaking them to a halter and lead.

Joe kept a close eye on his brother and she wasn't sure what he expected. Seth seemed content to live in the bunkhouse with the cowboys, even though she had asked about moving him to the main house. After all, Joe slept there. Did Joe expect Seth to run off, or perhaps steal a loaf of bread from Bonita's windowsill like he had once done?

Sky tried to get Seth to talk while they worked, but the youngster didn't seem inclined to spill the family secrets. Either that or he truly didn't remember his past. He was as close-mouthed as Joe, which frustrated her no end.

Life would have been idyllic if not for the disturbing report that day from the cowboys riding the range.

"Earmarks of another butcher," her father said that night at supper.

"How many this time?" Joe asked.

Sky had learned since Joe's return that her father spoke to him more often than to her about the ranch. He didn't exclude her exactly, but he valued Joe's opinion. That had been one reason he had made Joe foreman.

Now, her father shook his head. "Hard to tell since the cattle free-range, but Culpepper said there was enough blood to account for several head. And they found horse tracks. He's not much of a tracker but thinks they're several days old. I hate to think that the Indians are raiding again."

"Daddy, it could be wild animals," Sky protested.

"Not when there's no trace of the cattle," her father replied. "Any wild animal would kill and eat its fill. It isn't going to haul off the entire cow."

"But—"

"Your father's right," Joe interrupted. "It may not be Indians," he hurried on when Sky scowled at him, "but it's definitely human. There have been reports of the Horner gang being in the area, although I have to wonder if they'd take the time to butcher and haul off an entire animal. They'd more likely steal the cattle to sell for cash."

"You found Seth with them, didn't you?" Sky asked, having overheard Joe talking to her father when they first returned from Eagle Pass.

Joe's eyes narrowed, but he didn't reply. Damnit, Sky thought, getting information out of him was like prying a bone away from a hungry dog. One way or another, she was going to discover the mystery surrounding Joe Dawson.

"I need to replenish the supplies in the line shack." She casually changed the subject as she pushed her sweet peas around on her plate.

"Damnit it, Sky. You can't be going up there alone," her father said, as she had expected, "especially after what the men have found."

"You know I have nothing to fear from the Kickapoo, and if it was an outlaw gang that butchered the cattle, they would be long gone by now. No one steals another man's cattle and hangs around to be caught."

Her father didn't say anything for a minute, contemplating his beef steak. Sky was surprised Joe hadn't immediately protested, considering he was always trying to tell her what to do.

"I could take Seth with me." She finally broke the silence. "He's been very helpful with the horses, but I know he doesn't have a regular job with the cowboys."

"He's got his chores to do," Joe spoke up quickly. "And Patch is teaching him how to cook so he can help out in the bunkhouse."

Joe took a long drink of his water. She recognized his expression of resignation when he finally gave a huge sigh. "I reckon I could ride out with you. It would give me a chance to look for any tracks coming from west of the Indio Creek."

Sky didn't change her expression in the least, not in protest or agreement, but inside her heartbeat quickened and her mind cheered in victory.

They decided to ride up to the line shack the next day, but Joe wanted to take a look at a sick mare first. Sky was inside the barn currying Stormy. When she heard boots on the wooden floors, she spoke without turning around.

"Are you ready?"

"Sugar, I've been ready since the day I got here."

Sky turned quickly, almost colliding with Darin, one of the ranch hands. Before she could step away, he grabbed her by the upper arm and dragged her against him.

"Let me go." She pushed hard but couldn't get loose. She had never liked this particular cowboy, but her father kept him on because he was a good bronc buster. He was cocky and conceited, and she had overheard him a time or two bragging about his exploits in town. Although he had made suggestive remarks to her in the past, he had never dared lay a hand on her.

Now, the more she struggled, the tighter he held her. "Yeah, that's it. I like a woman with fight in her." He nuzzled her neck and Sky gagged.

"I'll scream," she threatened.

"Nobody in here 'cept you and me." He reached one hand down and squeezed her fanny. "You sashay around all day in them tight pants, I just bet hoping someone will grab you. Well, today is your lucky day." He pushed her back against the stall. Stormy snorted and shifted, pawing the straw. Sky was more concerned with what Darin was doing than whether her horse got loose.

His hands roamed at will across her back and hips before he loosened his hold enough to get a hand between them.

"Wait. Oh, my, just give me a minute to catch my breath." She gasped as though in pure ecstasy.

Predictably, Darin took a step back, tobacco stained teeth showing in a nasty grin. In the next second, Sky lifted her knee with all her strength and struck him hard between the legs. With a groan, he dropped to the floor.

"Hmm," Sky murmured as she stepped over him, leading her mare out of the stall. "It does work."

"What the hell?" Joe had walked up and now stared at the fallen cowboy, hands clutched between his legs and rolling slowly back and forth. "Is he sick?"

"Not exactly," Sky replied as she led Stormy past him. "Remember that time I accidentally kneed you while we were swimming?"

"Yeah. I couldn't walk straight for a week. What does that have to do wi—?"

"This time it wasn't an accident." Sky could tell the instant Joe understood what she had done, and probably why.

"Why that son of a bitch." He started back to the stall but Sky put a hand on his arm. "I seriously doubt you could do any more damage."

"Oh, I definitely could," Joe grumbled but followed Sky out of the barn. "I'll fire him."

"Daddy probably won't let you, because he's too good with the horses." She stopped and turned in front of him, pressing her palm against his chest. "And especially since we're not going to tell him what happened." She narrowed her gaze. "Right?"

With a sigh, Joe shook his head, then swung up into the saddle. "You really do need a keeper, Skyla Tate."

And you are it today, Joe Dawson. She didn't dare say it out loud, but Sky was very happy Joe was accompanying her. He hadn't tried to kiss her again, darn the man. Then again, they hadn't had a chance. It might seem like coercing, but she was determined to get him alone and explore the feelings he evoked in her with a single glance.

* * *

Joe wasn't in a happy frame of mind as they left the ranch behind. Even if Coop wouldn't fire Darin, Joe would make the cowboy's life a living hell. No one touched Sky that way unless she returned the interest. And he knew for a fact, she did not. He fell behind as she kicked her mare into a gallop and raced across the grassland, a musical laugh floating back to him on the breeze.

She was a beautiful, happy woman, and it shouldn't have surprised him that men would seek her attention. He just didn't care for the way it happened, although apparently Sky had kept it from going too far.

As he rode, he considered his own circumstances. Last night, he finally came to the conclusion that what had been a slight infatuation with Sky when he was nineteen had never fully faded, even when he left the ranch. Now, being around her day after day, watching her work the horses, and seeing how kind she was to his brother made him realize that instead of waning, his feelings had grown.

He still wanted to find his family. He needed to fulfill that promise. But he also needed Sky, some days with desperation akin to a drunk needing his next glass of whiskey. So until he figured out how to balance the two different parts of his life, he would simply enjoy her company, her laughter, and her friendship. Signaling to Critter, he raced his horse to catch up to where she had stopped alongside the creek that ran close to the shack.

"Isn't it amazing?" She turned to him, her smile bright enough to take the gloom from his mood. She stretched out her arms. "All this land, the beautiful mountains, the waters clear to the Rio Grande. Great-Grandpa Tate got a land grant, and every generation since has taken care of it, improved on it, and prospered from it."

Cooper Tate owned thousands of acres, and while Joe wanted a spread of his own one day, he could do with something smaller. Besides which, word had it that the land was being bought up quickly. Even though Texas was the biggest state in the Union, it was fast becoming populated.

And Sky had had the run of it for her entire life, Joe thought. He wasn't jealous, but he wondered if Sky knew just how fortunate she was. It wasn't just the land. She had family, loved ones who looked out for her.

As though she read his mind, she turned in her saddle toward him. "I don't take my life for granted, regardless of what you may think. And I'm trying to give back to those who lost so much."

"The Kickapoo?"

Her chin lifted in defiance. She didn't think he understood what it was like to have everything taken away. But he did, in a way that was impossible to describe.

"Do you really think they're responsible for the raids?" Her bright face shadowed.

Joe gave a look around. "This land's not much good for farming, but at one time it was good hunting ground and now it's not accessible to the Indians. I can see why they would try to regain their freedom and the land that was once theirs. But I'm afraid it will cost them too much in the process."

"That's just not right," she said, then sighed. "I know it wasn't the Kickapoo, but since that's one of the reasons we came out here, you'd best look for tracks while I replenish the shack." She turned her mare toward the building.

Joe didn't care for her to get too far out of his sight. "Don't wander from the cabin," he called as he swung down from Critter.

He squatted to study tracks, barely discernible in the rough ground and sparse grass. Horses, about a dozen from what he determined, had crossed the creek here. He walked along the bank, keeping his eyes to the ground. He found the place where they had crossed back over the creek, but couldn't tell from the tracks if they were shod or not. He rose and stared across the water. Anyone could have crossed here and still been on Double T land until they reached Eagle Pass.

Or they could have walked the creek to some point downstream before exiting on the opposite side. The small section of Circle C land to the southwest, bordering the Rio Grande, had been where the cattle were butchered. And directly across that river was the Kickapoo reservation.

He couldn't tell what had happened. All he could do was suggest to Coop that they keep the cattle closer to the main ranch house. That would work as long as the grass stayed green but when the cattle were moved to higher pastures at the base of the Anacacho Mountains, they would have to send more men on patrol.

He found Sky behind the line shack, picking blackberries.

"Caught you," he said, and she spun around, juice dripping down her chin. He longed to lick the sweetness, and her, especially when she sent him a grin.

"Every year we pick them, and every year I've forgotten how sweet they taste." She dropped a few more into the bucket at her feet.

"You were sitting at the table eating a blackberry tart when you saw me take that loaf of bread off Bonita's window," Joe recalled as though it were yesterday. "You tattled on me."

"I though sure Daddy would do more than holler at you all the way to the barn. I never did understand why he let you stay instead."

"I was just an orphan, and he felt sorry for me." Joe shrugged. "I was happy when he let me work at the ranch instead of turning me in to the sheriff."

"We had some fun back then, didn't we?" Her smile faded as she took a step toward him.

Joe's heart began to pound when she looked up at him with large eyes shimmering with tears.

"You broke my heart when you left." Her bottom lip trembled.

He couldn't help himself. He reached out a hand and gently rubbed his thumb along her lip, feeling her breath against his skin.

"That wasn't me," he said softly. "That was a scared kid trying to keep a promise he had no business making, wanting something he didn't understand."

"And now?" Her tongue peeked out and touched his thumb, shocking them both with the heat that flashed. "Do you know what you want now?"

Joe reached out and pulled her to him, lowering his mouth to hers. "God help me, but I do."

Chapter Nine

Sky surrendered with surprising quickness and Joe took full advantage. Slanting his mouth across hers, he tasted the sweetness of the blackberries, the wonder that was Sky. He couldn't hold back this time, and he needed to be sure Sky understood what he wanted.

"I want to make love to you," he whispered against her mouth. "I need you like I need the air to breathe." He kissed his way across her cheek, nibbled on her ear, and trailed his lips down her satiny neck. He felt her heart beat at the base of her throat, thrilled that it pulsed as rapidly as his.

Sky wiggled closer, pressing her breasts against his chest, moving her hips back and forth until Joe thought he would explode.

"I'm on fire," she panted, returning his attention with her own foray of nibbling kisses down his chest. She popped the buttons of his shirt open and her hot lips were everywhere. She slid her hands inside his shirt and circled his waist. Her tongue trailed heat across his chest to a nipple, laving it before sucking. Joe longed to do the same to her. When she raised a leg to hook it behind his, he'd had enough. He needed to have her spread beneath him and naked for all the things he'd imagined doing to her.

He caught her under the knees and lifted her off the ground, cradling her against his chest. Before she could stammer a word in surprise, he was striding around the shed to the door. The cabin was cool but he couldn't take time for a fire. Besides, they would soon be heating up the small interior just fine. He kicked the door shut behind him.

The slamming of the door brought Sky to a certain stage of awareness, but she was determined not to completely surface. She snuggled her face into his neck, breathing in the scent that was uniquely Joe. Her heart pounded as her breath came in gasps. The wonder of his kisses had been so much more than she had dreamed and she wasn't about to let him stop anytime soon. She wrapped her arms around his neck and held on. When he tried to lower her to the small bed in the corner of the cabin, she clung to him, bringing him down on top of her.

She fought her way back to his mouth, kissing, exploring with her tongue until he finally opened to her and she delved deep. He tasted hot and sweet and mysterious. She moved beneath him, spreading her legs so his hips fit between them. The ache in her nether reaches increased, and she gasped.

"Slow down," Joe whispered urgently. "Sugar, we have all the time in the world and some things do not need to be rushed."

He took her hands and levered them above her head as he leaned on his elbows to look down at her. She had memorized his face all those long years ago, but as her gaze roamed, she noticed differences. He was older, certainly, and the years had carved his features as though by a sculptor's hand, with passion. There was a ruggedness in the handsome angles with tiny lines fanning out from his eyes, more lines bracketing his mouth. The mouth she longed to kiss again.

Though he held her hands, she lifted her head to nibble his chin, rough with a day's growth of whiskers. From there she tugged his bottom lip with her teeth until he groaned as he lowered his head to kiss her again. They rolled back and forth on the narrow bed, neither getting satisfaction—Joe knowing what was to come and Sky longing for the unknown, always just out of reach. Finally, Joe rolled to the side and slid his hand down her shirt front, undoing buttons as he went.

Joe deliberately slowed his breathing as he undressed Sky. She was more than he had ever thought to have, and he wanted to take his time and savor every inch of skin he exposed. She wore a silk chemise beneath her shirt and as he slid his hand over it, his callouses snagged the fragile fabric. He pulled back.

"No, don't stop." Since he still held her hands with one of his above her head, she could do little more than wiggle. It still tantalized him.

"My hands are too rough. I'm too rough for you."

"No," she cried, pulling until he released her. She caught his face in her hands, her thumbs gently sliding across his lips. "You are giving, and gentle. Do you think I want a man with hands as soft as lilies to prove he never did a day's work in his life? I'm Texas born and raised, Joe, and I'm tougher than you think."

"What you are is beautiful," he breathed softly as he bent to kiss her again. He would savor her slowly, for he didn't know what tomorrow would bring, and once he had loved her, she might very well decide she wanted someone with more manners, more money. But for today, she was his, and he proceeded to lavish her with attention.

She laughed nervously as he sat at the edge of the bed to pull off her boots, then his own, but he didn't give her time to cover up. He quickly dispensed with her shirt, his own, then slowly lowered her pants down long tapered legs. He kissed every inch of exposed skin, stopping to nibble behind her knee. He kissed bare feet before trailing his tongue back up one leg. He paused just briefly at the juncture of her thighs, inhaling her female scent, but knowing she wasn't ready for him to taste her. Not yet.

He left his Levi's on although the pressure against his manhood hurt like the very devil. She wasn't ready for that yet, either. Instead, he continued up her stomach, sliding her chemise up until her breasts sprang free. He stopped and stared at the sheer beauty of her creamy skin; the high rise of her breasts; the rosy sight of her nipples, peaked in anticipation. He was not disappointed.

Sucking one into his mouth, he flicked the tip with his tongue as his hand cupped the other. She was full and heavy, just right in his hand. The more he sucked and squeezed, the more she squirmed and moaned. He wanted desperately to ram into her heat, but forced himself to go slowly, knowing she had little if any experience with men.

"Joe?" His name, a litany before, now came out as a question. He raised his head to see her expression of wonder.

"Is there more?" She asked. Her innocent question nearly broke him.

"Oh, baby, we haven't even begun."

Sky had been kissed before and sincerely thought she had some experience with the male species, but Joe was turning her inside out and every nerve in her body vibrated. She ached low in her stomach, a kind of anticipation but for what she did not know. When she looked up at Joe, she saw stars. When he kissed her so intimately on the breast, she thought she would expire from the delicious torture.

And then he had said there was more. She couldn't imagine anything finer than this, but finally gave herself up to the sensations, determined to savor them all. This was what she had wanted, had waited for since the moment Joe had disappeared from her life. When he started to pull away, she circled his waist, determined to hold him close.

"No, don't leave me," she whimpered.

He gave a hoarse chuckle. "I gotta get these pants off before they strangle me."

She rolled to her side when he stood. She knew basic male-female anatomy and the physical ritual of mating, having been brought up on a ranch, but when Joe tugged down his trousers and his male organ sprang free, she was in awe. He was so beautiful. Muscles rippled across his chest and down a flat stomach to his groin. There, within a nest of dark hair, he was stiff and long.

"Can I touch you?" she asked, even as she reached out a hand, but he grabbed her wrist.

"Not this time," he muttered, keeping her hand captive as he lowered to lie beside her on the narrow bed. "If you touch me, I'll explode."

"Is that a bad thing?" she questioned.

He kissed her forehead then hot breath fanned her skin as he chuckled. "No. It would be a good thing any time but now. Now is for you."

He slid a foot up and down her leg then hooked his heel behind her knee, gently spreading her legs. His hands were all over caressing, gently squeezing then soothing but always creating heat everywhere they stroked.

Sky had always laughed when women friends mentioned swooning, thinking the entire idea was preposterous. And yet, as her body trembled and her senses were saturated, she realized if she weren't lying down, she'd be a puddle on the floor.

Her hands roamed freely across his back, feeling the muscles quiver. Emboldened by his groans, she slid her hands down to his buttocks. How different he was from her, she thought. Hard where she was soft, rough to her smooth.

She tried to slide her hand between them when suddenly he turned away, rolling to the side of the bed and sitting up, his back to her.

"Hell and damnation! What am I thinking?" Joe cursed, not at Sky but at himself for letting things go too far. She was Coop's daughter—his boss's daughter—and he was just a cowboy. He had no right to touch her, let alone finish what they had started.

He stiffened, sucking in a harsh breath when he felt her breasts against his back, the heat searing clear through him. She wrapped her arms around him, her hands splaying across his chest. He knew she could feel his heart pounding.

"Let go," she whispered the words close to his ear, her breath like butterfly wings against his skin. "Don't be afraid…just let go."

Afraid? Joe was petrified. Not of what Sky was doing to him with her hands, her mouth and tongue caressing the sensitive skin behind his ear. What had him literally shaking in his boots was the fear that he would lose his heart to her and forsake his quest. And that he could not afford. He still had only one of his family back. He wanted them all.

99

"Please?" Sky would beg if she had to. Though she wasn't sure for what, she inherently knew only he could give it to her. She gently tugged on him until they once again lay side by side on the narrow bed. She found his hot mouth, kissing him, holding him tight until she felt his surrender as he deepened the kiss.

Her legs quivered as he slid a hand down her stomach and between her thighs. All the heat, the fire centered in her very core and she spread her legs, giving herself totally.

The weight of him felt magnificent as he rolled on top of her. She lifted her legs and wrapped them around his waist. When he entered her, she sucked in a breath. He was so big, so hot, the sensations made her lightheaded. There was just a pinprick of discomfort as he steadily pushed deeper. She tried not to tense, but he must have seen something on her face because he stopped with a groan.

"Are you sure?" His voice shook, and she opened her eyes, willing him to look into them to find her answer.

And then there was no turning back. He filled her completely then paused again resting his forehead on hers. She nudged him with her heels, urging him closer still. With a rough chuckle, he pushed deeper then withdrew, again and again.

Each time he meshed his hips with hers, she tightened around him, the heat spiraling through her almost too much to bear. When he gradually increased his rhythm she reached above her, grabbing the bed rails, sure she would fly off into space, so acute were the sensations.

He braced himself on his elbows and caught her face with his large hands. "Look at me," he whispered, his breathing as ragged as her own. She stared into his eyes, the gray gone molten silver with the heat of their passion.

"You are so hot, so tight. I can't hold on. Come with me, Sky. Let me take you to heaven and back." His hips quickened.

And suddenly she was there, weightless, flying through the clouds, her muscles tightening in uncontrollable ecstasy. The sensations shot from her woman's core up her spine and down her legs. She cried out in amazement as he kept moving within her, harder and deeper. Just when she thought she could take no more, he shifted the rhythm, rubbing a little higher, and she came again.

As her muscles clutched around him, he gave a shout, pushed hard and stopped, tucking his face into her neck. His arms quivered around her, his male member throbbed within her. She locked her legs around him to anchor herself, fearing she would fall right off the edge of the earth. She couldn't seem to move, didn't want to move and have this moment end.

"I'm smashing you," Joe said, levering up on his elbows.

Her gaze caressed his sleek body bathed in the light streaming in through the uncurtained window. A light sheen of sweat glistened on his broad chest and she managed to lift her head enough to kiss him, right over his heart. Her head dropped back, and she looked up at him, realizing tears misted her vision.

"Regrets?" He reached up and caught a tear with his thumb and brought it to his lips, making her a part of him.

She smiled. "Never. I've always...." She didn't finish. She loved him, had always loved him, but he wasn't ready to hear that. He had demons to exorcise. When the time was right....

Time? She glanced toward the window, just then noticing the shadows. "Oh, Lordy, Daddy is going to have a fit."

She began squirming, trying to get out from under him but he suddenly tensed and now held her captive.

"You're going to tell him?" His voice was incredulous and his expression was downright dangerous.

She pushed against his chest with both hands but his hips pinned her down. "Good heavens, not about this. It's simply that we've been gone a long time and he'll be wondering what happened to us. Especially with what has happened lately."

She didn't have to explain further. With a curse, he rolled away and onto his feet, grabbing his pants. She dressed as fast as he did, then quickly made the bed. They secured the cabin and saddled up.

As the sun sank they galloped for home. Sky gave the cabin a last glance, her heart singing in remembrance of their stolen time there, then thudding as she wondered what was to happen between her and Joe.

They rode toward the ranch at dusk and right into the middle of chaos.

Chapter Ten

They heard the shots a mile off—rapid gunfire, a pause, then more as they kicked their horses into a run. As they raced toward the ranch, a cloud of dust warned them that riders were coming their way. Joe pulled his rifle from its sheath and glanced over to see Sky doing the same. The area was flat and open with no place to hide, and he hoped they weren't too outnumbered.

It was only when the horses veered off to the left that he realized they were unmanned. While he was relieved, his heart continued to pound with the thought that someone was raiding the Double T and releasing the horses so no one could follow. He bent low, urging Critter to more speed as they raced the final distance into the ranch yard.

"Daddy!" Sky screamed, jumping off her horse before it had fully stopped and running toward her father, who was slumped against the house.

"Do something." She turned back to Joe. "It's Daddy!" Her voice was perilously close to hysteria, something Joe had never heard before.

He cursed himself for not being there when the attack came, but at the same time giving thanks that Sky had also been gone. Taking the porch steps two at a time, he knelt beside Coop. He jerked off his bandana and pressed it against the man's shoulder to stop the flow of blood that stained his shirt bright red.

He looked around. Men were running everywhere trying to catch the few remaining horses and Joe realized nobody seemed to know exactly what to do. He yelled when he saw Patch, his bowlegged gait eating up the ground.

"Patch! Grab a couple of guys and get over here."

"Why isn't he awake?" Sky fell to her knees on the other side of her father. Joe felt for her, but didn't have time to deal with it right now. Someone needed to be in charge.

"Paul, tell Bonita we need her in Coop's room." Two of the men carefully lifted Coop and carried him inside. Sky scrambled to her feet, still clinging to her father's good hand as the men took him away.

"Patch, how many are hurt?"

"Two, boss—Darin and Mick—but nothing bad. Darin got winged and Mick took a lump on the head. I'll see to 'em until Bonita takes care of Coop."

"Seth?" Joe hadn't seen him in the chaos.

Patch shook his head. "We was in the cook house so he's fine." He paused as his eyes drifted to the front door of the ranch house.

"We'll take care of Mr. Tate. You see to the others." He raced into the house, the door slamming behind him. By the time he got to Coop's bedroom, Andy and Matt already had him stretched out in bed and Sky was holding a towel against his shoulder.

Coop was awake and livid. "God damn cowards, running off before I could even get a shot off."

"Daddy, hush now." Sky's lips trembled as she unbuttoned his shirt and peeled it away from his shoulder. Coop hissed, and she gasped at the ugly sight of the gunshot, but when her hands started shaking, Joe gently cupped her shoulders and pulled her away.

"Get some hot water and more towels. I'll do this." He had seen plenty of gunshot wounds in his time and Coop's wasn't fatal. The wound was high on his shoulder and the bleeding had already slowed. Still, he was sure it wasn't an easy sight for a woman, especially the man's daughter.

By the time Bonita came in, he had the wound cleaned. He let her take over and stood by Sky as Bonita packed herbs onto the raw flesh, then wrapped a long bandage over the shoulder and chest.

104

Coop cursed through the entire affair. He refused the tonic Bonita offered and instead insisted on a whiskey. When Joe started to pour some into a glass, he growled.

"Give me the bottle, damn it." He took a swig and then another before Sky pried his fingers off the bottle and set it back on the dresser. "The attack came out of nowhere, right when most of the men were just hanging around the corral and bunkhouse getting ready to eat. I had just gone inside when I heard thundering hooves and a lot of hooting and hollering. I grabbed a rifle and came out on the porch as Indians raced through the yard.

"The men were scattering everywhere, diving to the ground but returning fire. Don't think they expected return fire, so they busted out the horses in the corral and as quickly as they came, they were gone." Wearily, Coop dropped his head against the pillow. His face was pale, and with the loss of blood, it didn't surprise Joe to see his eyes drift shut.

"You're in charge, Joe. Take care of her. She's my most precious possession." With a sigh, he gave in to the effects of the whiskey.

Out of the corner of his eye, he saw Sky flee the room. With a last glance at Coop, Joe turned to follow. He found her on the porch, but when he reached out to touch her arm, she whirled on him, fury in her gaze.

"You are not taking over the ranch, no matter what my father said."

"You little idiot. He was talking about you, not the ranch."

She brought a trembling hand to her mouth and looked at him with tears in her eyes. "He's not going to die, is he?"

"No," he stated emphatically. "No, he'll be fine." He opened his arms and with a cry she fell into them. He held her tight and inhaled her sweet fragrance. He wanted to kiss her, or do more, but overriding that was his guilt for not being here. He owed it to her father to take care of her, and the ranch, so he contented himself with rubbing her back and placing a kiss on the top of her head.

She stiffened in his arms, then pushed away. "Those bastards. I'm going to find them and shoot every last one."

"We can't do anything tonight but the Indians aren't going to be difficult to find. I'll send some men out tracking first thing in the morning."

"The Kickapoo didn't do this. Chief Black Thunder has always been father's friend," she hesitated, then added, "and mine."

"You heard what your father said, Sky. They may not be Kickapoo, but they're renegades, deposed of their land and angry. Apparently, they've decided to fight back."

She shook her head. "No, you're wrong." Tears came again and Joe was helpless to fight her. He tugged her against him again and for now, let her have her way.

* * *

By dawn, Joe had all able bodied men spread out in every direction. He sent two to Fort Duncan and Eagle Pass to report the incident, two more to the surrounding ranches to warn Cazneau and Winstead, and the rest set to tracking the intruders.

Sky stayed by her father's side most of the day, and the last time Joe went in to report, they were having an argument. Coop wanted up and Sky was trying to coerce him into eating the broth Bonita had fixed.

"Don't need any damn soup," he growled.

Joe quickly rattled off his report and beat a hasty retreat.

Late in the afternoon, most of the men had returned. No one had tried to raid the Circle C or the Cross S ranches, for which Joe was thankful. Matt indicated that Fort Duncan soldiers were going to patrol the area, but there was just so far they could go. But it was Andy's report that had Joe's head spinning.

"Disregarding the tracks due west, which you said were probably our own horses, we picked up some tracks further away from the ranch, up north and heading for the mountains." He stopped to take a sip of coffee. Hesitation flickered in the young cowboy's eyes.

"And…?"

"All the tracks—every single one of them—were made by shod horses." Andy shook his head. "This weren't no Indian attack."

"But the men everyone saw?"

Andy shrugged. "Easy enough to stick a feather in your hat and whoop it up. The way the sky had darkened and with everybody running for cover, it would have been hard to identify a body, be him white or redskin."

Joe began to think that Sky was right. In his mind's eye he recalled the chaotic scene when they had arrived at the ranch. When he talked to the men later that night, they described men in buckskin and denim. Not unheard of for the Indians, but more often they were in leather leggings.

He stood on the porch contemplating the men's reports when Matt approached.

"Sorry, boss, but I forgot to give you this when I got back from Eagle Pass." He handed Joe a folded paper, sealed with wax and his name scrawled across the front.

Joe popped the seal and scanned the contents, his heart pounding as he read the note from his Aunt Karah.

I ask everyone who stays here about your kin. A recent boarder, passing through from Carrizo Springs, mentioned seeing a red-haired girl there. I doubt she is your sister, Joe, because, well, he saw her at a place called Sugar's. I am not sure, but from his reference, I gather it is not the place for a young child of fifteen.

Affectionately,

Aunt Karah

Joe sucked in a breath. He knew Sugar's. While he hadn't frequently the whorehouse while patrolling as a Ranger, he had been befriended by its owner and she had been helpful in capturing a few outlaws visiting her girls.

His head ached as he went inside to talk to Coop. He couldn't—wouldn't—leave the ranch until he knew his boss was out of danger, and yet he ached to saddle up and head out that very night. Regardless of his aunt's hesitation that it might not be Mary Elizabeth, he had to go to Carrizo Springs and check it out.

He found Coop in the den, arm in a sling and a whiskey in his good hand.

"Just about to settle down for supper, Joe." He lifted his glass. "Join me in a drink while we wait on Sky."

Joe should have known Coop wouldn't stay in bed to recuperate. He declined the drink and stood, hands braced on the mantle, contemplating the empty fireplace hearth. Coop knew his story, but Joe still found it hard to bring up his family.

"Matt brought a note from Aunt Karah," he began as he turned around.

Before he could say more, Coop waved away his explanation. "You go do what you've got to do. We agreed on that from the very beginning. Paul and I can handle things here."

Joe raised a brow when Coop groaned as he got to his feet. The old man shot him a warning glance as Sky entered the room. She fussed with his sling, then reached up to peck him on the cheek. Coop grumbled but Joe could tell from his expression that he doted on his daughter's affection.

"Where are you going?" Sky questioned, apparently having overheard part of their conversation. "If it's Eagle Pass, I'll ride in with you. I have some things to get for Bonita."

Joe shook his head. He wasn't ready to tell her about his family, but more than that, he needed to know she was close at home where there were more than a dozen men to protect her. He knew, though, if he said that, she would insist on accompanying him just to be contrary. Instead, he said simply, "I have some business to see to."

Sky took her father's arm as he led her into supper, but Joe didn't miss the look of disappointment on her face when he didn't tell her what he was about.

* * *

Joe stuffed clothes and provisions for several days on the trail into his saddlebags. He told Seth he was going to be gone, but not the reason. He knew his brother would insist on going and he didn't want him disappointed if the girl wasn't Mary Elizabeth. They had begun to form a bond in the time Seth had been at the ranch, and he wanted to protect him as much as he did Sky.

The sky was clear and blue, the air not yet hot as dawn broke. He looked back once as he rode away from the Double T. It seemed that he was always leaving, and, where at one time that hadn't bothered him, things had changed. Even with the quest that seemed to haunt his every waking moment, he now carried visions of Sky in his head along with the images of his kin.

It took longer than he would have liked traveling south through Double T land before entering Cross S territory. He camped one night on Southwind land with Winstead's men, who were patrolling to keep an eye on the cattle grazing the open range. It had only been a few days since the raid, and while there hadn't been anything further occurring in the area, men still kept watch every night.

Three days later he approached Carrizo Springs, situated near the Nueces River. Texas was a huge territory and towns were few and far between, but thanks to Joe's time with the Rangers, he knew the lay of the land. Like any other small town, Carrizo Springs had one main street lined with wooden structures housing mercantile, feed stores and the like.

A small, white-washed church stood at the end of Main Street, separated by a patch of dusty brown grass. It was as though the good people of the town wanted to distance themselves from the usual rabble of saloons and whorehouses that habitually sprang up in most towns along with the array of shops.

Yet, unlike some towns where the working girls lived above the saloons, Sugar had established her own house on the opposite edge of town from the church. Gentle lady folk didn't care for the business of prostitution, but again, it seemed to be part of life and just about every town Joe had ever been in had at least a few working girls.

He didn't bother getting a room at the hotel, knowing Sugar would put him up for the night. Besides, he was anxious to find the girl his aunt had mentioned and couldn't have slept, anyway. He strolled down the hall to Sugar's office, knocking on the door before entering. She sat behind a large desk, writing in a ledger. A smile quickly formed as she rose to meet him.

"Why, Joe Dawson, as I live and breathe." She grabbed his hands and stood on tiptoe to kiss his cheek. "I heard you were shot. Whatever are you doing back here?"

As he lowered his weary body into a plush red velvet side chair, she poured him a drink. He rubbed his aching thigh, realizing he had spent too many long hours in the saddle. He took the glass and raised it in salute before downing a large swallow. The strong spirits hit his empty stomach, and he winced.

"Don't say a word until I get some supper ordered." She hurried over to the door and yelled down the hall for a tray.

Joe watched as she returned and leaned against the front of her desk. She was short, only a little over five feet, but she ran her establishment with a firm hand and most men frequenting the house said "yes, ma'am" when talking to her. She was naturally pretty, not overdone like many of the girls in the saloons. Her blonde hair was in a neat upsweep and her dress, a deep blue satin, was fairly modest. It was always good to see Sugar. Early in his years of wandering, she had worked in one of the saloons and staked him to a poker game. At the time, she had told him if he didn't win, he would owe her his soul. Perhaps he had believed her; perhaps he knew, even at twenty, that her sultry eyes and lush curves would never belong to any one man.

Regardless, he tripled her stake that same night, and she used her share of the money to start her own business. They remained friends and whenever Joe came to town, she offered him a hot meal and a clean bed, nothing more.

A knock on the door immediately stopped Joe from explaining why he was there. After the maid put the tray on a side table and left, Sugar motioned him over and they ate, rehashing old times. She wouldn't pressure him to say anything. As with Coop, she was one of the few people who knew his real story and had held his confidence all these years.

When he couldn't eat another bite of the beefsteak, he sat back with a sigh. "You still have that great cook, Maria?"

Sugar smiled. "I keep telling her it's time to retire, but she says there's nothing to do elsewhere when all she's ever done is cook. More than once, those dang cowboys have tried to woo her away, but she likes it here and she takes good care of the girls."

"That's what I came to see you about." Joe decided it was time to get to the point of his visit.

Sugar's eyebrows lifted. "You want my cook, or one of my girls?"

He shook his head. "No, but I am looking for my sister and heard she might be here."

She narrowed her gaze. "If I remember right, your sister would only be about fifteen." When he nodded, she continued, "You know I have rules against anyone that young working for me."

"I know, but…well, she has red hair and a pretty face. Her name is Mary Elizabeth."

"I remember you telling me that," she nodded, then pursed her lips. "I have some young maids and an assistant cook, all color of hair, but no one by that name. Joe, how on earth would she have ended up here?"

Joe's shoulders slumped in defeat. He had been so hopeful. "I guess she wouldn't have. It was just a rumor, and I had to check it out." He rubbed his hands over tired eyes.

Sugar stood. "Come. You need to get some sleep." As she opened the door, piano music drifted upstairs. "It already sounds like it'll be a busy night. Tell you what. I'll visit with my girls and some men in town and see if anyone knows of a young girl by that name."

She tucked her hand into the crook of his arm and led him down the hall to her bedroom. "You can stay here as I'll be up all night, anyway. I'll get George to bring up a tub and some hot water. Wash the trail dust off yourself and sleep. We'll talk again in the morning." She pecked him on the check and sashayed out, leaving behind the faint scent of lavender.

Joe tossed and turned most of the night. He dreamed of Mary Elizabeth snuggling on his lap as a tiny girl, listening to him tell them all stories at night. He saw her taking care of Rebecca, taking over for her when her mother had been too sick to look after the twins and Seth. Then his dreams turned to nightmares as he searched and searched. He'd point to his badge, saying *See, I'm a Texas Ranger*, expecting everyone to tell him what he wanted to know.

He finally fell asleep toward dawn and woke hours later when one of Sugar's girls brought him a tray of breakfast.

"I remember you," she said coyly as she settled the tray on a table. Putting her hands on her hips, she cocked a knee so that her silk wrapper opened to a long leg. "Do you want me to keep you company...while you eat?"

Joe sensed what she was suggesting and politely declined. He ate quickly, shaved and washed, then packed up his saddle bags. He figured he'd check with Sugar once more before heading back to the ranch.

He walked down the hallway and turned the corner, bumping into one of the girls at the top of the stairs. The dim light didn't allow him a good look at her, but she appeared clumsy and rather more plump than the women Sugar normally hired. There was barely enough room on the narrow stairway to maneuver and as he shuffled to get around her, she tripped over his boot. Her weight bumped against his hip as she tilted and began to fall.

"Easy, little lady." He dropped his saddlebags and grabbed, holding her securely as he spun around to brace his back against the wall. When his head cleared from the sudden movement on his bad leg, he released the girl slowly to make sure she had her balance.

"You okay?" He ducked his head and reached out to brush her hair from her face.

Her eyes were wide and frightened as she sucked in a breath and stiffened, backing away from him.

What little light the hallway window allowed glinted off her red-gold locks, reminding him of Mary Elizabeth. It had been so many years. He closed his eyes in resignation as his gut twisted in a hard knot, wondering if every girl with red hair would remind him of his sister. Even so, before he could stop himself, he whispered her name.

"No," she said with a wail, flinging herself away and hurrying down the stairs out of his reach.

In that instant Joe knew. In his heart that voice was Mary Elizabeth's, crying when he had left that night. His bad leg nearly buckled as he raced down the stairs after her. He rounded the corner into the parlor and came up short. Several of the girls lounged in sheer silk wrappers, relaxing after a busy night. But his gaze zeroed in on only one.

He couldn't see her face, but a red-gold head hid behind Sugar.

"Joe, Lizzy. What on earth is going on?"

"Lizzy?" Joe choked on the name. Mary Elizabeth had hated the nickname her brothers had given her. He took a step, his hands shaking as he reached for her, but she cowered behind the madam.

"Mary Elizabeth?" he questioned softly.

All he saw was the fierce shake of her head. Sugar turned toward the girl, blocking his view. She spoke quietly, soothing her hands over the girl's head and finally lifting her chin. Tears streaked down her face and he broke, grabbing hold of a chair to keep his knees from buckling.

His own eyes burned. Her face blurred as he unabashedly started crying, holding out his hand. Still she hesitated, and he held his breath.

"Go on," Sugar said softly.

With a wail, the girl flung herself at Joe, knocking them both sideways. "Joe," she sobbed into his neck as he

113

cradled her in his lap, sitting right there on the floor of Sugar's parlor.

He couldn't speak, couldn't even say her name, so overwhelmed that he had found her. Instead, he just sat there rocking her. Long minutes later she settled down and the crying quit. Still, she didn't lift her head from where it rested against his chest.

When he rubbed a hand down her arm in comfort, he became aware of her womanliness. Her arms were longer, softer. In his mind, she was still only eight, and he had to get used to the idea that she had grown up in his absence. It wasn't until his arm accidentally brushed across her stomach that he realized just how much she had grown up.

"Holy Mother of...." He unintentionally jerked her away from him, for the first time getting a good look at her rounded belly. Before he could question her, she covered her face with her hands.

"I'm so ashamed," she whispered, and he heard the depth of her anguish.

"Shh, baby. No." He didn't know how to comfort her, what words to use that would hide the shock of seeing his little sister huge with child. "Are you married, then, and I never got an invite to the wedding?"

His words only made her cry harder and Joe could only assume there was no husband. He shot Sugar a lethal scowl as she came back through the doorway after shooing the girls out. He opened his mouth to yell at her but a slight shake of her head and he snapped it shut again.

"Lizzy? Mary Elizabeth," she corrected, placing a hand on her shoulder. "Tilly is going to take you to your room while I talk to your brother. All right?"

Joe glanced at the older woman who stood beside Sugar, but he only tightened his hold. "She stays with me." He wasn't about to let her out of his sight, not when he had just found her. And because she had run from him on sight, he wasn't sure she wouldn't do it again.

"Tilly will stay with her." Sugar answered his unvoiced question as she helped Mary Elizabeth stand and Tilly took her by the hand to lead her away.

Mary Elizabeth looked back over her shoulder from the doorway. "You won't go away again, will you, Joe? You won't leave me just because...." Her voice trailed off.

"No way, sweetheart. Not in a million years." His voice cracked with emotion but he waited until she was beyond hearing before he turned the rage consuming him toward Sugar, whom he thought was a friend. He rolled up from the floor and took a menacing step toward her, his fists clenched. Afraid he might do bodily harm—and he had never struck a woman—he swiftly turned and began pacing.

"You let one of those men use my sister." It wasn't a question.

She never lost her composure. "No, Joe. You know I wouldn't allow a man with a girl that young, even though I never knew she was your sister. She wouldn't tell me her last name, only *Lizzy.*"

"Then how the hell did she get...like that?" He flung an arm out, gesturing toward the doorway.

"Would you like some coffee, a whiskey?"

"No, I don't want any damn coffee. I want answers."

"It's not a pretty story."

"There's never been much pretty in my life. Just tell me." Defeated, Joe fell into a straight chair, elbows on his knees, face in his hands. All he could see was his baby sister, whom he had practically raised, her belly swollen with some man's child.

"Judge John Boone brought her to me some months back, just when her condition became apparent."

"I know him," Joe said. "He's lenient on lawbreakers if they can pay him off and I've heard he's rough with the ladies."

Sugar nodded in agreement.

"That bastard! I'll kill him for this."

"I don't know the true story, for though I think what he told me is a lie, I can't prove it and Lizzy refuses to say."

"What?" he asked impatiently.

"She was a maid at their home, and he *said* she had gotten herself in trouble with one of the boys down at the

115

blacksmith's shop. No one in town would take her, of course, because of her condition, and his wife refused to keep her, implying she would disgrace their family, even though she was just a servant."

"Just a...." Red hazed Joe's vision, and it hurt to breathe. How could someone belittle one of his family, regardless of the circumstances?

"But you kept her in a brothel, for God's sake."

"Joe, the man tried to *sell* her to me. What was I supposed to do? If I hadn't taken her in, he would have sold her somewhere else. I didn't know quite what to do with her, but she begged to work here so I let her stay on." As Joe flashed her a fierce scowl, she hurriedly continued. "I really didn't let her work, just the lightest of duties because she insisted, and Maria made sure she ate well to keep up her strength."

"Did the boy ever get questioned?"

She shook her head. "No one would say anything."

"Then I go after the judge." Joe stood, reaching to the floor where his saddlebags and holster still lay. His gut told him the judge was responsible, if not for Mary Elizabeth's condition, then for not protecting her.

Sugar stepped forward and put her palm to his chest. "Judge Boone is the most powerful man in Carrizo Springs, probably in most of West Texas. He owns the sheriff and everyone in town is afraid of him. You can't go up against him."

"The hell I can't. If you recall, I have some powerful friends of my own." Before he had left the Rangers, there was talk of removing several of the area law enforcement and judicial authorities. For Texas ever to become settled, a fair justice system needed to be in place. Judge Boone was just one example why.

"Joe, think about it. You have just found your sister, who is in a delicate condition and feels she has shamed her family. Do you want to get in trouble with the law and perhaps go to jail, or have all that sordid laundry out on the line for everyone to see?"

116

He wanted to deny it, but she was right. "What am I supposed to do? I don't know anything about having a baby."

"Yes, you do. You told me once that you helped bring your brothers and baby sister into this world and practically raised them when you were just a boy yourself." She stroked his cheek and looked deep into his eyes. "You know what to do."

Joe's shoulders slumped as the weight of the world descended on them. Rage surged through him—at Preacher Burke and the Sheriff of Camino for taking his kin, at the unknown farmer for abusing Seth and Joe Horner for almost turning him into an outlaw, for the man responsible for raping his sister. And then he turned his anger on himself for his inability to do anything to change the past.

He rubbed his hands over gritty eyes. As much as he wanted his family back together, he wondered if he had the patience and strength to deal with a brother who thought he was a man and a sister who had been forced to become a woman long before she should have.

He couldn't wish Mary Elizabeth's trouble away and only hoped, as Sugar suggested, that he had the know-how to deal with it. Even so, he needed help, as much as it pained him to ask. If he couldn't shoot the judge right through the heart, there was only one thing he could do.

Chapter Eleven

Joe had been gone over two weeks and Sky was beside herself. After what happened at the line shack, she thought their relationship had changed. She *knew* it had changed and nothing would ever be the same. Every night she curled up in bed, a pillow hugged to her stomach, reliving those precious moments when he had taken her. No, when she had freely given herself to him. He had always had her heart, now he owned her body and soul.

Perhaps that was what frightened her. Something dark remained hidden in Joe's past. She knew he had a brother but felt there was more. No matter what she said or did, he wouldn't explain it to her. Now she wondered if his past had caught up with him and he was gone from her life again.

She pounded the pillow, refusing to accept that. Regardless of what Joe had done or the secrets of his past, she inherently knew he would not have made love to her and then left her. Every day she questioned her daddy, but he either didn't know or wouldn't say where Joe had gone. All she could do was wait, but oh boy, was Joe going to get an earful when he returned.

Uncle William came over one day to make sure all was well at the Double T and to inform them the soldiers had returned to Fort Duncan as there had been no further trouble.

"The captain is still convinced it's the Kickapoo," Uncle William said as they sat at the table enjoying Bonita's hearty meal. "He's keeping his men on patrol along the Rio to make sure they stay put."

"It's not them. You know it's not," Sky protested.

"Now, Sky," her father said, a note of warning in his voice. It seemed he was the only one who believed her, regardless of the original reports about the raiders having shod horses.

She bit the inside of her cheek to keep her thoughts to herself. It was too dangerous for her to try to visit Two Feathers, not with the soldiers so close, yet she wondered how they fared and worried about them.

"Even without the Indi...renegades to worry about," Uncle William continued when Sky scowled, "it's time to get those cattle moved. There's still water in the Rio, but our range has been chewed 'til there's nothing left but dust blowing through the mesquite." That was one of the reasons he and several of his cowboys had come over.

Her father nodded. "We've had some rain, but it's not enough with the numbers we're running. We need to move them north and closer to the Chaparrosa. There's still plenty of water coming down that creek from the Anacacho Mountains. The grass is high, and with only a little over a month before we send them to the railhead, we need to fatten them up. If there's not enough grass in the Oklahoma Territory, they'll lose too much fat before we get them to Abilene. Have you talked to Winstead?"

Uncle William laughed. "He swears we should go east toward the Nueces River. Claims there's still plenty of grass on his land, but the high ridge will be easier on the cattle. It's cooler and there's more cover than just the mesquite and chaparro we have on the range."

"I agree," her father concurred. "I'll have Paul send word to Charles. He'll go along with us, or he'll have to run his herd himself." He chuckled. "And you know that won't set well. Besides, going north now just puts us that much closer to San Antonio."

Uncle William frowned. "Have you thought any more about using the Goodnight-Loving Trail and going to Denver instead?"

Her father shook his head. "The Chisholm Trail is familiar and predictable." He stood, as did William, their voices trailing off as they moved to the den.

Sky sat for a moment longer, her mind not on the fall cattle drive but on the missing Joe. She could only assume he would be back before then, as she didn't think he would leave her father without notice or the help he had come to depend on. Besides, Seth was still here.

Instead of joining the men, she left them to their whiskeys and wandered outside. The evening sky was clear, with thousands of twinkling stars. She stood for a minute picking out a few of the constellations Patch had taught her as a child. The air was hot and still, and although the temperature had dropped slightly, it was a typical Texas summer. The flowers along the porch looked a sorry sight, their blossoms wilting. She took time to pump a bucket of water and pour it over their droopy heads.

"Well, look who's paying a visit," Patch greeted her when she knocked then entered the cookhouse. Dinner was done, and the cowboys had wandered back to the bunkhouse as morning came early on the ranch. Only Seth remained, and she was happy to see him as he made her feel closer to Joe. But one look at his face and she knew he didn't return the sentiment.

"Joe back?" he asked immediately, frowning as he scrubbed one of the cook pots.

He wasn't so much angry as worried. She shook her head.

"Do you know where he went?" The boy stared at her, searching out the truth in her face.

"No, I'm afraid I don't. I thought perhaps you did." She sat at the table and accepted the cup of tea Patch set in front of her. Regardless of the strong, constantly available coffee on the cook stove, she preferred tea.

"Thought maybe he went after…." Seth's voice trailed off, and he turned back to the sink.

Sky looked from him to Patch, who shrugged and shook his head. It seemed no one quite knew where Joe had gone, or why. As much as she tried to pry information out of the youngster, Seth was as closed-mouthed as his brother.

Another two days passed before Joe rode in from the west, whereas he had left going south. Sky watched him from the porch, heart beating rapidly, as he climbed down near the corral . She moved toward the steps, but something in his face kept her from going farther. He looked terrible; a growth of beard covered his chin and even from this distance she could see the shadows under his eyes. In addition, the minute he dismounted, he grabbed the saddle horn to keep on his feet, one hand reaching down to rub his thigh.

Her heart ached to go to him but what could she say, especially with other ranch hands nearby. Shoulders slumped, he never even looked her direction as he slowly limped toward the barn with his horse. If he didn't want to talk to her, fine, but she would let him know she was thinking of him. She entered through the kitchen door and asked Bonita to have one of her boys get the bathing tub to Joe's room and have it filled with hot water.

Bonita nodded with a grin. "I am happy to see our Joe has returned to where he belongs." She had always claimed him as her own, just as she did Sky.

* * *

Joe dragged his weary body up the back porch steps. He was so tired he could hardly see straight and felt like he had ridden to hell and back. It had taken forever, crossing the Southwind Ranch at an angle from Carrizo Springs and heading for Eagle Pass. He had gotten a buckboard and Sugar gave them plenty of blankets to pad the back to make the long ride more comfortable for his sister. Still, they had to camp out along the way, and Joe was on constant guard to make sure they weren't attacked.

For at least part of each day, Mary Elizabeth rode up front with him, asking him hundreds of questions about his life and her brothers and sister. It saddened her immensely when he told her he had only found Seth.

"Not the twins or baby Jessica?" she asked tearfully.

He reached over and grabbed her clutched hands. "Not yet, but I will."

"I'm so very sorry," she continued crying. "You told me to keep Jessica with me but I couldn't." Joe squeezed her hands. "The judge's wife didn't want a child, or children. She only wanted a servant. So the preacher took Jessica away from me."

He reached over and hugged her close to his side. "It's not your fault." *It's mine*, he thought again about not being able to keep his family safe.

And so the days had gone, until they neared Eagle Pass. Mary Elizabeth hadn't told him much about the seven years they had been separated, but her current condition was all that concerned Joe.

"I didn't know we had an Aunt Karah," she said as the town came into view.

"Well, actually, she is my aunt, my mother's sister."

"Oh my goodness, Joe, you can't take me to her. Why, she's not even a relation and...well, look at me." She rubbed her palms across her stomach.

"Sweetheart, she's a kind and generous lady and she will love you and take care of you in a heartbeat. She has a daughter, too, whom I'm sure you'll like, so you'll have company."

"But, but...."

"It'll only be for a little while," Joe tried to reassure her, just as he had Seth. And look how that turned out, he reminded himself. But Mary Elizabeth was a girl, and she didn't belong at the ranch. She needed to be with other women, especially during this difficult time.

It nearly broke his heart to leave her there, even with Aunt Karah, who of course immediately opened her arms to his frightened sister. When he left, she cried openly until Susan gently led her back into the house. Even though Aunt Karah assured him everything would be all right, Joe couldn't help but wonder what he had done in his life to have God punish him and his family like this.

Now, Joe dropped his saddlebags inside the door to his room, finally letting down his guard. His body hurt, his heart ached, and yet he knew he would have to get right back to work in the morning to earn the money he would need to take care of his family.

The steam from the tub finally hit him and he couldn't get his clothes off fast enough, only having the presence of mind to lock the door before he climbed into the hot water. It would be just like Sky, or Bonita, to come looking for him. Sky would be worse.

Sometime later, he woke to the knock on his door, sloshing water as he jerked upright in the tub. The water had cooled, and he had no idea how long he slept.

"Joe?" Sky's voice was hesitant. "Supper is almost ready."

"Go away, Sky. I'm tired."

"You have to eat." She persisted.

"Not tonight." It was all he could do to get those few words out.

"I'll have Bonita's boy bring you a tray."

He rubbed wrinkled hands over his face. He knew she wouldn't let him rest in peace.

"I'll talk to you tomorrow." Her heels clicked down the wood hallway as he toweled off and pulled on his long johns. When he fell face down onto the bed, he didn't hear another sound until morning.

Bright sunlight warmed his face and the normal, everyday sounds of ranch life washed over him when he woke, still face down across his bed. Although a groan escaped when he turned over, there was only a dull ache in the muscles of his thigh, not the tearing pain that usually accompanied long hours in the saddle. Stretching slowly, he rolled out of bed. Regardless of his troubles, it felt good to be back. As he shaved the heavy whiskers off his face, he thought that perhaps getting back to his job as foreman was what he needed.

And then he glanced out the window at the sound of a woman's voice and saw Sky, helping Bonita hang out some wash. Rich brown hair framed her face and her lips tilted into a smile as she lifted her face to the sun. Maybe it wasn't the work he needed, he realized, wiping his face and tugging on a shirt. He ached in entirely different places than when he rode a horse too long.

He had seen Sky on the porch when he arrived last night, seemingly waiting for him to return to the Double T. For an instant, he wanted nothing more than to go to her. Every night when he had been gone, he dreamed of her; of satin smooth skin and breathless sighs. They had shared heated kisses, and he thought again about the gift she had given him. But at the moment, he had nothing to give her in return.

He should never have made love to her, he thought as he jammed his feet into his boots. Should never have taken her innocence. His life was a mess, and whereas Coop had set him to rights when he had been just a boy, it wasn't fair to involve Sky in his troubles until he could keep himself on the right path and finish what he had started so long ago.

Knowing everyone had probably already eaten, Joe bypassed the dining room and went right to the kitchen. He grabbed a hot biscuit with jam and cup of coffee as he headed outside. Since he didn't see Coop, he had a quick conversation with Paul to get caught up on any new activity since he'd been gone. He raised a brow when he heard that Cazneau was at the ranch and that a message had been sent to fetch Winstead from Southwind.

"What's that all about?"

Paul just shrugged. "I can only guess they are ready to move the cattle."

Joe looked around and out toward the west pasture, visible over a small rise from where he stood. In the weeks he'd been gone, the grass had turned brown and now that he thought about it, the range he had driven through was beginning to look parched. If he hadn't had Mary Elizabeth with him and so much on his mind, he would have paid more attention. That was his job.

He set his coffee cup on a stump and headed toward several cowboys working the horses. Time was slipping away. Not only did the cattle need to be moved to better range for the remainder of the summer but before too much longer they would be getting ready for the long trail drive north. Every man riding the trail would need at least five to ten horses, and that meant making sure they were all trained to be good cow herders. His thigh ached with just the thought of months in the saddle.

He didn't see Sky all day and wasn't sure if he was happy about that or not. It wasn't like they had time for a tryst in the hay in the middle of the day. Why should it bother him that she didn't seek him out? Was she mad because he had been gone so long, or that he hadn't told her where he was going or why? It wasn't her business, anyway.

By evening, he was in a grouchy mood and more than once barked orders instead of simply stating what he needed from the men. He was the foreman, damn it, and they should do what he said. Even when he thought that, he knew he wasn't being fair. The men worked hard and deserved his respect. He was the one who had been gone over two weeks, slacking in his duties, and yet they continued to follow his instructions.

This was all Sky's fault.

When he washed up for supper and came into the house, he found William Cazneau, along with Charles Winstead and his son Mason in the den with Coop and Sky. He felt a punch to the gut at how pretty she looked in a ruffled, pale blue blouse and dark skirt. And she was hanging all over Mason Winstead, damn it to hell. He poured himself a drink without Coop's invitation and scowled at the room in general and Winstead in particular.

He listened but didn't participate in the men's discussion. He was just the hired help. He tried to ignore Sky's lilting voice and happy laugh as well, but without much success.

"What do you think, Joe?" Coop asked.

"Beg your pardon, sir, but what?"

"We keep having this discussion about whether to take the Goodnight-Loving or the Chisholm Trail?" Coop raised a brow, probably wondering where Joe's head was.

Joe turned away from where Sky held Mason's attention near the mantle. *He* didn't appear to be paying attention to the discussion either.

"The Chisholm is closer to a rail head, and there's at least three rivers running across it to water the cattle along the way," Joe answered. He hadn't been on a cattle drive in four years, but things wouldn't have changed in that time. "Besides, getting the steers to Abilene is that much closer to the slaughter houses in Chicago."

The dinner bell rang, and the men rose, leaving the discussion in the den. Before Joe could take a step toward Sky, Mason crooked his elbow, and she laid her hand on his arm, giving him a dazzling smile and ignoring Joe as she walked past him.

Joe hardly tasted the beef steak and fried potatoes on his plate. He couldn't believe Sky was so flighty that she would give herself to him and then take up with Winstead. It all just stirred the madness already simmering beneath the surface.

Talk around the table centered on the recent activity at Fort Duncan. It seemed there was more unrest farther north along the Rio Grande near Del Rio. Nobody seemed sure if it was Indians or Mexicans, and soldiers at the fort had been spread pretty thin patrolling the border. Joe tried to follow the conversation instead of thinking about Sky.

* * *

Sky tried hard to flirt with Mason to make Joe jealous, but throughout supper he didn't seem aware of her. He just frowned down at his plate. She wanted to see him last night when he returned, but he locked his door to keep her out. She knew, because she jiggled the knob long after her Daddy had gone to bed.

When Mason's hand touched her thigh beneath the table, she choked, covering her mouth with her napkin when the other men looked her way.

"Sorry," she said, waving the cloth in front of her flushed face. "A bite went down the wrong way."

Her father raised a brow, Joe scowled more than he had already been doing, and Mason laughed, squeezing lightly. To keep from embarrassing herself by slapping him, she quickly excused herself to help Bonita with the pie and coffee for dessert.

Much later, she paced her room, stopping often to press an ear against the door. She still heard the men's voices down the hall in the den. Were they never going to bed? Flopping down before her dressing table, she cupped her chin in her hands, elbows propped on the dark wood and tilted her head this way and that.

Had Joe ignored her all day because he found someone else while he was gone? She was sure during his time with the Texas Rangers he had seen beautiful women; had probably even consorted with them. Had he taken up with one of them again? Wasn't she pretty enough? Since she had given herself to him, was that all he wanted? Her stomach clenched at questions for which she had no answers.

She had no idea what a man thought after making love to a woman. Shouldn't it mean he would marry her and they would live their lives together? Some of the men went into town after payday and caroused with the women who worked in the saloons, but she felt in her heart that Joe wasn't like that.

Giving up on thoughts that were sure to drive her crazy, she began unbuttoning her shirt to get ready for bed. She paused when the shuffling of boot heels stopped near her door.

"Night, sweetie." Her father's gravelly voice came to her through the heavy wooden door. He sounded slightly drunk.

"Good night, Daddy." She held her breath as he moved farther down the hall to his room. She tilted her head and kept listening, finally hearing another set of boots, this time firm and steady. They didn't stop at her door, but she knew it was Joe, whose room was just past hers.

The rest of their guests were in another wing of the house, away from the family rooms.

She quietly heeled out of her boots, undid yet another button on her shirt, and ran her fingers through her hair. In stocking feet, she silently slipped out of her room.

Chapter Twelve

Joe whirled around at the creak of the door. "What in hell are you doing here?"

The slight moonlight filtering past the curtains illuminated Sky in the shadows. Even from this distance he could define the curvy shape of her, the swell of her breasts between her unbuttoned shirt.

Unbuttoned? Joe's heart beat erratically and other parts of him began to throb.

"You can't be here," he choked out as she inched toward him, hips swaying. "Your daddy will kill me."

Her silvery laugh sent shivers down his spine. "Daddy sleeps like a log, especially when he's been drinking with Uncle William."

"Regardless, you can't just—" He never finished as Sky pressed her chest against his naked one and wrapped her arms around his neck.

She tilted her head and covered his lips with her hot mouth and he was lost. He circled her waist with his arms, drawing her closer. When she pressed her tongue against the seam of his mouth, he couldn't help but groan and let her in. Their tongues dueled and he sucked her deeper. She responded by rubbing her hips against his groin, a small feminine moan erupting.

He didn't know where she had learned to kiss like that but it quickly drove him mad. Then he recalled her flirtations with Mason Winstead at supper and red hot anger seared through him. Grabbing her upper arms, he pushed her away.

She immediately pouted and glanced up at him with huge, luminous eyes. He could get lost in those eyes. She placed her palm flat on his chest and her touch washed away his anger.

"I've missed you, Joe. You were gone so long, and no one would tell me where you went or why."

He ran a hand through is hair. "I never saw you the whole day. And you sure didn't appear to have been missing me at supper tonight."

She tilted her head to the side as if in question. "I didn't want to interrupt your work, and I surely couldn't just run up and kiss you in front of all the men." Then a full smile lit up the room. "Are you jealous of Mason?"

"No." His reply was instant.

She twisted free of his hold and moved in again. "Maybe I wanted to make you jealous. After what happened up at the line shack, then you disappear for weeks on end. I didn't know what to think." She hung her head.

Joe reached out and tilted her face to his. He put a gentle kiss on the tip of her nose. "One thing has nothing to do with the other."

"Then what? Why won't you tell me?"

He moved from her nose to her eyes, to her mouth, each kiss soft and gentle. His initial intent of stopping her questions changed to a push for her surrender. "I can think of better things to do than talk."

He took her hand and led her to his bed. When he stumbled trying to toe off his boots, she laughed, turning and pushing him down. "Let me do that." She slapped his knee and when he raised his leg, she tugged one boot off, then the other. Then she reached for the button on his trousers, her fingers sending goose bumps across his stomach. He leaned up on his elbows and watched her, fascinated by the play of emotions that crossed her face.

She tugged off his pants then moved between his legs. With her tongue just peeking out between her lips, she reached a hand out to touch him.

Joe sucked in a breath. "Easy," he hissed when she circled his shaft and squeezed.

"You are so beautiful," she whispered, her gaze drifting up his torso until she held his captive.

"Cowboys aren't beautiful. I've got scars and hair…."

She shook her head. "Your muscles tell me you are strong and not afraid to work hard. Your scars are a sign that you're not frightened of getting hurt helping other people." She lightly ran a finger down the ragged scar on his thigh. "All of this makes you a beautiful person."

"You're the one who's beautiful," he countered, sitting up to see her better. His hands shook as he finished undoing the buttons on her blouse and sliding it from her shoulders. He couldn't believe she was his.

He kissed along the edge of her chemise that concealed her pebbled nipples. Pulling her straps partway down her arms, he captured one breast in his mouth while a hand came up to cup the other. She arched into him, urging him closer.

Joe moved from one breast to the other while Sky ran her hands through his hair and down his back, fingers massaging his shoulders.

"I'm on fire," she panted. "Please, Joe, now." She tried to push him back on the bed but he held his ground.

"We're taking it slow tonight. Sweet and slow…." And then he lost his train of thought as she reached between them and touched him again. With a groan, he pulled her down and rolled her beneath him.

Sky tried to wrap her long legs around his waist, forgetting that she was still half-dressed.

"Wait a second." She pushed him and he levered up on one elbow. She quickly slid her skirt down over her hips, followed by her petticoat. His eyes glittered with anticipation. In the next instant, his mouth was on her, kissing every inch of her skin, lingering at the sensitive underside of her breast.

When he went lower, Sky held her breath. His tongue was hot, igniting nerve endings in all her private places. He stopped at her stomach, tickling her belly button with his tongue before continuing down her inner thigh. He pushed her legs wider, and she opened to him, her face heating when he kissed back up her thigh, very close to her womanhood.

"Joe?" Her hand tugged at his hair and she tried to squeeze her legs together.

"Shh, it's okay, sweetheart. Let me show you." The words were muffled against her skin, but she heard them in her heart.

The minute his fingers delved deep, her hips arched off the bed. Exquisite waves of heat, and shock, raced through her and she whimpered.

"Does that hurt?" His breath was hot against her hip.

She couldn't speak, could only shake her head. When he started to withdraw, she stilled his hand. "No." How could she explain the divine things just his touch did to her?

"More?" He questioned, but she didn't have to answer. His fingers gently parted her folds and then she felt his hot, raspy tongue lathing, his mouth sucking, and she soared.

Joe hadn't realized how sensitive Sky would be, surprised as she quickly climaxed. Even when her inner muscles clutched around his fingers, he wouldn't let her go and continued to suck the tiny pebble of arousal at the tip of her entrance. When he felt her tighten again, he slid between her legs and buried himself in her hot sheath. Her gasp echoed his own.

He stilled, bringing his hands up to cup her face. She looked at him in wonder, and Joe felt that at long last, he had done something right with his life. He kissed her eyes, her nose, before settling on her lips in a kiss as tender as it was intense. Never had he felt this way, and for an instant wondered if he wasn't giving her his heart.

The thought drifted away as he began to rock his hips. It took her little time to catch his rhythm and even when he moved faster, she was right there with him. She grabbed his wrists to hang on, wrapping her legs around his waist to draw him deeper.

She climaxed yet again, and her contracting muscles ignited Joe's own release. Locking gazes with her, he refused to free any part of her from focusing entirely on them, on the ride that had them soaring together across the plains, racing the wind.

When Joe caught his breath, he tried to roll off Sky, but she latched on and refused to let him. So instead, he rolled to the side, bringing her with him, hitching his leg over her hip and cradling her head on his chest. He was still buried deep inside her tight passage, and though they had just finished making love, he felt he could take her again.

"I love you," she whispered into his neck and planted a kiss where his pulse still throbbed.

Joe bit back a groan. Though he had a tender spot for Sky, he didn't know anything about love. He certainly hadn't experienced it before. He thought about feinting sleep but that wouldn't be fair to her.

"I thought you hated me," he countered, remembering the scene at the pond when he first arrived back at the ranch.

She didn't raise her head, but he felt her sigh against his skin. "I hated that you left me three years ago, that I wasn't the center of your world like you were mine. But that's all changed now."

Joe couldn't answer.

"Hasn't it?" This time she did raise her head to gaze at him. He knew what she wanted, and he hoped that his desperation didn't show.

He reached a hand up to brush her hair from her eyes. Trying to be as honest as he could, he said, "I'm just a cowboy, Sky. There are things in my past, things I have to finish. Besides, I have no prospects, nothing to give you."

She drew a circle on his chest around where his heart lay. "All I need is your heart."

Joe knew she already held that in her petite hands. She had probably taken it clear back when he was nineteen and neither of them knew what they were about. Sky flicked a fingernail against his nipple and he swelled again inside her. Rolling back over, he settled between her legs. He didn't have the words she wanted. For the moment, all he could do was give her his body.

Joe's last thought was that he had died and gone to heaven.

"Joe, time to rise and shine!" Rapping knuckles followed in a sharp tattoo that caused both Joe and Sky to jerk upright in bed.

Sky's gaze flew to his face as Joe slapped a hand over her mouth in time to muffle her squeal.

"Sky, girl. We've got work to do." The pounding continued on the door next to Joe's.

Neither of them dared draw a breath until they heard Coop's boot heels echo farther down the hall.

"Oh, good God." She splayed a hand across her bare chest. Joe hurriedly pulled the sheet over her nakedness as he climbed out of bed.

"That was entirely too close," he said, jerking on his pants. "We can't do this again."

She followed him out of bed and began to dress, more slowly than he because she kept staring at him. His muscular body was not without flaws, she thought as he grimaced while balancing on his wounded leg. His hair was too long and rather shaggy, and a shadow of beard darkened his cheeks. But he was hers and she couldn't believe how wonderful making love to him had been. And to sleep in his arms was pure heaven.

He bent to tug on his boots, and she longed to rub her hands over his backside. More than that, she would have given anything to fall back into his rumpled bed with him on top of her.

Instead, she finished buttoning her blouse. "I'm a woman grown, Joe, and my daddy really doesn't have anything to say about my actions."

Joe shook his head in disagreement. "You are his daughter and you live in his house." He stomped on his other boot. "And he has a gun strapped to his side more days than not."

She looked at him in shock. "Well, he certainly wouldn't shoot me just because we made love."

"It's not you I'm thinking would get a bullet."

She watched as he strolled to the door, jerked it open, then slammed it shut again. Turning, he gave her a look that she had no idea how to interpret, but before she had time to take a breath, he was back in front of her. Grabbing her around the waist, he pulled her against him as his mouth captured hers in a searing kiss. Just as abruptly he turned her loose.

"Make sure the hallway is clear before you go prancing back to your room."

And then he was gone, leaving Sky staring at the door while her heart refused to slow down to a normal beat.

He hadn't returned her confession of love last night, she recalled as she slowly pulled on her skirt. She shouldn't have expected he would. But when she licked her lips, still tasting him, she smiled. He might not have said the words, but his actions told her the truth.

Peeking both ways in the hallway, she hurried to her room, quickly washed up and donned fresh clothes. She was only minutes behind Joe, but he had already eaten and left the house by the time she entered the dining room. Her father and his friends lingered over coffee, and from the gist of the conversation, they had reached an agreement as to where to move the cattle.

"It shouldn't take more than a week to get all the cattle up to the foothills. The valley is protected, and will act as a natural corral ," her daddy said.

"Still a good idea to have the herd looked after by our boys," Uncle William replied.

Charles Winstead concurred. "We sure can't afford to lose cattle this late in the season, and I don't trust that the soldiers can keep those renegades confined."

Sky started to object, but her daddy coughed loudly, catching her attention. He gave her a wink.

"Once we get the herd moved, we'll divvy up the watch," he said. "I'll have Patch put some grub in the chuck wagon and set up camp near the Chaparrosa Creek. Even if the boys rotate in and out, we can't leave them out there with hard tack and jerky."

"Let's get moving," Uncle William said. "It'll take a couple of days for our boys to get those steers rounded up and headed north. We'll meet there." He, Charles and Mason nodded at Sky and left.

She had made a point of not sitting anywhere close to Mason and hadn't looked him in the eye, but somehow she felt his gaze on her. Did she look different? Could anyone possibly guess that she had spent the night with Joe? Feeling her cheeks warm with the idea, she switched her thoughts.

"I'll ride with Patch in the chuck," she said as she nibbled on a fresh biscuit spread with jam.

Her father shook his head as he stood. "It's hotter than hell this time of year, darlin'. There's no sense you being out there."

He came around the table and kissed the top of her head. "Stay here and help Bonita with...something."

She couldn't believe he said that. "Daddy!" She jumped up and followed him out of the room. "You're going and your shoulder isn't healed."

"I'm fit as can be." He strolled off the porch toward the corral , waving his arm in the air to prove his point, and leaving Sky fuming.

Sky was partially pacified that evening when she heard that her daddy and the Double T crew wouldn't leave for a day or two. That meant Joe would be here, even if he hadn't shown up for supper. She squirmed through the meal, then made excuses to her daddy instead of settling with him in the den for a game of chess. As the night quieted, she paced her room. If she only had a few days before Joe left yet again, she wasn't about to waste them sleeping.

Chapter Thirteen

Two days later, her father, Joe and most of the cowboys left the ranch. Patch had headed out the day before to set up camp at the base of the Anacacho range. Joe's brother, Seth, went with Patch, leaving no one with whom she could visit. She had argued again with her father about going, but for the first time that she could remember, he actually became angry with her insistence. Not wanting to upset him further, she pursed her lips and held her peace.

Even though it was barely dawn, heat waves shimmered in the distance. It hadn't rained in weeks, and the pastures close to the ranch were nothing more than dried grass and tumbleweeds. While she would never admit it, perhaps she was better off staying home instead of enduring the hot, dusty conditions on the trail.

A few men stayed behind to tend the remaining horses and see to the protection of the ranch, but since one of them was Darin, Sky would steer clear of the barn and corrals.

Not wanting to retreat into the silence of the house, even if the cool interior of the adobe provided relief from the heat, Sky sat on the porch swing and stretched out her legs. She closed her eyes and pulled up memories of the past nights. She had impatiently waited for her father to retire before sneaking into Joe's room. He had launched an initial protest, but it only took a few heated kisses before he willingly opened his arms to her.

Each night brought a fresh awakening of the woman within. He taught her how to pleasure him, and in return, he took her to the heights of ecstasy again and again. She hadn't known about the rapture she could find being on top with him buried deep within her. She had ridden him as he bucked like a wild horse, sending her soaring.

In the aftermath, he held her close, her head on his chest as she listened to his heart thunder. They didn't talk, although there were still questions she wanted to ask and things she wanted to tell him as she dreamed about a life together. Instinctively she knew he didn't want to hear any more proclamations of love, and so she kept the words in her heart.

The back door slammed, jarring Sky from her daydreams. As long as she was stuck here, she might as well do something useful, she thought, pushing to her feet and rounding the side of the house. Bonita was out in the garden, pathetic sight that it was. As much as they tried to keep the vegetables watered, the summer heat wilted all but the hardiest of plants.

"Might as well dig up the rest of the potatoes and turnips," Bonita stated as she bent over with a short-handled shovel. Sky joined her and together they filled one bushel basket then another.

"Paul will get these to the root cellar," Bonita said as she stood, rubbing the small of her back. "He maybe wanted to not work so hard, but he's driving me loco wandering around the house. I should have chased him out with a broom and sent him with the rest of the men. A few days on the hard ground would make him appreciate my bed."

Sky knew she didn't mean her harsh words. She always felt Paul and Bonita were family, not employees of the Double T. They had the kind of relationship she wanted—love, friendship, family. They shared a special bond that grew deeper as the years went by. Her father and mother had also loved intensely, and Sky had feared losing him when her mother died.

That was how she felt about Joe, if she could only make him see. She wanted to give him everything she had; everything she was. And perhaps if she wished hard enough, he would learn to love her and to trust her with his secrets.

Late in the night, she awoke with intense cramps. Swearing, she got up to take care of the problem. She hated her monthlies and often cursed being a woman, even after her mother explained her bodily processes the first time her courses came.

"If not for the way women are made, there would be no procreation, no babies," Mama had told her.

"I don't want to have babies," Sky had stated emphatically at the time. "I want to run the ranch and raise horses."

Now she curled on her side in bed and thought about having a child of her own, about having Joe's child. Her emotions soared at the idea and just as quickly plummeted. She wasn't having his baby, and if she thought rationally, that was probably for the best. She would never try to trap him with a child, and would only ever marry for love. At the moment, Joe didn't seem inclined to give her his heart.

* * *

Joe tossed and turned on his bedroll, cursing the hard ground, the heat lingering long after the sun had set, and his life in general. He thought of Mary Elizabeth and her predicament and hoped she fared all right. He hadn't told Seth about finding their sister yet, but he couldn't put it off for long.

Overriding his thoughts of family were images of Sky as he had left her that last night at the ranch. She had lain naked on his bed, moonlight bathing her skin, and the image had turned his body hard as a rock even though they had just finished making love for the third time.

His body now responded to his thoughts, and he reached beneath the light blanket to adjust his trousers. He couldn't get her out of his mind. She gave herself so freely to him and had been eager to learn everything about pleasing him. Each time they loved, a little more of his heart opened until she filled it completely and he knew there would never be another for him. He just didn't know what to do about it when there were so many other things he had to finish.

She owned his heart—of that he was sure—and he was honest enough to realize it was more than just the physical ache to be buried inside her. If the constant thoughts of her, the need to be with her and to hear her voice, the urge to protect her at all costs, meant he was in love, then he guessed he was smitten. But would she understand his need to find his family? And if he could locate the remainder of them, would she accept them into her life along with him?

Knowing he would get no sleep, he struggled to his feet, stomped into his boots, and went to relieve the night watch. He cursed the fact he had told Coop he would stay out with the herd for the time it took the other ranchers to arrive with the remainder of the cattle.

* * *

Sky was beside herself and while she stormed around the kitchen, Bonita nodded and murmured in Spanish. Sky understood enough to know she was offering sympathy, but it wasn't enough.

"Why did daddy let the others come back and not Joe?" The majority of cowboys had returned to the ranch, but Patch, Seth, Joe, and her father remained out on the range. Even though she understood the need to have someone out there with the cattle, why did it have to be Joe?

Maybe he didn't want to come back. Maybe he was tired of her and didn't want to tell her. Maybe....

"Augh!" She spun around and practically ran Bonita down as the petite woman moved around the counter, rolling out pie crust.

"You are in love, but you will make yourself sick if you do not quit worrying," Bonita said as she patted the crust into a pie pan, seemingly unconcerned with Sky's dilemma.

"I'm not in love...." Sky started to deny what she knew was the truth as Bonita raised a brow. The woman had always known things even without Sky telling her.

"Well, if I fell *in* love with him, I can certainly just fall *out* of love." She pouted.

"Si," Bonita agreed.

Sky fell into a chair, deflated. "I can't. I've loved him all my life. Why can't he see that and love me back?"

"Men, they have minds of their own. They do not see love as we do."

"Then what am I to do?" Sky watched as Bonita put the pie in the oven and then began to clean up.

"Find something to keep you busy so you not think about him all the time."

Easier said than done, thought Sky. The garden was finished; the ledgers her daddy let her keep were balanced. She had no one to talk to except Bonita.

She jumped up. "I'm going to town to see Susan. Besides, the trail ride starts before long and Patch will need plenty of supplies, so I might as well get them."

"You cannot ride to Eagle Pass alone," Bonita admonished.

"All right. You and Paul can go with me. We'll take the buckboard for supplies and I'll ride Stormy." What she didn't say was that she would send the two of them back with the supplies and she would stay in town a day or two with her friend. It would serve him right if Joe returned and found her gone.

There would be enough time to get to town and load supplies before dark, but not return, so when she saw Paul, she bribed him with a night in the hotel with his lovely wife. He eagerly agreed to harness the buckboard while Bonita's pie finished baking.

Sky threw a few things in her saddlebags, grabbed her rifle and ammunition from the rack in the den, and hurried to the barn to saddle Stormy. Paul also had a rifle under the buckboard seat when they left the ranch. She didn't expect trouble, but one didn't leave the protection of the ranch without a weapon. There were wild animals and snakes, along with the stray person or two, always drifting through the area.

The ride into town was uneventful and the closer they came, the more excited Sky grew. For a small West Texas town, Eagle Pass bustled with new construction and people. Used to the cowboys on the ranch, Sky soaked in the colorful dresses of the ladies and the carriage or two that were so different from the standard buckboards. She even glanced covertly at the few saloon women in their frilly dresses and matching parasols. She knew many men preferred those fancy ladies and wondered about getting a new dress. While Joe definitely realized she was a woman, she wondered if he would prefer that she dress the part. She would have to ask Susan Morgan.

She had known Susan all her life and longed to confide in her friend. Hurriedly handing over her supply list to Thom McGuffy, she gave instructions to Paul to return in the morning with the buckboard. Paul would see to the horses, so she grabbed her saddlebags and hurried down the boardwalk to Karah Morgan's boarding house.

"Sky, what a pleasant surprise." Susan immediately enveloped her in a hug after opening the door.

"I hope I'm not intruding," Sky said, stepping into the parlor and noticing several men sitting there, some reading while others played cards.

"Of course not," Karah Morgan added to her daughter's protests, hugging Sky in turn. "We've just finished supper, but there's some left on the stove if you're hungry."

"Come." Susan took her hand and led her down the hall to the kitchen. "We'll have some tea and talk. I hope you plan to stay, for I haven't seen you in ages and there's so much to catch up on."

"Everyone is out on the range, moving the cattle to greener pastures." Sky sat and accepted the plate Karah handed her. "I couldn't stand being there alone." She didn't mention hating to be there without Joe. That was a story she would share with her friend later.

"Why didn't you go with them?" Susan poured them each a cup of tea and sat across from her. "You were never one to be a house flower."

Sky looked across at her pretty friend who had always favored frilly dresses over the denim jeans and plaid shirts that Sky habitually wore. Susan wore her long hair in a fashionable bun and Sky kept hers short. They were as unalike as any two people could be but had become friends in grade school when Sky knocked Bobby Calhoun down for taking Susan's lunch pail. At that time, they lived in town while her daddy built their ranch house.

"Daddy said I was to stay home and help Bonita." She frowned in remembrance.

Susan laughed. "Oh, I'll bet that went over well."

Karah excused herself when a feminine cry came from the back room. Sky didn't think much about it as Susan kept talking. The boarding house catered mostly to men travelling through, but Sky didn't doubt Karah had a woman boarder now and again.

After Sky finished eating, Susan grabbed a bottle of wine and with a finger to her lips, she waved Sky to follow. She snatched up her saddlebags and tiptoed down the back hall to Susan's room. The boarders all slept upstairs, which was probably a good thing, because Susan and Sky sat cross-legged on the bed, drinking wine and telling secrets until late in the night.

"So are you going to marry Bobby Calhoun?" Sky asked, surprised, and yet not, to hear that the onetime bully now courted her friend.

Susan dreamily smiled. "In the spring, when Mama's garden is in bloom." She reached over and grabbed Sky's hand. "You will stand up for me, won't you?"

Sky nodded, happy for her friend. Really she was. But here she was, twenty years of age and not married. Most of the girls their age were married and had children. At least Susan had a beau.

Susan easily read her face. "What's wrong?"

"Joe Dawson's back."

Susan didn't act surprised. "I know. I didn't see him at your birthday party, but he's been here to see Mama. Did you know she is his aunt, on his mother's side?"

Sky was surprised, totally taken aback that Joe hadn't told her. "I didn't think he had any family except Seth."

"Why, of course he does. He has Mama and Seth and…." She paused. "Wait a minute." She narrowed her gaze and Sky knew she could read everything on her face.

"Oh, my goodness. How could I forget how infatuated you were with him when he first came to the ranch? And now he's back, so…?"

Sky told her friend everything. Somewhere in the middle of the telling, Susan poured them more wine, but she didn't interrupt. Her eyes grew wide when Sky said she had confessed her love to Joe.

"And he didn't say it back to you?" she finally asked when Sky grew silent.

Sky shook her head.

"Not even when he took your virginity?" Susan tried to sound shocked but Sky heard something else in her voice.

"Are you terribly disappointed in me for not waiting until I married?"

Susan giggled. "Heavens, no. You always were more daring than me. Here I am engaged and I can't get Bobby to do more than, well, not that anyway. Is it wonderful?"

Sky couldn't help but sigh. "It is the most wonderful feeling in the world. Every time is better than the last."

"Every time? You mean it happened more than once?"

"Once we started, it was hard not to want him all the time." Sky's eyes filled with tears. "I really do think he loves me, but there's something in his past that haunts him. He won't tell me what it is, even though I ask." The wine made her morose and more tears came, obscuring her vision so that she didn't notice Susan's frown.

"Things have a way of working out," she said cryptically, taking the tipping wine glass from Sky's shaking hand. "I think we've had enough for tonight. Mama will be in here after us if we don't settle down to sleep."

Sky was tipsy enough to allow Susan to help her undress and don her nightgown. She slipped beneath the covers and was asleep before Susan joined her in the big feather bed.

Chapter Fourteen

"We should tell her," Susan's voice carried to Sky as she walked down the hall toward the kitchen.

"It is not our business," Karah replied in agitation.

"But she loves him," Susan's heartfelt reply made Sky wonder who they were discussing.

"Good morning," she mumbled as she entered the doorway. Both Susan and Karah looked guilty, but maybe she imagined it. Her head was fuzzy from the wine she had the night before and her stomach roiled as if it would heave at any moment.

"Hello, dear," Karah chirped cheerfully.

Sky winced. She really should have known better than to drink so much. She made her way to the table and gingerly sat. Susan put a large glass of water in front of her.

"Drink this. It will help your head."

Sky had the glass half gone when she heard a cry from the direction of Karah's bedroom. Karah hurried out of the kitchen and Sky looked to Susan in question.

Susan wouldn't meet her gaze. "One of the boarders is…indisposed," she murmured. "Mama thought she would be better off down here."

It was unusual for Karah to give up her room for a boarder, Sky thought. Before she could form a question, Karah hurried back.

"Where is Timmy? You said he would be here right away."

"Mama, I left a message with Timmy's mother and she said she would send him straight away." As she spoke a knock sounded at the back door and Karah hurriedly opened it.

"Ma'am." The youngster tugged off his cap as he nodded at Karah, then at Susan and Sky. Timmy was the preacher's son and was about Seth's age.

She wondered what was going on, but didn't feel it her place to ask, so she quietly continued sipping her water.

"Timmy, I need you to ride out to the Double T and fetch Joe Dawson. Do you know how to get there?"

The mention of Joe's name brought Sky to attention. "He's not at the ranch. He's out in the north pasture foothills."

"Oh, dear. That's even farther, and we need him right away." Karah twisted her hands in worry as yet another cry sounded from the back room.

"What is going on? Can I help?" Sky stood, wobbled, and sank back into her chair.

"You're in no condition to ride," Susan said. "Timmy, do you know how to get to where Joe is?"

"Yes, 'um," the youngster nodded. "My paw let me go out and watch the round up last spring."

"Well, get on your way and be quick about it," Karah instructed. "Tell Joe to get here as fast as he can." She drew a bowl of water from the pump at the sink, grabbed two fresh towels, and disappeared through the doorway to her room.

Timmy scurried out the back, leaving Susan and Sky, who tried to make sense of the happenings. When Susan looked at her helplessly, she decided to find out for herself. Normally she wouldn't interfere in another's business, but somehow this concerned Joe.

She stood, bracing herself against the back of the chair until her head stopped spinning, then made her way toward the back bedroom.

The sight of the young woman lying on a cot in one corner of Karah's room rocked what was left of her composure. Her back was to Sky, and all she saw was her small form and a long braid of bright red hair, but she couldn't shut out the cries of pain.

She hurried over to the cot. "I can do that," she said to Karah as she dipped a cloth into the bowl of water.

145

"This probably isn't something you should see," Karah commented, "not being married."

But Sky was close enough to get a good look at the woman and she gasped. "Why, she's just a child, poor thing." At her voice, the girl turned, striking her speechless. From the girl's tear-streaked face and soft rounded cheeks, Sky couldn't think her to be more than fifteen or sixteen, yet her belly was swollen with child.

"Oh, dear God," she whispered, not wanting to frighten the girl more than she already appeared to be.

"Who in the world…?" she started to question and then saw the silver concho hanging on a thread around her neck. "What does Joe have to do with this?" She turned and whispered to Susan, who had come in behind her.

Susan hesitated, glancing first at the girl, then her mother, before finally resting her gaze on Sky. "She is Joe's—"

"Joe's?" Sky interrupted with a shriek, which she made no effort to muffle. She looked back at the cot, slapped a hand over her mouth and ran from the room. She barely made it out the back door before depositing the contents of her stomach in the dirt. She continued to heave even after her stomach was empty, gasping for breath between the convulsions.

Blindly, she stumbled out the gate and into the trees that lined the back edge of town. When she was far enough away from the boarding house not to be seen, she sank to the ground behind a tree and began to cry, great heaving sobs that tore at her heart. When she thought she had no more tears, she leaned her head against the rough bark of the tree.

All the secrets Joe harbored—the years he was gone from the ranch—she would never in her life have thought he was married and was about to have a child. Her heart broke knowing he had lied to her.

It had all been a lie—the tender lovemaking, the heated kisses. The longer she sat there, the more fury rose within her at his deception. And while she might think she should have had a declaration before giving herself to him, she

146

wasn't about to take the blame. *He* was the one with a family. *He* was the one who had deceived them all. How *dare* he take what only she could give and then trounce on her heart this way.

She couldn't go back and face Susan, not after what she had told her friend last night. She began crying again, the tears sliding silently down her cheeks. Emotionally drained, she curled into a ball, tucked her arm beneath her head and closed her eyes.

Sky didn't know how long she had lain there, but thundering hoof beats roused her. She peeked cautiously around the tree just in time to see Joe vault from his horse and race for the house, followed closely by Seth. All the anger and grief over his deception rose in her again, and she jumped to her feet. There was no time like the present to confront the low-down, two-timing cowpoke.

* * *

Joe barged in the back door of Aunt Karah's without knocking, glancing wildly around in search of Mary Elizabeth. Although Timmy hadn't told him why Karah had summoned him, he knew in his gut it had to do with his sister.

A feminine scream echoed through the doorway to his right, but as he turned in that direction, Susan emerged and blocked his way.

"You got here fast, Joe," she said as she shuffled back and forth in front of him to keep him in the kitchen.

"We were already on the way to town when Timmy intercepted us. What's going on?"

He reached for Susan's arms to move her out of the way when yet another shriek came, this one so full of pain, Joe's knees buckled.

Seth scooted a chair under him before he hit the floor. "Mary Elizabeth?" His throat felt raw, and he swallowed, trying to get his head around what he knew was happening.

Susan confirmed it. "Her time is here, although she fears it's too early for the baby."

Mary Elizabeth screamed again.

"Jesus Christ! Isn't there something you can do?" Joe rubbed his face with shaking hands. When his vision cleared, he noticed Sky standing stiffly at the back door, arms crossed over her chest and shooting daggers at him.

He started to reach a hand out to her, but was paralyzed when another cry reached him. This time, he recognized not the sound of a woman giving birth, but the cry of a baby. Sometime later, Aunt Karah came out of the room and smiled when she saw him.

"You can see her now, if you want."

Joe shot out of his chair, all else forgotten as he stepped into the room. Soft afternoon light filtered through the curtains and Joe's gaze swept over Mary Elizabeth, looking for signs of pain. Instead of his baby sister, he saw a young woman's face aglow with happiness.

Joe knelt by the cot, taking his sister's hand in his. "Aw, sweetheart. This is all my fault. I should have tried harder to stay with you all. I'm so sorry you had to go through this."

"No, Joe, look." Mary Elizabeth folded back the blanket covering the bundle at her side and Joe stared in wonder. "Isn't he beautiful? I think he looks like a Dawson, don't you?" Before he could form a coherent thought, she continued. "I want to call him Joey, if that's all right with you."

If Joe hadn't been so enthralled with the miniature person wrapped in his sister's arms, he would have noticed the gasp from the other side of the room, and the hurried footsteps as someone left. Instead, he carefully picked up the bundle and rocked back on his heels as he turned to his brother.

"Joey, I'd like you to meet your Uncle Seth." Seth's gaze flew from the baby to Mary Elizabeth's face.

He had told Mary Elizabeth about Seth, but not the other way around and it took a minute for Seth to recognize his sister and realize the connection.

"Holy shit!" He exploded, but Joe wasn't about to jump on him at that particular moment. The three of them laughed and a weight lifted from Joe's heart that he'd carried for the last seven years.

While Mary Elizabeth and Seth peppered each other with questions, he gazed down at the precious gift he still held. He had helped Rebecca bring his brothers and sister into the world, but it hadn't been the same. He gently touched the satin soft skin of Joey's cheek and gave his silent pledge that he would forfeit his life before any harm came to this innocent.

It wasn't until Aunt Karah shooed them out of the room so Mary Elizabeth could feed the baby and rest that Joe realized Sky wasn't in the kitchen.

"Where did Sky go?" he asked Susan.

Timmy, who had stayed in the kitchen eating cookies, piped up. "She went tearing out of here like a wild steer was chasing her tail." He grinned at the image, but Joe frowned.

"Why would she leave?" He turned to Aunt Karah.

She bit her bottom lip in thought, but instead of answering, she asked a question. "Joe, you haven't told her about your family, have you?"

"Well, no, except for Seth since he's out at the ranch now. What does that have to do with anything?" Even as he asked, a knot formed in his stomach.

"Honey, she doesn't know Mary Elizabeth is your sister. I fear she thinks there's a more…intimate connection between you."

"What?" Joe sputtered. "That's crazy. Why would she…?" His voice trailed off as he thought back over the past few hours and how it would look from Sky's viewpoint. His ignoring her in favor of Mary Elizabeth, his visible anxiety over her predicament, what he had said about it being his fault.

"Well, hell." He muttered, forgetting to beg his aunt's pardon as his concern turned to fear that in her anger, Sky would try to get as far away from him as she could. He grabbed his hat and stormed out, banging the door hard enough to shake it on its hinges.

"I'm coming with you." Seth dogged his heels.

"Stay with Mary Elizabeth." Joe grabbed the reins and mounted Critter in one swift movement.

"Ain't staying in no house full of women."

Joe didn't take time to argue, instead turning his horse down the main street of Eagle Pass, stopping first at the stable to see if her horse was gone. When the blacksmith said she had headed out of town directly east, Joe took a breath, thankful she hadn't gone south toward the Kickapoo reservation. While she might be on friendly terms with the tribe, he would be an unwelcome intruder.

"Dawson!" He hadn't gotten far when Sheriff Warren hailed him. Anxious to pick up Sky's trail, he slowed his horse before the sheriff's office but didn't dismount.

"Sheriff." He gave a curt nod.

"Heard the Horner gang is close by, probably up to no good. Before they cause trouble here in town, I'm rounding up a posse and bringing them in. You can ride with us."

Joe glanced at the group of men milling around. "Looks like you've got yourself enough men, Sheriff. Besides, I told you I'm not with the Rangers anymore." Then it hit him. "Where'd you say they were?"

"Didn't say, but I figure they're camped out near Indio Creek."

Son of a bitch, Joe thought. Sky could be riding right into a nest of outlaws. He wheeled his horse in a tight circle as he yelled at the sheriff. "Sky Tate is riding to the ranch. I'm going after her and hope to God she doesn't run into Horner. Get your damn men together and catch up with me, fast!" He took off at a gallop, figuring Seth could keep up or not; it didn't matter. All that mattered was getting to Sky before the temper that had her running off landed them both in a pot of trouble.

* * *

He should have known better, Joe thought sometime later, as he and Seth slithered forward on their bellies behind an outcrop of mesquite, watching the horror unfold in the small clearing beyond.

150

"Damnit to hell and back," he cursed as he watched Sky struggle against her captor. "You stay here. I'm going in. If all hell breaks loose, you get Sky and ride like the devil back toward town. The sheriff should be at our backs, but just in case, you'll run into him and have protection."

When Seth didn't answer, Joe turned his head to where Seth gazed wide-eyed, holding his breath.

"Seth! You hear me?"

He blinked, then turned and nodded, but Joe saw the fear on his face.

"He can't hurt you anymore," he said softly, referring to Seth's time with the gang. To reassure his brother, and possibly himself, he reached over and squeezed his arm. He stood and made his presence known only when he had weapons in both hands.

"Let her go." His deadly voice carried across the expanse separating him from the outlaws.

The tallest of the group spun around, his weapon already in his hand.

"That's a good way to get yourself killed, mister."

Joe slowly moved forward from his hiding place, careful to keep one gun trained on the outlaw holding Sky, the rifle aimed in the general vicinity of the other two men.

"Joe," Sky breathed, barely above a whisper.

"Joe?" Horner raised his gun higher. "The only Joe I heared of, 'sides myself, is that Ranger, Joe Dawson."

Joe eyed the odds, thinking fast. He hoped Seth had his rifle trained on the group. He didn't count on the sheriff getting here in time.

He would have to bluff. "Dawson, hell, you think I'd run around the country using that as my real name?" At their questioning look, he continued. "Any of you go by your real name?"

The three men took a minute to eye each other before looking back at Joe.

"I go by Joe, and if any fool wants to think it's Dawson, then that could very well be their problem." To add credence to his story, he shrugged. "'sides, I heard

151

Dawson got himself killed in a shootout nigh on to three weeks ago."

While the outlaws might have believed his story, the one holding Sky seemed suddenly to remember her mention of his name.

"So how's it that this little filly knows you?" He spoke as he tightened an arm about her waist, pulling her closer in front of him and nuzzling her neck. Sky squirmed and tried to stomp his foot, but he just laughed.

Joe saw red. He clenched and unclenched his jaw, bringing his temper under tight control before answering. *Never give anything away*, he remembered Captain Armstrong saying on more than one occasion. *Act like you have the cavalry at your back.*

"She's riding with me, that's how. Wandered off while I made camp."

"Well now, maybe she decided to look for a better *provider*." He gave a raucous laugh.

"She's mine 'til I say otherwise." Sky was shaking, and it was not fear, but anger. He laid it on even thicker. "She ain't got no say in the matter."

"If she's yours, prove it." The outlaw flung Sky towards him as he and his cohorts laughed.

Sky fumed, anger flashed in her eyes. At the moment, it didn't matter if it was aimed at him or the men who had captured her. He knew how these men proved a woman belonged to them and only hoped, despite her anger, that Sky would cooperate. He holstered his gun but kept his rifle trained on the men.

"Play along," he whispered as he grabbed her wrist. She immediately resisted.

"Damn it, Sky, do what I tell you or you'll get us both killed," he hissed, jerking her close, bending her arm behind her back, not hard but enough to end her struggle.

Before she could object further, he sealed any protest with his lips, forcing her mouth open. He knew the instant she capitulated. Her body softened against his. In that same instant, Joe was the one in trouble. Not from the outlaws, but from the spitfire he held in his arms.

He lifted his head from the kiss, still keeping his eyes, and rifle, trained on the outlaws. Sky leaned into him, burying her face in his shirtfront, her hands fisted in his shirt.

"That don't prove nothing," one of the men said. "Hell, any woman would kiss like a fool if her life depended on it."

"Yeah, well, that's all the show you're going to get. I say she's mine, she's mine." He pulled Sky behind him and began to inch backward. "Get on your horse," he ordered over his shoulder.

"Hey, where you think you're going?" Horner took a step forward, hand on the butt of his gun.

"We're not staying," Joe stated flatly.

"Maybe I say you are. Maybe I want to make sure you're not the law and sneak back to kill us in the middle of the night."

Joe snorted. "Hell, Horner, if I was the law, you'd already be dead." The sound of several rifles being cocked caught on the breeze and all three men spun in circles, trying to locate the intruders. Joe kept backing up, feeling Sky's hands clutching his sides as she stayed directly behind him.

By the time they reached the cover of the trees, the sheriff and his posse had the three surrounded and Warren was issuing orders to get the prisoners tied up and the horses gathered. Seth found Sky's horse and they mounted. As far as Joe was concerned, the sheriff could handle the rest of it. He grabbed Sky's reins, kicked his horse into a gallop and headed for home.

They weren't a mile along the trail before Sky started in on him. "Would you let go of my reins?" She jerked on the trailing ends, trying to take charge of her horse.

Joe let go of the control that had kept him focused for the past hour. He drew the horses to a halt, tossed her the reins, and exploded, "What in hell were you thinking? What kind of idiot would just ride out of town across miles of land without a thought to her own safety?"

"We're on Double T land." She jutted out her chin.

153

"That didn't make any difference to the Horner gang, now did it?" His shoulders dropped in defeat; his heart thudded at the thought of what might have happened to her. "Christ, Sky. Do you have any idea how I would have felt if I hadn't gotten there in time? Don't you know what you mean to me?"

The last came out without conscious thought, but he couldn't take back the words. However, the minute he said them, her entire demeanor changed. Her spine straightened, her eyes flashed fire and her pretty lips flattened. "You have *no* right, absolutely *none*, to say that to me."

For an instant, he thought he saw tears shimmering in her lethal gaze, but before he could question her further, she gathered her reins and spurred her horse into a gallop. Critter was tiring, and it was all he could do to keep up with her. Even when they stopped to water the horses, she stood apart from him and Seth, refusing to meet his gaze much less talk to him. When he looked at Seth in question, the boy shrugged. It would appear neither of them knew just what to do with a woman in a temper.

Chapter Fifteen

Sky didn't say a word the rest of the ride home. Her mind was in turmoil, her body hurt from the outlaw's rough treatment, and her heart ached. How could Joe possibly care for her, as he said, when she had watched as his baby was born? Oh, she wasn't naïve enough to think that all men were loyal to only one woman, but she thought Joe was different. For the first time, she left the care of her horse to Matt, who happened to be in the stable when she rode in. She didn't even grab her saddlebags as she hurried toward the ranch house. And she certainly didn't turn when Joe called her name.

She found her father in the den, poring over his ledgers. He looked up in surprise. "Hello, sweetheart. Bonita said you wouldn't be back for a few…." His words were cut short when she fell to her knees at his side and buried her face in his lap. "Whoa, there. What the hell?"

"I want him gone, Daddy. You have to fire him and make him leave the ranch," Sky sobbed.

"Who, Sugar?"

She didn't have time to answer as Joe stormed in. "Sky, you're going to listen to me, if I have to throw you down and hogtie you."

She stood quickly and moved behind her father, who would protect her at all costs. She glared defiantly across the room at Joe.

"Get out! I hate you." She threw the words at him and felt a sense of satisfaction when his arrogant expression changed and his steps faltered, if only for a heartbeat. The next instant he was leaning over her father's desk, his large hands planted firmly on the surface.

"You said you loved me. Are you going to listen to me or just be a fickle woman?"

"Me?" She squealed. "After what you did, then I find out you're…you're—"

His glare froze her on the spot. "After what *we* did, sweetheart. I didn't force you."

She gasped; her father growled as he stood.

"Joe Dawson, I told you once you'd better not ever hurt her." He took a menacing step around his desk and Sky crossed her arms over her chest and smirked.

"Coop, you know that would never happen, but she won't listen to me so I can explain what you already know."

His woeful expression had Sky wavering. He looked like a beat down puppy.

Her father turned and spoke sternly. "Looks like the two of you should have been doing more talking before things went too far." As quickly as he had defended her, he now took Joe's side. "Skyla, you sit your fanny down and listen to this boy before you go making rash statements."

"But Daddy…." She couldn't believe her own father would take Joe's side.

He held up a hand to silence her. "After you hear him out, if you still want me to fire him, he'll be gone before sundown." He walked to the door and left, leaving her to face Joe alone.

She kept the desk between them because he looked as if he truly would sit on her. She wasn't afraid of him, for she knew he would never physically hurt her. But the damage had already been done to her emotions, and she didn't think she could stand any more heartbreak. She watched as he paced to the fireplace and back, his back rigid, hands shoved in his back pockets. She refused to break the silence.

Finally, he began. "I have a family, but it's not what you think."

"How would you possibly know what I think?" As much as her heart ached, she wasn't going to make this easy for him.

He gave a short laugh. "I know everything about you, Skyla Tate, probably even things you never realized

156

yourself. That's what comes from watching you grow up, studying you harder than I ever did my sums when Miss Tianna tried to teach me."

She felt herself weakening and sank into her father's chair.

Joe scrubbed a hand through his hair. "I dreamed about you all those years I was gone, wondering how you were doing, hoping no man at the ranch or elsewhere had caught your eye, dreaming of the day I could return."

"Then why did it take you so long?" she whispered. All those years of longing, wasted time when they could have been together.

"Like I said, I have a family. I was only fifteen when my paw died, leaving us alone on a dirt farm near Camino. I tried to keep us together, but the sheriff threw me in jail and gave my sisters and brothers to a passing preacher, who in turn sold them to whoever had a silver dollar or two."

She gasped at the injustice even as her heart melted. "You could have brought them here."

He shook his head. "I didn't know your father then. I wandered, looking for them and ended up here. I'm not sure what would have happened to me if your father hadn't taken me in and given me a job. As soon as I'd earned enough for tack and a good horse, I joined the Rangers, not so much out of loyalty to the Republic but as a way to search for my family."

Sky began to understand why Joe left the ranch those years ago, why he still periodically left. "You found Seth, but you're still searching, aren't you? How many are there?"

"Five, six counting me. Seth is the next oldest boy, and I found him with the Horner gang after he ran away from a farmer who wanted nothing more than a work horse."

"Oh, Joe." She went to him, taking a hand and leading him to the settee. They sat, side by side, and she continued to clasp his hand with both of hers. "And the others?"

"Twin boys—Michael and Matthew—who were only two at the time, and Jessica, who had been born that spring.

My stepmother, Rebecca, died giving birth to her while my father was off getting drunk."

The bitterness in his voice made Sky wince. She had always felt loved and cherished by her parents and couldn't conceive of a father not taking care of his own.

But that only accounted for five children, and it suddenly dawned on Sky who the other child was. "Mary Elizabeth is your sister, isn't she?"

When he nodded, Sky cursed herself for her unfounded conclusions, thoughts and actions that had nearly gotten them shot by outlaws.

"She got sold to a judge over in Carrizo whose wife wanted a maid, not a daughter. Although I have no proof and Mary Elizabeth won't speak of it, someone—and I think it was the judge—had his way with her."

Tears ran down Sky's cheeks at all the terrible things that had happened to Joe's family. She ached for Mary Elizabeth—a child having a child—for Seth who could very well have been on the wrong side of the law when his brother was a Ranger hunting outlaws. She even felt for the children he had yet to find.

"Oh, Joe, I have been such a fool. I thought—"

He stopped her with a kiss. Warm and firm, his lips caressed hers as if she were the most fragile thing alive. When she would have deepened the kiss, he pulled back, his gaze still caressing her face, and she saw love in his eyes before he got up and moved to the hearth, putting distance between them.

When he spoke, his words contradicted the look she had seen. "I can't give you what you want, Sky, what you deserve. It was my fault. I was the oldest and should have been able to take care of them. If I couldn't do it then, how can I trust myself to take care of anyone now?"

She went to him, circling his waist with both arms and laying her head against his chest. "You aren't to blame, Joe. You were just a boy, yourself." She stood on tiptoe and nipped his chin.

"I love you," she whispered.

He didn't repeat her words. "Everything I ever thought I loved was taken away from me. I have this huge hole in me." His voice choked on the words.

"We'll find them, Joe, all of them." It was an enormous promise and one she didn't know how to keep, but there was nothing in this world she wouldn't do for Joe. He had spent almost half his life alone, searching, not allowing himself any happiness, and Sky was determined to change that. Together, they would find his brothers and sister, and together they would make a family again.

* * *

Sky's faith in him humbled Joe, and that night, as the moon peeked in and out of the clouds and the coyotes howled in the distance, he laid her down on a blanket by the pond and tried to show her with his body what he felt.

It wasn't easy keeping the words of love inside. She had taught him how to love, how to give more than he took. But saying the words out loud meant a commitment, and he had things yet to do.

For now, he showered her with tenderness, slowly removing her clothes, kissing every inch of exposed skin. Each time the moon appeared, he paused to gaze at her, to caress skin that glowed like the finest pearls.

"You are so beautiful," he murmured as he kissed one breast then the other. He heard her gasp as he took the tip into his mouth, sucking gently, then harder, until it pebbled beneath his tongue. He slid a hand down her flat stomach until his fingers tangled in the curls hiding her womanhood. He continued exploring until two fingers were deep inside her, his thumb pressing on the tiny nub at her entrance.

"Now," she whimpered.

But he wasn't done and continued to discover new ways to pleasure her, and himself. He knelt between her legs and lifted her hips, taking her with his mouth until she was writhing, crying out his name as she exploded around him. And still he wouldn't release her from his touch, instead kissing down the inside of her thigh and back, letting her recover only to take her again.

This time, when her climax came, he lowered her hips and slid into her, almost exploding from the force of her clinching around him. Propping himself on his elbows, his forehead resting against hers, he gasped for breath. She circled his hips with her slender legs and urged him deeper.

"Wait," he gulped for air. He wanted the moment to last, but she was making it incredibly hard to hold back. While he fought for control, her fingers wandered over his back, down his hips, massaging taut muscles and creating havoc with his brain.

"Love me, Joe." Her breath tickled his ear. She lifted her hips against his and he was lost.

I do, he thought, *with all my heart and everything I am.*

Together, they moved to a rhythm older than the stars that winked down from above. When she came, a wildness seized her movements and the keening sound she made was Joe's undoing. He pushed harder and deeper, wanting to become one with her, riding the crest with her into the unknown.

Sky's slight shiver roused Joe, and he grabbed the edge of the blanket, tossing it over them as he hugged her closer. It was late; the moon had disappeared below the horizon, and yet he couldn't force himself to move. He didn't want the world to interfere with this perfect moment. He almost scoffed at his sentimental thoughts, but Sky had caused such an upheaval in his life, some days he didn't know up from down. All he knew for sure was that since he told her about his family and his need to find them, he felt more at peace than he had in over seven years.

"So, Uncle Joe." Her voice held humor as she ran a finger down his chest. "What do you intend to do now?"

"Uncle?" The word caught him by surprise but as he tested it on his tongue, he found he liked the idea. "I don't see it as much different than being the oldest. He's my responsibility as much as any of the others." At least now he was older, wiser, and had some money saved, though not near enough to buy a spread and build a proper house.

Sky wiggled until she lay half on him, her chin propped on her fist. "Well, I think Mary Elizabeth and Joey should come out here to the Double T." Her eyes twinkled.

"To live?"

She gave him an exasperated look. "Of course, to live. I know Karah Morgan is kin, and I'm sure she would take very good care of them, but you have to admit she doesn't have all that much room for a new mother and baby. And what better place to grow up than the ranch."

"I'm not sure your daddy would want a crying baby in his house. Besides, Mary Elizabeth needs a womanly influence. She didn't have much of one growing up, although Rebecca tried."

Sky struggled out of his grasp and knelt beside him. She scowled, and her chest heaved in indignation, but all Joe saw were her glorious breasts. He reached a hand to one, and she slapped it away.

"Joe Dawson, in case you haven't figured it out, I am a woman."

She was so indignant, Joe laughed and when she tried to slap his chest, he grabbed her wrist and tugged, rolling so she was under him. "Sweetheart, there is nothing about you that I haven't figured out, and believe me, I sure as hell know you're all woman." He kissed her soundly to keep further protests at bay, but eventually had to come up for air.

"I have Bonita to help." She raised a brow and Joe knew she wouldn't give up.

One more kiss to her pert nose and he rose to dress. "I'll talk to Coop. If your father agrees, I'll see about moving her out here. Now, get your fanny dressed so I can get you back to the house before daylight or your father might keep Mary Elizabeth and kick me out."

* * *

Joe felt he had barely fallen asleep when pounding on his door jarred him awake. From the position of the sun he could just see from his window, he realized that to be the

161

truth. Sky hadn't gotten dressed when he asked, instead enticing him to take a swim with her. One thing led to another, and they had loved the night away.

He groaned as he stood. She was worse than a hangover. Getting drunk only affected his head. Making love all night on the hard ground made his body feel like he'd been run over by a herd of wild horses.

Staring blurry-eyed at his reflection in the shaving mirror, he grinned. If given a chance, he'd do it all again, and again.

The minute he walked outside, he knew trouble was brewing. The air was charged, hanging heavily over the ranch. Though the sun was shining, in the distance, he saw rolling black clouds. The wind picked up, stirring dust into little whorls as Coop met him half-way to the corral.

"Storm brewing up in the mountains." He didn't have to explain further.

Late summer storms were unusual and their effects were most often disastrous. The ground was parched and whereas a gentle rain would soak in and revive the pasture, what looked to be a frightening downpour would simply run off, overflowing the shallow creek beds and flooding the valley.

"How much time do we have?" he asked as they headed to the stable.

"About enough to get our men up to the herd." Coop shook his head. "There's no time to get word to Winstead or Cazneau, so we'll just have to take what we got and ride hard."

When he got to the barn, Seth already had his horse saddled.

"You're not going," Joe said, passing his brother without stopping.

"Mr. Tate said he needs everybody. I can help," Seth protested.

Responsibility weighed on Joe. Seth was on the verge of manhood and didn't take kindly to being told what to do by his brother, even when that brother was older and wiser.

"You can't swim, remember? Chances are those cattle are going to stampede and every man out there will be caught between the Nueces River and Chaparrosa Creek, trying to keep them contained."

Seth's face blanched, as he likely remembered his near drowning earlier that spring.

Joe hadn't intended to make Seth feel bad, so tried to soften his command into a request. "There're chores to be done here as well as out there, and I need a good man to see to the horses. Can you do that?"

Seth's shoulders straightened, and he looked him right in the eye. "Of course. Ain't nobody better with the horses 'cept maybe Matt."

It didn't take long to gather the men and a few supplies and head north. While they had left a half dozen or so men up there to keep an eye on the herd, it wouldn't be enough if this storm got as bad as it looked. Every man on the ranch knew the danger of the cattle stampeding when a thunderstorm struck.

Even as he thought it, the sky lit up around them. *Heat lightning*, they called it. Instead of streaks, the entire sky flashed with light, making the hair on his arms stand on end. It was hard to tell the direction of the storm, he thought, just before a streak of lightning flashed in the distance and a loud rumble shook the ground.

Chapter Sixteen

Sky peered out of one eye, wondering what time it was. Her windows were open to catch the breeze, but she heard no activity. There was no bright sun, yet she instinctively felt it was time to rise. Padding barefoot over to the window, she pulled aside the curtains and realized it was later than she thought. Though the sun wasn't shining clearly, a ray or two sliced through heavy black clouds.

Finally, they would get the rain they desperately needed. There was nothing she liked better than a good storm. She quickly washed and pulled on a pair of Levi's, her chemise and a bright plaid shirt. After running a brush haphazardly through her curls, she grabbed her boots and trotted down the hall. Finding the dining room empty, she walked around the long table and through the door to the kitchen.

"Good morning, *'mija,*" Bonita called over her shoulder from the stove. "You sleep late this morning. It makes me wonder what you were doing in the night."

Sky refused to let her teasing bother her, especially when she saw Seth at the work table, devouring a blackberry tart. He barely spared her a glance as he gulped down a glass of milk.

"Where is Daddy?" Sky asked, pouring herself a cup of coffee.

"They went to the cattle. Paul said a storm is coming, and they are worried the Anacacho spirits will bring the rain too quick." Bonita clasped her hands at her bosom and glanced toward the heavens in benediction.

It was well known that most of their water came as a result of runoff from the mountains, and it was usually contained in one of the three creeks that ran through the Double T. But a severe storm where the rain came too rapidly to soak into the ground would cause flooding in the valley at the base of the mountain. Her thoughts were interrupted when a clap of thunder rattled the windows.

"He must be worried that the cattle will stampede," she murmured. Something like that could be disastrous, not only for the cattle but for the men trying to keep them relatively quiet. Even a good cow horse couldn't insure there wouldn't be injuries.

At that thought, she couldn't help but ask, "Did everyone go?"

"Joe's foreman, he's gotta go." Seth looked at her suspiciously, even though she hadn't asked specifically about Joe.

"Well, of course he does," she said carelessly. "That's leaves you and me to see to things here. We need to get as many of the horses as we can into the barn and secure the doors. They can get just as spooked as the steers."

"Already done that." Seth gave her a look that clearly said, *what do you know?* He then turned his attention back to the plate of tarts. He slid his gaze to Bonita's back while one hand crept across the table toward the plate. Quicker than a rattle snake strike, he snatched another tart and bit into the warm pastry.

Sky couldn't help but smile. He was so like Joe when he first came to the ranch. He was not just starved for *growing food*, as her daddy called it, but he had a huge sweet tooth. And Bonita made sure he had a ready supply of sweets, just as she did now for Seth. It wasn't like she didn't know how many tarts Seth ate, Sky mused, as she took one herself. Bonita had eyes in the back of her head.

Thunder cracked again, and the rain began, pounding the tiled roof. There didn't seem to be much wind behind it, which was unusual. She topped off her coffee and turned to Seth.

"Let's watch from the porch." She walked past him and lowered her voice. "Besides, if you eat many more tarts, Bonita will be giving you her tonic for a belly ache. And believe me, it won't taste near as good as a tart."

Rain poured off the porch roof so rapidly it formed a curtain, obscuring the stable and corrals. It had cooled the heat of summer, which was always welcome. Sitting on a chair against the house, she sipped her coffee and enjoyed the moment.

"Is it dangerous out there?" Seth broke the silence and she glanced over to where he sat on the swing, his brow furrowed.

He worried about his brother, as did she, but there wasn't much either of them could do except wait. She tried to reassure him. "The men know what they're about, but there's always some danger to their work, whether from a storm or roundup or the trail drive north."

"Joe says I get to go." The frown disappeared and now Seth spoke enthusiastically, "I'm going to make so much money when we get to Abilene and the herd is sold."

Ah, the innocence of youth, Sky thought with a smile. "And what do you intend to do with your fortune?"

He answered immediately. "I'm going to buy horses, good ones, and train and breed them."

He must have been thinking about it for some time and it didn't surprise her that he would plan on building something for himself. Again, she considered how like Joe he was.

"And where will you keep this wonderful herd of yours?"

His face fell, but just as quickly brightened. "Well, I'll just have to buy some land, too."

It all seemed so simple when he said it, and Sky wasn't about to disillusion him. "Sounds like a good plan," she said instead.

Beyond the curtain of rain, she could make out more dark clouds and wondered how long the storm would last. While she was safe here, she worried about Joe, her father, and all the men out in the wet weather. Cattle were simple critters, and if spooked they'd run right into the overflowing creeks, trying to climb over each other, causing any number of steers to drown. After the long, hot summer trying to put some weight on them before market,

166

none of the ranchers could afford to lose even part of their herd.

"You going to marry Joe?"

Seth's question came out of nowhere and Sky choked on her coffee. She carefully set her cup on the porch, taking time to compose herself.

When she glanced over at Seth, he gazed steadily at her, his expression somber.

"Well, I think that's between Joe and me, don't you?" While she wanted nothing more than to marry Joe, it wasn't entirely up to her. And it seemed too complicated to explain to a thirteen-year old.

Seth frowned and was silent for so long, Sky hoped the subject was dropped.

"He's my brother," Seth said, "and I gotta look out for him."

Sky pursed her lips to keep from smiling. Here Seth was only a boy and wanting to look out for his older brother. Regardless of the years that had gone by, family blood ran deep.

"Don't you think he's old enough to see to himself?"

Again, Seth gave her that *what do you know?* look, shaking his head. "He's so busy trying to take care of me and Mary Elizabeth, and to find the rest of us, he don't pay no attention to his self."

"Taking care of family is what makes a good man," she said, knowing that was one of the qualities she loved in Joe.

Seth *tsked* just like an old lady. "I can take care of myself. Mary Elizabeth, now, that's another story, 'specially now she's got little Joey."

Sky leaned forward, elbows on knees. "I promise, Seth, that I want to help Joe, and you, find the rest of your family."

"That ain't what I asked." He wasn't going to let her off the hook.

"Okay, here's how it is," she said with a sigh. "I love your brother, but it takes two people to love each other mightily before they can make a good marriage. And I

167

won't settle for anything less than a marriage like my parents had."

He seemed to think about that for a bit, then rose and walked to the edge of the steps. "All right, then. Rain's letting up, so I figure Patch and me will have plenty of hungry fellows to feed for supper. 'Sides, I gotta go see to the horses."

Sky remained on the porch, listening to the last of the rain drip from the eaves. She knew Joe loved her, even if he wouldn't say the words she wanted to hear. He had this terrible need inside to right a wrong from the past before he would ever quit wandering and settle down. She wished she knew how to hurry that along.

Since sitting and stewing didn't do much good, she tossed the cold remains of her coffee out into a puddle and went back inside. She found Bonita in the kitchen, a pile of mending in the basket by her chair. Since several of the items were hers, Sky dragged up a chair and was soon tacking a patch onto the backside of her denims.

"Might as well throw those in the rag bag as to put another patch on the ones already there," Bonita mumbled, a needle in her mouth as she cut a thread.

"I just got them broken in."

Bonita chuckled. "'*Mija*, you been wearing those long enough. Besides, a lady should be wearing skirts, not pants."

"Ha. The best thing ever invented were these Levi denim pants, though I doubt Mr. Strauss ever thought to see women wearing them." She neatly folded the pair she had finished and put them aside. Until she discovered the pants at McGuffy's, she had worn split skirts when riding. While they were comfortable, they weren't near as durable or versatile as the Levi's, which served her well working on the ranch. Sky didn't use her position as the boss's daughter to get out of work that needed done. Next to her daddy, she knew more about the running of the Double T than anybody because she was always in the middle of it.

Once the mending was done, Sky wandered into the den, telling Bonita not to bother with supper until the men

168

showed up. She ran a finger along the spines of the books on one shelf, pulled out a favorite book of poems and settled down to read.

She dozed, awaking with a start sometime later. There was no light from the windows, yet she hadn't heard her daddy or Joe come in. Rubbing the crick out of her neck, she rose and put the book back on the shelf.

The storm had long since passed as she went down the hallway to her room. She had hoped Joe would return tonight, but wasn't surprised that he would stay out with the other men. He took his job as foreman seriously, not expecting the cowboys to do anything he wouldn't.

Those thoughts didn't lighten her mood as she got ready for bed. She missed him, plain and simple. When she crawled into bed, her thoughts of him lulled her to sleep, thoughts that turned into dreams of heated passion.

The bed squeaked as a weight came down, the covers lifted so that a cool breeze caressed Sky's back. She tried to snuggle deeper into the covers, but they were replaced with a chilly arm circling her and an even colder hand caressing her stomach.

"My lord, you're cold," she murmured in her sleep as she tried to turn.

"Lie still and just let me hold you," her dream lover said. "You're soft and warm." He nuzzled the side of her neck and she felt her womanly parts start to throb. Dreams couldn't replace the real thing, she mused, but it was all she had at the moment.

He curved closer until they touched from shoulder to toe. Sky placed one hand over his and reached around with the other to rub along his hip, more than willing to share her body heat.

He moved, then a heated kiss fell on her cheek before he sucked the lobe of her ear. The throbbing grew stronger.

Even in her dreams, she heard his husky voice. "All I could think about out on the range was that I didn't want to spend the night on the soggy ground." His hand moved upward to cover her breast, his thumb and forefinger pinching the nipple lightly.

She groaned, trying again to turn in his arms, but he held her firmly. So firmly that she felt his rigid manhood rubbing against her bottom.

"Bend your knees," he whispered, nudging her legs, following them with his own as she pulled them up.

She gasped as he slid into her from behind, her eyes popping open but seeing nothing in the dark. It was no dream, for this was beyond her experience, and beyond her wildest imaginings. When he pushed his hips toward hers, she pushed back, and when he slid his hand down to finger her, she became crazed.

She wanted to kiss him, lick every inch of skin until he was as hot as she, but he kept her pinned from behind, ramming into her until she was on the brink. Then he stopped.

She whimpered.

"Shh." He stilled her complaint, biting lightly on her neck. She had visions of horses mating, the stallion biting and marking the mare as he took her. She felt that with Joe now; his mark was already on her heart.

"You feel so good," he whispered softly. "I want it to last."

He throbbed inside her; his control was as fragile as her own. She tried to slow her breathing but her lungs were on fire along with the rest of her. She knew from experience they could make love more than once in a very short time, so she didn't want to prolong anything. Besides, he pushed his thumb against her nubbin and there suddenly was no waiting.

"Finish it," she commanded, bumping her hips back.

He scooted his other arm between her and the mattress, snugging her tightly to him as he began once again to move inside her. She grabbed his arm to try to anchor herself, pushing back against him to take him deeper.

"Oh, god," she gasped as her climax came, stronger than any she had experienced. Fire shot up and down her legs from her center; muscles tingled and her womanhood clutched. Her climax triggered his and as he shot hot and strong inside her, she came again, taking all he had to offer.

Exhausted, they both lay there, not moving, not talking, just trying to breathe. When she felt she could move, she turned in his arms, hoping to talk to him, ask about the cattle and whether her father had come home with him.

His eyes were closed and his chest had settled into a steady rhythm. She wasn't outraged that he had fallen asleep right after they made love. Thrilled that he had ridden in the dark just to be with her, she leaned up and lightly kissed his lips.

"Home," he murmured in his sleep, pulling her closer to his side.

Whether he realized it or not, he had made a declaration and Sky's heart swelled.

Chapter Seventeen

Joe arched his back and stretched as he sipped the last of his coffee on the porch. The sun was shining, the air clear, and for once he wasn't worried about what the day would bring. In fact, even though there was a hell of a lot of work to do before the cattle drive north, he was eager to begin.

"What's the plan, boss," Andy asked when Joe sauntered to the corral. He, Mick and Matt had let the horses out and they milled in the corral.

"First, thanks for giving up your sleep to work the cattle last night." Almost all the men on the Double T had been out in the valley, continuously moving around the cattle during the storm to keep them contained. Even so, there had been some wild ones running amuck.

"What do you think the damage is?" Matt asked.

"Tom said he'd come by with a count on his way back to the Southwind," Joe said, "but I'm thinking we might have lost a dozen head, all told."

The men shook their heads. Losing any cattle this late in the season was never a good thing. The drive north to the railhead would take some as it was. Lack of good grazing, high water and sickness would all take their toll on the herd.

"Can't change what is," Joe stated. "Might as well get ready for the next move. Some of these horses still need saddle time before they're worth a damn on the trail. The bosses have decided since the herds are already north of here, we might as well head them over to San Antonio and pick up the Chisholm."

"Not as much water as following the Nueces River on the Goodnight-Loving," Mick, who had been on more drives than the other two, commented with a shake of his head.

"Not my call," Joe replied. "I just take orders like the rest of you." For the first time since he arrived at the ranch all those years ago, Joe wasn't looking forward to the cattle drive. Getting the steers to the railhead in Abilene was a necessary evil of being a cattle rancher in West Texas, but it was a long haul.

Truth be told, he thought, as he walked away from the men, he didn't want to be away from Sky for the length of time it would take to get the cattle to market. His body constantly ached for her. He craved her warmth and giving nature so much last night, he had ridden home in the dark and the final splatters of rain just to be with her. If not for his horse, he probably would have ridden right into the river.

Now, as he entered the kitchen and poured more coffee, he heard her talking, presumably to her father. Following the sound of her voice, which often came to him in his dreams, he found the two of them as usual in the den. He thought there was a formal parlor somewhere in the house, but damned if he knew where, as they seemed to spend all their time in Coop's domain.

"Morning." He tried to sound casual as he walked in, but just the sight of her made his heart pound and other parts of him swell uncomfortably. The Levi's she wore followed her curves like a second skin; her checked shirt outlined her breasts and trim waist. He tried to swallow but couldn't and thought to tell Coop she shouldn't be out and about on a ranch full of men in that attire. *He* might like it, but he sure as hell didn't want the other men staring at her.

One look at her face and he knew that *she knew* exactly what he was thinking. Clearing his throat, he turned his gaze to Coop, but that wasn't any better. The old man stared intently in his direction, one brow raised, as though to say there would soon be a reckoning for Joe's behavior toward his one and only daughter. He was sure Coop would be much happier once Joe left with the rest of the men on the cattle drive.

"I was telling daddy about Mary Elizabeth, and that we should bring her out here to live." Sky spoke up.

Joe's desire faded immediately. He frowned. "I told you I would talk to your father. I don't need you interfering in my business."

Sky's face fell and he might have felt bad about sounding so gruff, but damn it, he didn't need some woman—any woman—taking care of what was his responsibility.

She opened her mouth then snapped it shut again. Glaring at him across the distance, she squared her shoulders. Her heaving breasts made Joe mentally groan.

"Well, that's just fine, then." She stomped past him and through the doorway, leaving Joe staring at her rigid back.

He swung his gaze around at the sound of Coop's cough. His boss looked like he was having a hard time holding in his laughter and in fact, it burst out when he looked at Joe, who imagined his face showed his confusion. Unable to speak around his chuckles, Coop waved a hand to the chair Sky had recently vacated.

"What?" Joe asked, befuddled as he sank into the soft cushions.

Coop's eyes twinkled as he finally spoke, "Son, you haven't learned much on this ranch if you haven't realized that women make it their mission in life to interfere with ours."

When Joe continued to look confused, Coop shook his head. "Are you planning to marry my daughter?"

Joe choked on the swift change of subject. "Sir, you know I have things—"

"I know, I know. You have family to find and a spread to buy. But one of these days you're going to have to settle down and there's no reason why it should be elsewhere. I always figured someday it might be you and Sky running the Double T, seeing as I never had a son."

Joe had never thought about a future on the Double T. "I don't know what to say."

"Do you love her?" Coop asked and when Joe didn't answer, he continued, "I don't want you two getting the cart before the horse, so to speak, and I won't have my girl hurt if your intentions aren't honorable. I told you that once before."

If Joe thought it strange having a conversation like this with Sky's father, he couldn't say, but Coop deserved the truth. Still, he cautiously looked toward the doorway.

"Yes," he said in barely a whisper. As everything he had ever loved had been lost, he glanced around as though expecting the sky to fall.

"Good." Coop blew out his breath, slapped his knees and stood. "I don't intend to be interfering, but if I were you, I'd let her know before Mason Winstead gets a hankering to marry her and haul her off to Washington, DC. Can't say as I dislike the boy, but I don't want my gal that far away."

Winstead? Just the thought of him touching Sky made Joe itch for a fight.

"One more thing in case you haven't figure it out yet...." Coop stopped at the door as they strolled out. "I may have spoiled Sky some growing up, and probably more so after her mother died, but she has a kind and generous soul. She'll do anything for someone she cares about, sometimes whether they want her help or not."

Joe remained where he was as Coop sauntered down the hall and into the kitchen. He heard him greet Bonita, then they both laughed, the sound lingering after the back door closed.

He hadn't thought about marriage, at least not in any tangible way like the day-to-day life on a ranch. He had spent so much time in the saddle wandering from place to place, he wondered if he had what it took to settle down.

It didn't take a second to recall crawling into bed with Sky last night, her body warming him and taking them both to the heights of pleasure. What would it be like having her by his side every day, every night? She loved the ranch and wasn't afraid of the work it entailed and ranch life was all he knew. He had shared his story with her and she hadn't backed away. She already had his heart; he was sure of that, but could he give himself totally?

Joe didn't have time to look for Sky outside. There were horses to be worked or shod and tack to clean and mend—all the things that needed to be done on a daily basis to keep the ranch running smoothly. There would be hell to pay if any of the men ended up out on the range with a lame horse or a slipping saddle girth.

His thoughts were interrupted at the sound of thundering hooves coming around the bend. Even after all the rain, small clouds of dust rose from the horses' hooves as three riders approached. He shaded his eyes and let out a groan when he recognized the sheriff in the lead. Since he was half way between the ranch house and the corral, Joe saw no sense in trying to evade the man, so he stopped where he was, tugging his hat further down to shadow his eyes.

The man reined in his horse barely two feet from where Joe stood. For some strange reason, the sheriff didn't like him, and the feeling was mutual.

"Sheriff Warren," Joe said in a barely civilized voice.

"Where's Mr. Tate?"

No greeting, no acknowledgement. Joe could do the same, so he simply thumbed to the right without another word. When he turned his horse in that direction, his deputies right behind him, Joe followed them to where Coop stood by the corral. He wasn't about to let the sheriff talk to Coop alone, regardless of his business here.

The sheriff dismounted, still scowling at Joe, but Joe stared right through him, hooking a boot on the bottom rail next to Coop.

"Sheriff," Coop nodded in greeting. "Rounding up more outlaws?"

Coop was just making polite conversation, but as the sheriff's scowl deepened, it suddenly dawned on Joe as to what caused a burr under the man's saddle. It had been Joe who had found the Horner gang, with the sheriff coming in as back up. Admittedly, Joe had been trying to find, then rescue Sky, but for some reason, the sheriff held Joe's status as a former Texas Ranger against him. And that made Joe grin at the sheriff's discomfort.

"Just wanted to give you an update, seeing as you were shot and all," the sheriff grumbled.

"By outlaws, or the Indians?" Coop questioned, and Joe knew exactly to what his boss was inferring. Everyone in the area, especially the sheriff, accused the Indians of staging the raid, and even when told different, many still weren't satisfied.

The sheriff cleared his throat, looking everywhere but at Joe and Coop. "We took those outlaws over to Fort Duncan, as there was to be a judge coming in. When the captain went through their gear, he found what appears to be feathers and skins."

"Appears to be...?" Coop started but Joe interrupted.

"Feathers and skins?" he repeated. "As in headdresses and warrior shirts?"

"Well, yeah," the sheriff said with a disgruntled look, and Joe could only assume that he didn't like to be found in the wrong.

Joe couldn't help but rub it in. "So the Horner gang was riding around raiding, dressed like Indians while you and the soldiers at Fort Duncan were busy accusing the Kickapoo."

"Let it go, Joe," Coop said quietly.

Sheriff Warren took a menacing step forward. "Look, Dawson, just because we don't wear a damned Texas Ranger star don't mean we can't take care of our own. That gang figured if people thought it was the Indians, they'd all hurry into town for safety, leaving their cattle and homes unprotected. Easy pickin's for a group of thieves, until you...we caught them."

Joe didn't miss the sheriff's need to put his stamp on what had gone down, but it really didn't matter to him. He was no longer a Ranger, in fact, no longer had a lot of use for those of Warren's ilk. Little good the law had done his sister. He turned on his heel and headed for the stable, determined to ride out and find Sky.

* * *

Sky was in a huff so she saddled Stormy and rode out to the pond. The recent rain had filled the pond to the very edge of the grass where she sat, and the water was crystal clear. The air was warm, the sun beating hot on her back, and she thought idly about swimming if for no other reason than to cool her temper. Instead she sat shredding a strip of prairie grass and stared out across the water where sunlight shimmered and danced.

"I figured you'd be here."

Her heart skipped a beat at the sound of his voice. She turned, shading her eyes. He took a step to the side, blocking the sun, but she could still only see his outline.

"I didn't ask you to come looking for me."

He sat down, his shoulder brushing hers. "No, and I didn't ask you to talk to your father, either."

She frowned, her anger quickly returning. "I was only trying to help."

He gently bumped her shoulder. "I know, and I shouldn't have yelled at you. I'm not used to having people look out for me and mine."

"Well, maybe it's time you did." She turned to look at him. His eyes were shadowed and he hadn't shaved. He looked totally disreputable, and she loved him all the more. Giving up her anger, she laid her head on his shoulder and relaxed when he circled her waist and tugged her closer.

"I was being truly selfish, if you must know."

"How's that?" he asked, his lips brushing her forehead in a gentle kiss.

"I thought having her here would keep my mind off the fact that you weren't here. I can't stand the idea of you being gone for the next few months." She sighed. "What am I to do?"

"Sky, you have never gone on a cattle drive and this is the first time I've been back in seven years. What do you usually do when your father is gone?"

"Up until recently, I haven't had anyone to keep my mind busy." She slid her hand along his thigh to his crotch.

"Who's going to keep me warm at night?" She turned into him, kissing along his scratchy jaw until she found his warm lips. Before he could protest, she pushed him onto his back and slanted her mouth across his until he surrendered.

The feeling of power made her bold, and she continued her explorations, rubbing, squeezing until she felt him swell beneath her hand. When she licked along his lips, he opened to her and sucked her tongue in to duel with his.

"Damn, woman, it's broad daylight," he gasped when she lifted her head.

Her nipples ached for his touch and she rubbed against his chest, seeking relief. Just when she thought he would give her what her body craved, he pushed her back, forcing her to sit up.

"Shh," he warned, sitting again beside her and rubbing a hand down his pant leg. "Someone's coming."

He had no sooner spoken than Sky heard horse hooves pounding the ground, coming closer.

She started to rise, wanting her rifle which she had left with her horse, but Joe put a hand on her arm to stop her.

"It's only Seth," he said, unconcerned.

Sky glanced into the distance and saw Seth coming over the last rise. She turned to Joe. "How did you know that?"

Joe laughed. "He rides better than he did and he hasn't fallen in the creek lately, but he sure hasn't learned to be quiet."

Seth bounded off his horse, ground tied him and headed their way, a wide grin on his face.

"Told Patch I could find you," he said smugly, plopping down and tugging off his boots.

"What're you doing?" Joe asked.

"Figured I might as well take a swim while I'm here."

Joe snorted. "You can't swim, remember?"

Seth cocked his head to the side, eyeing the water. Sky thought he looked disappointed, but then he brightened. "Well, I can wade anyway."

Joe rose, tapping the brim of his brother's hat so it fell over his eyes. "Not a good idea, kid. Rain caused the pond

179

to turn, and there's all kinds of critters in there just waiting for some fresh food."

Seth grabbed his hat off, his eyes wide with surprise. "You're kidding, right?"

Joe shrugged. "Well, if the pond critters don't get you, there's always the snakes and scorpions wanting to chew on your toes."

Seth looked over at her and Sky shrugged, trying hard not to smile. She enjoyed watching Joe tease his brother. She had rarely seen him relax enough to do that, much less laugh. While she couldn't take the credit, being at the ranch made a difference in Joe's life.

"Come on kid. I'm sure there's work to be done." Joe held out a hand and pulled Seth to his feet.

"Yikes, that's why I came out in the first place." He looked longingly at the pond, sighed, then continued, "Patch said we'll be heading out with the chuck wagon in two days and the rest of you will be coming right along."

Joe frowned and when he looked at her, his frown deepened. Was he thinking what she was, that they only had days before they would be separated for months?

* * *

It took longer than Patch's predicted two days to get everything ready for the trail ride. Joe had talked to Coop, who had visited with the other ranchers and they all agreed it would be best to head north now instead of waiting another four weeks. Even with the recent rain, the pastures were gone. The nights had started to cool down, a sure sign that the seasons were changing. They not only had to get the cattle to market but needed to make it back home before winter hit up north. He wondered where the time had gone, but looking across the corral to where Sky talked with her father, he knew.

Days had been full of work, the nights with Sky. When he tried to suppress his feelings and not go traipsing to her room at midnight, she came to his bed, warm and willing, a force to be reckoned with. Where she was concerned, Joe had no will power.

He tried to come to peace with the idea of never knowing what happened to his brothers or baby sister. He had Seth and Mary Elizabeth, and now baby Joey. He had to be satisfied with that, although in the back of his mind he knew he would still hunt down any leads that came his way. But he could no longer let that mission rule his life. Sky was too important to him, and it was damn time he did something about it.

He headed in her direction but was interrupted when riders came into the yard. He instantly recognized Mason Winstead at the head of a group of cowboys. By the time he reached Coop and Sky, he caught only the tail end of the conversation.

"So Paw said it was up to me to ride trail and take care of Southwind's interests."

Coop nodded. "It's about time you young fellas took over. I'll be staying home, too." He nodded toward Joe. "Joe will ride herd on my boys and take care of business in Abilene."

Winstead eyed Joe before turning his attention to Sky. His smug expression told Joe what he was thinking—Joe would be out of the picture at the Double T for some time to come.

Well, cowboy, Joe thought as the couple walked away, *so will you.*

Joe would have liked to forego supper, but Coop had arranged a big barbeque for all the men as a sendoff. Though they all had trail cooks, and Patch was the best of the lot, there was nothing like Bonita's bread and pies to make the men think of home during the long nights on the trail. Even though they would head out at the crack of dawn, energy crackled in the air as the men joked and ate and joked some more.

Someone broke out a fiddle and another a harmonica, and the music drifted across the calm night. Most of the men were unmarried, so left no sweethearts behind; therefore Sky and Bonita were kept busy dancing from

181

cowboy to cowboy. They laughed and gave each man their full attention until he got shoved aside for a new partner. Paul finally led Bonita, and while Joe's palms itched to circle Sky's waist, he wasn't about to put himself out there in front of the men, even when Mason Winstead did.

She's mine tonight, he thought, already knowing the lack of sleep would make him grumpy in the morning, but he wouldn't give up one last night with Sky. He lingered by the barbeque pit as the neighboring cowboys pulled out bedrolls and settled down for the night. His men were in the bunkhouse; Sky had left some time ago, and now Coop and Winstead wandered toward the house. When he was sure the fire was banked for the night, he entered through the front door so his boot heels wouldn't echo down the guest wing of the house.

He didn't know if Winstead realized he slept in the main house, and though it was none of his business, there was no sense borrowing trouble. The man had hovered possessively over Sky most of the evening, frowning any time another man took a turn at dancing with her. At some past time, Joe might have done the same, but now he knew Sky belonged to him. And she had a right to know how he felt.

He washed off the camp smoke, shaved, and still she hadn't come to him. When he couldn't wait another minute, he quietly opened his door and walked barefoot to hers. She didn't answer his knock, but the door was unlocked and he slipped into the darkness.

He knew her room by heart and had no trouble finding the bed, dropping his trousers and slipping naked in beside her.

"Oh, no," she whimpered. "Go away, please."

When he tried to put his arm around her, she jerked away, edging to the far side of the bed, her back to him.

"Sugar, what's wrong?"

"I…we…" she stammered, and Joe was sure he heard tears in her voice.

"Come here," he said and gave her no chance to resist, tugging her close. She was as stiff as an arrow, and when he angled up on his elbow to see her face, she refused to look at him.

He brushed her hair away from her face then rubbed a thumb across her cheek, wiping her tears. He didn't need a light to see how upset she was. Her body trembled against his; her lips quivered as he gently rubbed his thumb over them.

"Have I done something?" He would have sworn he hadn't, but felt it better to take the blame.

She finally opened her eyes, tears still glittering at the corners. "Oh, no, of course you haven't. It's just that I...." Again she faltered.

"Tell me." It wasn't like Sky to be weepy, or to be reticent about speaking her mind.

His demand got her anger up and she pushed against his chest until he released her. "I'm a woman," she said by way of explanation as she sat up on the side of the bed. To Joe, it didn't explain a thing.

"Well, I do know that." He reached over to touch her back and she jumped out of bed. Clearly agitated she paced in the shadows to the window and back.

"Why did it have to happen tonight? Why have all the saints above cursed me with being a woman tonight?"

Joe bit his tongue. He had known Sky long enough to realize that the wrong words were worse than no words at all, but for the life of him, he had no idea what she was talking about.

"I wanted this last night to be perfect. I wanted us to be together in a way that you would remember all those weeks on the trail. And now, it's just too embarrassing to even think about telling you." She suddenly hugged her arms to her stomach and bent nearly double with a groan.

Joe was beside her in an instant, lifting her in his arms and carrying her back to bed. When he curled her against him, savoring her warmth through the cotton of her gown, she tried to pull away but he refused to let her. It finally dawned on his idiotic cowboy brain what was wrong with her.

The nightgown should have been his first clue, he thought as he spread his fingers over her stomach, massaging lightly. She was always naked when he came to her bed. He kissed the back of her neck, trying to sooth instead of arouse.

"Just let me hold you," he whispered and at last felt her relax. It wasn't the way he imagined tonight would go either, but the longer they lay there, the more content he felt. It didn't surprise him that while Sky could arouse him in the blink of an eye, he could also be satisfied simply to hold her. He supposed that was what love was.

She sighed softly, the kind of gentle *huff* that meant she still had something on her mind. "Spit it out."

She turned in his arms, pushing him to his back and then planting her chin on his bare chest. "Promise me you won't run off with some short-skirted floozy in a saloon in Abilene."

He would have laughed, but she looked dead serious. "Will you be here waiting for me, no matter how long it takes?"

Her answer was immediate. "Of course. I love you."

He kissed her, long and deep, hoping she would understand all he had yet to say. Then he tucked her into his side and pulled the covers over them.

"Well, all right then. I promise."

Chapter Eighteen

Sky couldn't believe how fast the time had gone since the cattle drive began. An autumn tang hung in the air, and although West Texas didn't have a dramatic change of seasons like Mason had told her occurred in Washington, DC, she relished the cooler days and even enjoyed a fire in the den on several evenings.

At the sound of a baby's laugh, she smiled. Joey was another reason the time had gone so quickly. She had politely *asked* Joe the morning he left if she could bring Mary Elizabeth and the baby out to the Double T. Men were so prideful, she thought. The difference in telling and asking garnered the same results, but Joe could still feel he was in control. So, no sooner had the men left than she talked her father into letting her take the old buggy into Eagle Pass to collect Mary Elizabeth and the baby. She had a pleasant visit with her friend, Susan, and Joe's Aunt Karah. When she tried to apologize to Susan for running off the last time, her friend brushed it aside.

"Mama said I wasn't supposed to tell you about Mary Elizabeth, that it was Joe's business. Then things just got out of hand when the baby came." Susan hugged her and smiled. "I take it you and Joe straightened things out?"

Sky felt her cheeks flush. "He asked me to wait for him, but I swear if that man doesn't say he loves me when he returns, I may just run off with Mason Winstead."

"Sky, you wouldn't," Susan admonished.

"Well, I will threaten to, anyway," Sky relented.

Now, she peeked into the den to find only her father sitting by the fire reading.

"Where's Mary Elizabeth?" she asked before planting a kiss on his brow.

"She went off to take care of the baby. That little one was squirming all over my lap." He chuckled. "He's going to be a terror when he gets to walking." She would have left him in peace, but he took her hand. "Sweetheart, you did good bringing them out here. It's been far too quiet in this big old house."

Sky wondered if he was thinking as she did, that it was past time for her to have a family, to give him grandchildren he could bounce on his knee and teach to ride a horse. She gave him another kiss and left him to his reading.

She tip-toed by the room they had given Mary Elizabeth, not wanting to interrupt if she was resting. That young woman had been another revelation to Sky, and she recalled their conversation on the trip from Eagle Pass.

The day had been warm and Sky was glad she had taken the buggy instead of the buckboard. The half canopy over their heads provided shade but the open sides allowed the breeze to waft through. Mary Elizabeth wasn't chatty, so Sky filled the time with stories about life on the ranch and about Joe's time there when he was younger, for she felt the girl was hungry for information about her brother's life in the time they had been apart.

While the baby slept in Mary Elizabeth's lap, Sky tried to keep the buggy on the smoothest part of the road. She had run out of things to say when Mary Elizabeth turned to her.

"Are you going to marry my brother?" she asked hesitantly.

Here we go again, Sky thought, and wondered if Mary Elizabeth would be more forthcoming than Seth had been when she'd had this conversation with him.

"First, I think, like most women do, that I would only marry for love."

"I'll never marry," Mary Elizabeth replied, staring off into the distance. "No man will ever want me after…." Her voice trailed off.

Sky reached over and squeezed her hand. "What happened to you was not your fault. Someday there will be someone who will love you and Joey."

She hadn't looked convinced. "Do you love Joe?"

"Yes, I do."

"Then you will marry him," she stated and Sky wasn't sure if her tone indicated approval or resignation.

"The fact of the matter is I don't know how he feels about that." While Sky knew Joe had feelings for her, especially since that last night when he promised to return to her, she couldn't swear he loved her.

"Joe probably wouldn't admit to loving anyone, not after what happened to us."

The baby whimpered in his sleep and Mary Elizabeth easily slipped him to her shoulder and patted his bottom. Regardless of her age, she had taken to being a mother. When she said no more, Sky wondered if Mary Elizabeth thought she didn't know about their background.

"I know about you and your brothers and sister, if you're worried about telling me something you shouldn't."

"You were there at Missus Morgan's—saw me and Seth—so I figure you know about us. It's not that part of the story Joe won't admit, but I could tell by talking to him that he's not over his anger and that's a worry to me."

"He blames himself for not being able to keep you all together, for losing you." Sky's heart still hurt thinking of Joe at that age.

"If anyone is to blame, it's me. After Joe, I was the oldest, and the preacher got rid of me first. I'm thinking he figured the little ones wouldn't give him any trouble."

Sky had never known such cruelty, and silently swore that she would make sure Seth, Mary Elizabeth and Joe had all they would ever need and more.

Mary Elizabeth turned, her face earnest. "It wasn't his fault. Joe has a lot of goodness in him. My maw was with child again almost as soon as she quit nursing me, then again and again. Seems Paw only came 'round long enough to get another baby on her afore he was off and drinking again. Joe took care of all of us, including my maw,

187

working from morning to night to make sure we had food, and we weren't even his kin, not really."

"I know he doesn't consider that so. You're his family as much as if Rebecca was his own mother."

"But she wasn't. He lost his maw years before. Then he lost his step-maw and his paw, then he lost us."

She looked so very sad, Sky pulled the horse to a stop and turned to embrace her. Mary Elizabeth sobbed into her shoulder and Sky strained to hear her words.

"He's lost everyone in the world that he loved, and those who loved him. Is it any wonder that he wouldn't admit to loving you, even if he does?"

Out of the mouths of babes, Sky thought and wondered why she hadn't already figured that out.

She pushed gently until she met Mary Elizabeth's gaze. "Well, that's changing every day. He found Seth and you, and he now has a little nephew who's going to follow him all over the ranch and love him to pieces." That brought a smile to her lips but Sky wasn't done, "And I love him more than life itself. So when he gets back from the cattle drive, we're just going to have to show him that and make sure he knows we are not going anywhere."

Now, as Sky thought back over their conversation, she hoped she hadn't exaggerated. Was their love enough to bring Joe the peace and security he seemed to need so desperately?

* * *

Joe settled his bedroll at the edge of a group of men, knowing he'd be up in the middle of the night for the pre-dawn watch. They had made good time, some days as many as fifteen miles, even with stopping mid-day to water the herd and let them graze. He was glad there was still grass en route, for the idea was to keep the cattle fattened so they fetched a better price at market.

He and Patch, riding ahead of the herd, had found a good spot to bed down for the night. A lazy creek ran nearby, enough water for the cattle but not wide enough to

188

cause any hazard when crossing in the morning. They were at the border of Texas and would enter Indian Territory in the morning.

Although he hadn't been this way in years, Patch and the others assured him the Indians wouldn't cause trouble. If anything, they would demand a toll and Joe and the other foremen already determined a steer each would probably suffice. There was little wild game—buffalo or deer and antelope—to sustain the tribes the government had forced into this no-man's-land. Offering them meat by way of safe passage seemed a fair exchange.

There was talk of railways being built from Kansas down to the east part of Texas, and eventually the cattle drives would divert to Fort Worth instead of having to ride all the way to Abilene. But the national government could no longer offer land grants and right-of-ways through the territory given to the Indians, so progress was slow. Even if the railroads got to northeast Texas, Double T cattle would still have to be herded over half way across the state.

He groaned as he sat on the hard ground and tugged off his boots. He was getting too old for this. Most of the cowboys were younger than his twenty-two years, although some days he felt far more ancient. He glanced over when Seth laughed at something Matt said. Seth was only going on thirteen, but his life had made him grow up fast.

At first hesitant to bring him along, Joe finally admitted that the kid pulled his own weight and didn't complain. In fact, a few days ago they came across a group of wild mustangs near the watering hole where they had stopped mid-day, and Seth had been in the middle of the group of men who had gone after them. They lassoed several, with Seth claiming at least two. They weren't fit as cow ponies, but would be trained back at the ranch this winter. For now, they were kept on long trailing leads along with the extra horses each man owned.

Joe blocked out the low voices as he pulled his blanket up and settled down for a few hours' sleep. Someone played a harmonica in the distance, the cowboy using it to lull the cattle bedded down not far from camp. The stars shone, the moon bright, and the crisp air told him more than a calendar that autumn had arrived. He hoped their travels would continue to be ordinary so he could get the herd to market and get back to the Double T before winter. Though West Texas received little snow, he didn't relish getting stuck in some Kansas cow town, or out on the range, during a winter blizzard.

He closed his eyes, but sleep eluded him as thoughts of Sky intruded. He thought of nothing else since leaving the ranch, some days swearing he heard her voice calling to him across the distance. He should have told her how he felt before he left. But he worried that saying the words out loud would bring him bad luck because he was out here with hundreds of miles separating them. Anything could happen. He could get thrown from his horse, get run over by the herd. She could get sick, outlaws could come to the ranch.

Joe swore as he flung aside his blanket and rose. He would go crazy thinking like that. Nothing was going to happen to either of them. He could take care of himself, had since he was fifteen. He stomped into his boots. If Sky would just stay at the ranch where her father could look after her, everything would be fine until he got back.

* * *

"But Daddy, we haven't heard anything," Sky complained at breakfast. "We need supplies anyway, so I'll just take the buckboard into Eagle Pass, then stop at Fort Duncan to see if they've received a telegram."

While the telegraph was a wonderful invention, transmission wires were sporadically placed and West Texas didn't have towns large enough to warrant train stations or telegraph offices. However, the government had made sure the military outposts were able to communicate rapidly, so most people went to Fort Duncan if they needed telegraph services. And even if Joe had telegraphed their progress, no one from the fort would bring the message out to the Double T unless it was an emergency.

190

Her father voiced those thoughts. "We would know if there were an emergency. Otherwise, we will see them when we see them."

"How long are they usually gone?" Mary Elizabeth asked as she juggled Joey on her lap, trying to get him to eat some mush that Bonita had fixed.

Joey promptly spit out each spoonful his mother tried to give him.

Sky made a face, sticking out her tongue. "You are entirely right, Joey. Mush is nasty stuff. Maybe he'd like a fritter." She held one out and he made a grab for it, but his mother got to it first.

"He can't eat that, Sky. He doesn't have any teeth."

"Well, he doesn't have any taste, either, if he eats that mush." She made another face and Joey laughed.

"All babies eat mush," Bonita said as she brought in more coffee. "Ground corn and milk is very good for them." She chucked Joey under the chin and retreated to the kitchen.

Sky thought how much things had changed around the ranch since Joey's arrival. His good nature was infectious and Mary Elizabeth had blossomed into a pretty young woman. She had asked Sky to help her with lessons when Joey slept, and together they began exploring the world through books her father owned. Just as Joe had been, Mary Elizabeth was hungry for knowledge. Like now.

"How long does it take to get the cattle to market and return?" she asked again.

"Depends on a lot of things," Sky's father replied. "In the past, we've made the run in as little as two months. If they'd ever get the damn railways finished, we could go to San Antonio instead of clear the hell to Kansas."

"Daddy," Sky *tsked*, rolling her eyes at his language.

"That boy may be smart enough not to like mush, but he sure doesn't know what I'm saying."

"Da," Joey babbled, and they all laughed while her daddy looked chagrined.

"I'm tired of sitting around," Sky said. "Winter won't be far off, and I know the Kickapoo could also use some

191

supplies." Before her father could object, Sky continued, "There have been no raids, ambushes or trouble since they captured the Horner gang. Seth's not here to go with me, but maybe I can talk Timmy's father into letting him ride shotgun. Town is close enough to the reservation that we can go in one day and return. Then I'll stay with Susan and come back within a few days." She didn't need protection from the Indians, but it would pacify her father.

"You give food to the Indians?" Mary Elizabeth's voice wavered.

"We have befriended them for years," Sky said. "Did you encounter Indians when the preacher took all of you?"

Mary Elizabeth shook her head. "I didn't, but in Carrizo Springs there was always talk about Indian raids, murdering travelers along the Camino Real."

"The Kickapoo don't raid," Sky stated emphatically, "and they certainly don't commit murder."

"Sky, Mary Elizabeth doesn't mean anything by what she said," her father commented. "You know it's common gossip when town people have nothing better to talk about."

Sky sighed. "I know. I'm sorry, Mary Elizabeth. I'm just tired of the Kickapoo getting blamed for every little thing. Why didn't they blame the Horner gang for all the mischief that was being done back when they were roaming the foothills?"

Her daddy shook his head and sipped his coffee. They both knew there was no answer. The government had relegated many northern tribes to the bleak territory between Texas and the state of Kansas even before the War Between the States. When conflict started, both the Confederates and the Union tried to use the tribes to fight their battles. Groups of Kansas and Oklahoma Kickapoo refused to be drawn into the conflicts and fled to their relatives across the Rio Grande. Even though many years had gone by, bitterness remained among many Texans, whereas the Kickapoo only wanted to live in peace and perpetuate the culture of their ancestors.

"All right. I can't change history or the minds of ignorant people. But I can help my friends."

Since only a few men had been left at the ranch with her father overseeing the chores, there was no one available to go with Sky, but she again assured him all would be well. She loaded the buckboard with some of Bonita's fresh baked bread for Karah and kissed her daddy good bye. She would get food stuffs at the mercantile for the reservation, but she packed her saddlebags with strings of beads, paper and pencils for the children. She would have to see if Mr. McGuffy had any new dime novels. The stories were tall tales and only loosely based on fact, but the children enjoyed it when she read to them.

Hours later, she left Fort Duncan in high spirits. A telegram had indeed arrived from Joe to her father, indicating they had arrived in Abilene in record time and would be heading home within days. After the herd was sold, Joe would pay off the cowboys and wire the rest of the money to her father's bank. Then it was every man for himself, as many would stay in Abilene and spend every last penny they had earned.

Some wouldn't come back at all. They usually carried everything they owned in their saddlebags, and many drifted from place to place looking for a better life. Her daddy paid better than most, so they tended not to lose as many hands as other ranchers. The ones who stayed would straggle in, two or three at a time, bemoaning the loss of their wages at poker tables or on loose women who plied their trade in the saloons. Then it was back to work as usual.

The telegram contained nothing of a personal nature and Sky hoped Joe would start back home with Patch, who in the past had always been the first to return, stating he was too old to waste his time and money on the perversions of the cow town.

She spent the night with Susan, but they confined their drinking to cups of tea as Sky wanted an early start. The next morning she sat in the kitchen when Timmy knocked at the back door. Karah and Susan were serving breakfast

193

to the boarders in the dining room, but Sky was the one who had requested he come by so she met him at the door.

"Good morning, Miss Sky." Timmy was always polite, snatching the cap from his head and grinning at her.

"You're up early, Timmy. Would you like to join me for some flapjacks?" She held the door open wider as he scooted in, sniffing the air.

"With maple syrup?" He peeked around her to the table.

"Of course." She laughed, reaching into the cupboard for another plate.

Timmy ate a stack of four flapjacks before Sky finished her coffee. He had barely swallowed the last bite before saying, "Paw said you needed me to ride with you to protect you from the Injins."

"Indians," Sky corrected gently. "And it wasn't for protection but to help with supplies. But since I spoke with your father, I have something else for you to do." At the crestfallen look that crossed his face, she said, "It's far more important and very necessary. We have received a telegram from our foreman, Joe Dawson, concerning the cattle drive. My father has been beside himself with worry about his men, so it would be very helpful if you could ride out to the Double T and deliver it to him." She didn't feel the least bad at embellishing her story to gain the boy's compliance.

When he seemed unconvinced, she added, "I can get Mr. McGuffy to help with the supplies, but I need someone who can ride a horse well to get out to the ranch and back without mishap."

His chest puffed up with importance and Sky knew he would do her bidding. Her father would forgive her for not taking the boy with her once he had the news that one more drive was complete and the money for another year was in the bank.

With that thought in mind, she put more supplies on her father's tab at the mercantile and the feed store than she normally would have. She wasn't frivolous, but would do without before she would let children go hungry.

There was no bridge crossing the Rio, but the water was low enough she had little trouble crossing to the other side. She never saw a brave, but the skin on the back of her neck tingled and she knew she was being watched as she drove the buckboard away from the river. It wasn't until the lodges in the distance came into view that a group on horseback approached her. She smiled broadly at Two Feathers leading his braves.

"It has been too long since you have come to visit my father," he said by way of greeting as he easily swung from his horse to the seat beside her. The minute he took the reins from her hands, she wrapped her arms around him in a hug.

"I've missed you, too."

He grunted as he put the horses into a trot and Sky grabbed the edge of the seat as they jostled along. "Why are we in a hurry? Is everything all right with your family, your father?" Chief Black Thunder was getting on in years and Sky often worried what would happen when he passed on, as he was the driving force within the tribe.

"All is well, *Numees*, but it is always better if patrolling soldiers do not see us close to the river border."

Numees—sister. She knew much of the Kickapoo language as well as Spanish, but since there was little opportunity to speak either, the words often sounded odd on her tongue.

The minute they entered the circle of lodges, children swarmed the wagon chanting *"Chepi, Chepi."*

She laughed at the endearment that meant "fairy" or "bringer of gifts." She didn't disappoint as she grabbed her saddlebags, dismounted, and distributed the trinkets she had brought. Black Thunder would forgive her for not greeting him first as he also had a soft spot for the children of his tribe—his hope for the future.

She left the wagon, taking only one loaf of bread. The good women of the tribe would see that the supplies were evenly divided. When she walked across the compound, she saw the Chief sitting in front of his lodge, watching her approach.

"Good day, honored Chief." She bowed slightly in front of him.

"*Oota Dabun,* come." He waved her closer, and she knelt at his side. He gently cupped her face. "You are as bright as the star for which we gave you the name, and as beautiful as the cactus blossom."

Sky blushed under his praise. "And you, great Chief, are still as handsome as the youngest of your braves."

He laughed at her flattery and gratefully accepted her gift of bread. Though the tribal women were excellent cooks, no one could come close to the taste of Bonita's stone ground bread.

"Does your honorable father know you have crossed the river?" His brow furrowed in concern.

"Yes," Sky said with a sigh. "But he only thinks I bring supplies, which I have," she added hastily when she saw his concern. "There is actually something else which I would like to speak with you about."

The chief sat quietly. It had always been his way to wait patiently, whether listening to his children squabble or to the elders' advice.

Sky fidgeted. She hadn't mentioned her real reason for wanting to come to the reservation, using only the need for supplies as a ruse to get here. Now, she hesitated to speak, wanting to be right, but so afraid she would be proven wrong.

"Can you tell me about the two young, blue-eyed boys who live with your people?"

His gaze met hers for a long moment before he spoke. "You have heard their story before."

"Perhaps you could tell me again."

Black Thunder looked into the distance. "They were maybe five summers when we found them, hiding among the mesquite along the river. My braves looked further and discovered a wagon, upside-down in the water. There had been much rain that year and the river was unsafe to cross." He shrugged. "Some are not wise in the ways of nature and do not know the danger of the water."

"You don't know to whom they belonged?"

He shook his head. "No one was near, no one was found. Perhaps the river took them. The young ones had not eaten in days and though afraid of my braves, they came along gladly with the promise of food."

"So your people gave them a home. How long has that been?"

"They have been with us four summers now."

Sky sucked in a breath. That would make them nine years old now. Could it possibly be true?

"Did they tell you their names? Do you know where they came from?"

"You are very inquisitive, my daughter. The boys did not speak at first, and when they finally did, it was in the Kickapoo tongue. They choose to remember little else." He rested his hand briefly on her head, then tipped up her chin. "Perhaps it is time for me to ask you a question."

Sky needed no prompting as she told the chief about Joe and his search for his family.

"And you believe Angry Dog and Little Fox are this Joe Dawson's missing brothers?"

"I believe they could be. I ask your permission to bring Joe here to make sure. But perhaps...." She bit her bottom lip.

Again, the chief waited patiently.

"Did either boy have anything with him when they were found? Something they thought would keep them safe, or that would identify them?"

"A talisman?" The old man frowned in thought. "Perhaps a silver concho hanging against their hearts?"

Chapter Nineteen

Joe was more than ready to be home. Funny that he now thought of the Double T that way. It was because of Sky. Could he leave the past behind and settle down? If it ever were going to happen, she would be the reason. She had always been his friend. Now she was his lover and confidant. She wasn't afraid of hard work, and there would surely be plenty of that in the days to come if he started his own ranch. Of most importance, she loved him and Joe had come to depend on that love and support. He no longer told himself he didn't deserve it, or that something bad would happen. Life was what it was, and he needed to take advantage of every day.

At the moment, those days were dragging, and if he were by himself, he would push Critter to cover more miles a day. But he refused to let Patch and Seth bring the chuck wagon back alone, even with the few men who had come along. In addition, they had the remuda. Some of the men had sold off a few of their cow ponies in Abilene because it would save feed through the winter, and the prices were high for well-trained animals. But since many of the men had also stayed in Abilene for a few wild nights in town, Joe had agreed that he and Seth would see to the horses on the return trip.

He had tried to talk Seth into selling the mustangs he had captured, but the kid refused. Joe wasn't sure the wildness could ever be tamed out of them, but Seth was adamant about trying. Joe admired his brother's gumption and told him so. Seth blushed under his praise and had worked all the harder on the ride home.

Joe had wired the balance of the sales to Coop after paying the men. He kept only a small portion of his own wages for the trip back, knowing Coop would settle up with him at a later date. He still wouldn't have enough to buy his own spread, but after what Coop had said, he figured perhaps he and Seth could use Double T land and pay Coop for grazing rights. With the use of barbed wire becoming more and more frequent, he wouldn't have access to the open grazing that had worked for the ranchers in the past.

"How long we got to get home?" Seth asked that night when they sat around the fire eating Patch's stew and biscuits.

"I figure another week," Joe replied.

"Leastways we got through Indian Territory with no trouble," Patch grumbled between mouthfuls. "Don't know what that government were thinking, forcing all them tribes to live where there's nothing but red dirt that cain't grow a turnip. It's no wonder they go after anyone crossing their land."

"You know, Patch, Texas is a state in the union run by *that* government."

"Texas is a republic regardless of who says different. Ain't nobody got more say in what's what than you do if'n you're a Texan."

It was an ongoing argument with Patch, who had been around before Texas was annexed into the American Union in 1845. Most Texans had been excited about the annexation because they felt homes and towns would be protected by a strong government. A government that would also see an end to marauding Indians and intruding Mexicans. That had not happened as expected, for Texas was a vast and sparsely populated state, and oftentimes, people wondered if the government in Washington even remembered their existence. Many Texans felt as Patch did and lived by their own laws.

"If you weren't so old and crotchety, maybe we should send you to Washington so you could set them straight on 'what's what'."

"I ain't too old, but young'uns like Mason Winstead be doing fine representing Texas folk."

The mention of the man's name set Joe's teeth on edge. Winstead had sold the Southwind cattle as quickly as possible and left town on an eastbound train, leaving his men to fend for themselves. Joe hoped he was heading back to Washington—far away from Sky—but if he made a connecting train in Kansas City, he could get to San Antonio and then home long before Joe and his traveling band.

It had been a lucky thing the three ranches' herds had been large enough that the trail bosses and cook wagons were spread across the distance during the drive. If messages needed to be exchanged, Joe had usually sent Seth or Matt, preferring not to see the man who curried Sky's favor.

"Get some sleep," he grumbled to Seth. "We're heading out at daylight." He stood and dumped his coffee cup. He was probably more anxious to get home than any of the others. Sky had said she loved him, but that wouldn't prevent Winstead from trying to turn her head with promises of a lavish lifestyle—something Joe was unable to give her.

* * *

Two days later Seth pointed. "What the hell?"

Joe would have preferred he not swear, but ever since coming on the cattle drive, Seth thought he was one of the men. He followed Seth's distant gaze.

They hadn't passed it on the way north but the more direct route home took them right by the huge formation. "It's called 'Enchanted Rock' or 'Spirit Song Rock' for native legends."

"Like what?" Seth asked.

Patch took up the tale. "It's said to be revered by native tribes as an opening to other worlds, and anyone spending the night on the rock becomes invisible."

Seth's eyes grew wide. "Are you joshing me?"

Patch shook his head. "Story goes that a Spanish priest fled to the rock pursued by native tribes and he disappeared. Seems he came back later to tell a tall tale

200

'bout falling into a cavern and getting swallowed by the rock."

Joe didn't recall much about the rock, so couldn't be sure if Patch was spinning his own tall tale. But he enjoyed the old man's stories.

"Seems, too, that he bumped into lots of spirits in the tunnels before he was spit out later."

"Spirits?" Seth asked. "Ain't that whiskey?"

"Guess some call it such, but these spirits are ghosts said to haunt the rock after they was slaughtered by a rival tribe."

They drew closer to the massive pink granite dome that protruded above the flat Texas plain like a gigantic lump on the head.

"Can we camp here and sleep on the rock? Maybe we'll disappear." Seth's voice held all the enthusiasm of youth.

Joe shook his head. "I'm not hanging around for days waiting for that rock to chuck you out again. Fredericksburg is about fifteen miles south, so how about we stop and have a bath and a good meal?"

"You saying you don't like my cookin' no more?" Patch grumbled from atop the chuck wagon seat.

Seth immediately took sides. "Don't be saying nothin' 'bout his cookin', Joe, 'cause I don't want to eat yours the rest of the way home."

Joe wasn't the greatest cook, but he sure as shooting wouldn't admit it to those two. "Just because I'm saying I want a good beef steak doesn't mean I don't appreciate your cooking, Patch." He then skewered his brother with a look. "As for you, if you don't start learning something from Patch, you'll be mucking out stalls instead of cleaning pots."

"Ah, now there's a good idea," Patch chimed in at the look of disappointment on Seth's face.

Joe continued in a different vein. "Besides, I could use a night's sleep on a fine feather mattress."

Patch gave a lusty sigh. "Ah, that would make two of us."

201

"What do you mean? You brought your bunk mattress with you." Seth teased the old man.

"Well, now, after months of it on the ground, it's got kinda lumpy. Just like your head's a-gonna be if you don't watch out." Patch shook his fist at Seth but the boy just laughed.

They made Fredericksburg before nightfall and after securing the horses at the town's corral, Joe got a couple of rooms at the hotel. While waiting for the other two, Joe slipped across the street to the barber for a trim and a shave. It felt good to get the whiskers off his face.

The evening air was brisk as they walked down the dusty street in search of a place to eat. While many saloons served meals, Joe didn't want Seth in one. The town wasn't that big, so it didn't take long to find the restaurant, cheerfully decorated with red checked table covers and white chairs. Joe hung his hat on a hook inside the door, then poked Seth, reminding him that hats were removed indoors.

Victoria Miller owned the restaurant and since it wasn't busy, took time to introduce herself and visit as she poured their coffee and took their orders.

"Where y'all heading?"

"Heading south a ways," Patch said as he dumped sugar into his coffee. They'd run out of that commodity several days back.

"Took cattle up to Abilene," Joe expanded as Patch fed his sweet tooth. "We work for the Double—"

"Mama, come quick. Papa has kittens." A little girl with bright red braids interrupted Joe as she scurried over to tug on her mother's skirts. She reminded Joe of a young Mary Elizabeth.

"It's not polite to interrupt," she said, then seemed to realize what her daughter had said. "Not in my kitchen, he'd better not." She hurried away, but returned in just a bit with their plates of beef steak and potatoes, refilling coffee cups. Seth dug into his meal and chatted with Patch, even when Joe reminded him not to talk with his mouth full.

Months on the trail with rowdy cowhands had undone any manners Joe had tried to instill in him.

The little girl, sensing someone closer to her age than the other customers, brought a kitten over to show Seth.

"Isn't she beautiful?"

"Yeah, I guess," Seth answered without even looking at the animal.

The little girl laughed at the face Seth made and it hit Joe hard. Her laugh was Mary Elizabeth's.

Joe cleared his throat and raised a brow.

"What?" Seth asked then sighed when Joe nodded toward the girl. He dutifully scratched the kitten behind the ears.

"My name's Isabelle Miller. What's yours?"

"Seth Dawson."

Joe heard a gasp and turned to see Missus Miller, her face ashen, one hand over her mouth and the other clutched against her stomach. He looked back at Isabelle, reminded again of how much she resembled Mary Elizabeth. His own stomach dropped.

"How old are you, Isabelle?" His throat was raw as he choked out the question.

"I'm seven," she answered automatically, more interested in the kitten that was trying to scramble up her dress front.

"Isabelle, quit bothering the customers." Her mother hurried over to the table.

"She ain't no bother, missy." Patch had been making faces at her and looked disappointed when her mother took the child by the arm and quickly led her away.

Joe stared after them, lost in thought and his supper forgotten. Saying nothing to Seth or Patch, he got up and followed the woman through a swinging door into the kitchen. He found her weeping in her husband's arms. She was a young woman with black hair and dark eyes, perhaps part Mexican. Joe took a good look at her husband and knew without a doubt there were questions needing answers. The man was Mexican through and through. Two dark-haired Mexicans would not have a red haired girl.

"Have you always lived here in Fredericksburg?"

His question brought the man's head up, but it wasn't anger at Joe's intrusion on his face. It was fear.

"We moved from Carizzo seven years ago," Mister Miller answered, then added, "I don't see what concern it is of yours."

Joe had no idea how far afield the preacher had taken his family after they left Camino. Mary Elizabeth had had no idea as she was the first to be foisted off and Seth didn't remember much.

"Is Isabelle your blood?"

"That certainly is none of your business," the husband said as his wife wept louder. "I'm asking you to go. You've upset my wife."

Joe's stomach was tied in knots and while it might be rude, he wanted answers.

"I think she may be my sister, Jessica, lost to me for seven years."

"No!" Victoria cried.

"She was born in 1870, in June," Joe doggedly continued.

Although Missus Miller violently shook her head, Joe saw the fear return. He reached inside his shirt and slipped the leather thong over his head. He held it out, the light glinting off the silver concho.

Victoria collapsed, her husband barely catching her before she hit the floor. He led her to a chair. She cried, while he managed to say, "We paid him good money to adopt her. The preacher couldn't tell us much about her, except her last name was Dawson. He said she was an orphan, that she had lost her parents."

"That much is true, but she still had me."

Mister Miller motioned Joe to join them at the table, then brought the coffee pot over and poured for all of them. As he did so, Joe told them his story, from the moment he had hung a concho around each child's neck with the promise to come back for them. Though the pain had lessened after so many years, Joe still choked up at his failure to rescue all his brothers and sisters.

Victoria cried throughout and her husband swore more than once. The man wasn't angry at him, but rather at the preacher, the lies and the circumstances that had torn apart a family.

When Joe finally fell silent, Victoria slipped a hand into her apron pocket, then reached across the table and turned it over. In her palm was the silver concho on a pretty pink ribbon. "She likes to play with it, but sometimes forgets where she leaves it."

Joe glanced from the shaking hand up to her teary face. Her lips quivered until she finally took a deep breath and pinched them together.

"Please don't take our daughter. We're all she has ever known."

Joe looked from one to the other, easily reading their love for a child, and he knew he would not be leaving with the little girl. He understood exactly what they were feeling, wanting to keep what they considered theirs, and he wouldn't destroy that. Unlike Seth and Mary Elizabeth, who had not had families when he found them, his baby sister was alive, safe, and had a happy life with loving parents—everything he could have hoped for her.

He asked for paper and pencil, and wrote his name and that he worked at the Double T, which was large enough that the Millers had heard of it. He listed each of his brothers' names, Mary Elizabeth's and their current ages.

"When she's older—if you ever think the time is right—would you tell her about us?"

"Of course." She gave him a fierce hug. "Thank you," she whispered.

* * *

When she wasn't doing chores, Sky paced the porch, anxiously watching for any sign of Joe. The excitement she had felt after visiting with Black Thunder built, but because she had no definite proof that their twin brothers were living with the Kickapoo, she had carefully refrained from mentioning anything to Mary Elizabeth. Yet some days she felt she would burst if she didn't say something.

Today, Mary Elizabeth came out to join her on the porch, settling little Joey on a blanket by the swing where she sat. "Are you this anxious at the end of every cattle drive?" she asked, tucking her feet under her skirts. "Or is it just Joe you are anxious for?"

Sky spun in a circle just in time to catch the teasing grin on her face. The young woman had matured rapidly with motherhood, and both of them loved Joe, albeit in different ways, so it was natural for them to form a bond.

"Except for Daddy, I've never had anyone particular before that I'm waiting for," Sky answered, "so it does make the days move slowly." She and Mary Elizabeth had talked, so it wasn't as if Sky had to keep her feelings toward Joe a secret.

"Although I seriously doubt I shall ever marry, I'll tell you right now it will be to a butcher or a baker or some such." Mary Elizabeth followed Sky's gaze down the lane. "I certainly cannot see waiting by myself for months for someone to come riding back to me."

"You are right," Sky said with a sigh as she plopped down beside her on the swing. "It's just that I have such news to tell him." Mary Elizabeth leaned forward, dangling a button on a string to catch the baby's attention.

The silver glittered in the sunlight. "That's the concho Joe gave you when he left, isn't it? The same as he gave each of you, even Jessica, the smallest."

Mary Elizabeth cocked her head, eyeing Sky. "Yes," she said slowly. "Why?"

"I know where there are two boys who I think are wearing the same token." She had wanted to tell Joe first, but Mary Elizabeth was also family and Sky couldn't keep it to herself any longer.

Mary Elizabeth gasped. "And you haven't told Joe?"

"I just recently discovered it when I visited the Kickapoo reservation. I have only seen them briefly a time or two on other visits to the camp and the talismans they wore could be any kind of medallion." Sky spoke rapidly.

206

"Besides, I don't know what the boys looked like when they were younger, and this last time, they were out fishing so I didn't have the chance to speak to them."

Mary Elizabeth frowned. "They're living with Indians? Surely not." She shook her head. "I know Seth was running with outlaws, but I like to think all the others have good homes with loving parents."

Sky tried not to be affronted, for not everyone understood the Indians. "The Kickapoo are a fiercely protective tribe, and their family ties are strong. Chief Black Thunder said these two boys had been with the tribe four years, and they have been treated well."

Mary Elizabeth worried her bottom lip, tears shimmering in her eyes. "I was nine when all this occurred, and sometimes I'm not sure if what I remember is true, or just a dream I've had." She reached over and grabbed Sky's hand, squeezing hard as the tears overflowed.

"I'm scared, Sky. Scared to hope. Is it bad of me not to want to run off to the reservation to see if it's them? Sometimes, it's hard to even remember the little ones' names, much less what they looked like. They would have only been two. Is there any chance at all they would even remember anything of life before all this happened?"

Sky gave her new friend a hug. There were no answers she could offer. All she could hope was that she and Joe would go to the reservation and perhaps help close the circle.

Chapter Twenty

Joe made sure their travels brought them to the Double T ranch in the dark, late enough to have missed dinner and all the chatter that always accompanied the end of a trail drive. There was only one thing—or rather person—he had any interest in seeing, and he wanted nothing to interrupt that.

He parted ways with the rest of the men at the pond. Regardless of the late autumn chill, he stripped down and dove under the water, coming up sputtering. As quickly as he could, he washed, shaved, and put on the last clean pair of Levi's he owned. His hands shook as he stuffed his gear back into his saddlebags, but it was not from the cold. Having dreamed of Sky for weeks on end, he now felt he might explode if he didn't get to her right away.

Luckily the house was dark when he arrived, and although he heard murmurs coming from behind one of the doors just past the den, he didn't stop. He doubted he could have stopped; his entire being was focused on only one thing.

Testing the knob to Sky's door, he found it turned easily. Slipping through, he stopped just inside the door for his eyes to adjust, although she had left a lamp glowing softly on her dresser. He toed out of his boots, stripped off his Levi's and softly crept to her bedside.

"I'd know you from half a mile away," she whispered softly and flung back the covers.

"Jesus Christ, Sky, you scared the pants right off me."

"I can see that."

Laughter rang in her voice.

His heart pounded, but he wasn't sure if it was the unexpected sound of her voice or the fact that she lay buck naked under the light blanket she had thrown aside.

Her skin glowed in the soft light and Joe found himself frozen in place, devouring her with his gaze. Her breasts, high and firm, jiggled slightly as her breath hitched. She moved close to him and he reached down and cupped one breast, his brown hand in sharp contrast to her milky skin.

She gasped at his touch and he started to withdraw, thinking his calluses were too rough, but she gripped his wrist to hold him in place.

"I have waited, night after night, for you to return." Her voice was as he remembered although perhaps more urgent. "Are you going to keep me waiting now?" She tugged on him and he lost all control, tumbling into bed on top of her, taking her mouth in a ravaging kiss.

He couldn't get enough of her, but her scorching lips gave as good as she got. Her tongue flicked out, dancing with his as they rolled back and forth on the bed. She wrapped her arms around his neck and her legs around his waist and he felt he was melting right into her. When he tried to lift himself slightly away, she murmured against his neck.

"No, no. Take me now." Her teeth bit into his skin, firing his blood and passion to a new level. He couldn't deny her what they both wanted.

With a groan, he pushed into her hot depths. She used her heels against his buttocks, driving him even deeper. Together, they paused to savor the intensity of their union.

"God, yes," she whispered, peppering his chest with kisses as he began to move.

He pulled out as far as he dared before ramming into her again and again. She met him stroke for stroke, urging him faster every time her hips rose to meet his. He was losing control.

"Are you with me, baby?" He barely got the words out but needed her to reach the climax with him, to find the pleasure just as he was. Almost powerless to hold back, his hips pumped faster and faster until he erupted, hot and strong, throbbing within her tight sheath.

She followed him over the crest and as she squeezed around him, he came again, amazed at a climax that didn't seem to end. His entire body shook and his heart pounded so hard he felt sure it would burst from his chest. He tried to focus on Sky, but she was a blur of light and heat and he finally let himself be consumed by the flames.

Sky had waited for months but what Joe had given her wiped away any memory of their previous lovemaking and replaced it with an ecstasy that was beyond her understanding. Was it possible for her to love this man more than she had before he left? As he cradled her gently to his side, she realized that while their lovemaking had been intense, there had been a quality about it that had not been there before.

She snuggled close against his chest, thoughts flitting around in her brain so fast she wasn't able to snatch one and examine it. He kissed the top of her head, softly rubbed her belly and cupped her breast in one large hand. He murmured her name and suddenly it struck her.

She had seen it happen before when a wild stallion had been captured. Constant love, attention, and work had finally tamed the animal. Not broken his spirit, but gentled it so he would accept what was being offered to him.

For whatever reason, Joe was content. She felt it in his breathing, in the tender way he held her. Her wild, rambling cowboy had finally come home for good. And still, she had a question.

"And did you visit any short skirted saloon girls?" she asked as she rubbed her palm over his chest.

"Well now, there was this little...ouch," he yelped when she pinched his nipple.

She found herself quickly rolled beneath him and began to giggle as he nipped her skin, then quietly groaned as he settled his mouth on her breast, sucking gently then with more intensity. She felt his manhood swell between her legs and pushed until he rolled over so she was on top. She straddled his hips.

"Don't I have a say in this?" he murmured in protest, although it was a very weak protest indeed.

"And if I said yes, would you deny me my pleasure?" She bent forward and rubbed her breasts against his hot chest. She tugged at his bottom lip with her teeth before slanting her mouth over his to stop any objection. Then she pushed against his shoulders, lifted her hips and slowly, so slowly, slid down until they were completely joined.

She watched his face transform, the lines fanning out from his eyes softening, his wide mouth forming a gentle smile. As she started to move, he sighed.

"I could no more deny you pleasure than I could stop breathing. You are my life, Sky, my heart."

* * *

Sky sleepily reached across the bed for the warmth Joe always offered, but all she felt were the cold sheets. Pulling his pillow close, she inhaled the lingering scent of wood smoke and pine ingrained in his being as much as his loyalty and work ethic. She should have known he would already be up, but a small part of her wished she could wake up with him every morning.

With a sigh, she quickly washed and dressed, then followed the sounds of laughter and found everyone already enjoying breakfast, even though it was barely dawn. She had known Mary Elizabeth would be up, for little Joey was an early riser, but she was surprised to see Joe, her daddy, and even Seth still at the table. Even more surprising, Joe was feeding the baby spoons of oatmeal, and he laughed every time Joey spit it back out.

"He wants steak," Seth said, talking with his mouth full of biscuit slathered with butter.

"He can't eat meat until his teeth come in," Mary Elizabeth said as she took over the feeding, allowing Joe to dig into his own breakfast.

Sky stood for a moment simply enjoying the sight of all the people she loved gathered in one place. When Joe looked up and caught her gaze, a flush rose to her cheeks.

She recalled his words of the night before—*You are my heart*—and knew he loved her. He gave her a smile so tender, she thought her legs would melt out from under her, and she barely managed to gain her seat.

"Seth, you look to have grown a foot since you left," she said as Bonita placed her breakfast before her. "Did everyone get back in one piece?"

"Most did," Joe answered. "I imagine the rest will be wandering in after a day or so. Their money won't last any longer than that."

"Ah, how I miss those rowdy days at the end of a drive," her daddy sighed from the far end of the table. "Drinking rot-gut whiskey, listening to an off-key piano…."

"Daddy, you never…?" Sky wasn't even sure what exactly happened, but had a fair idea.

"No, pet, I wasn't chasing loose women. I was usually the one paying the damages to keep my boys out of jail." He chuckled in remembrance.

"I managed to rope me some wild ponies," Seth said excitedly. "I'm starting my own herd." He nodded emphatically.

"Then you'd best be getting to work to earn more money for feed," her daddy told him.

Joe put a hand on Seth's arm as the youngster started to leave. "Before we all scatter for the day, I've got something to say."

Sky held her breath. Was he finally going to tell her he loved her and wanted to get married? She would have preferred for him to declare his love in private, but….

"I found Jessica." He wasn't looking at her, but at Mary Elizabeth, and for a moment Sky's heart plummeted at another woman's name on his tongue. But when Mary Elizabeth gasped and slapped a hand over her mouth as tears fell, Sky suddenly realized to whom Joe referred.

"Who's Jessica?" Seth asked.

"You were probably too young to remember," Joe said, "but she was, is, our baby sister. Your maw died shortly after she was born."

Everyone started asking questions at once, and Sky sat silent as Joe explained discovering the little girl, now named Isabelle, in Fredericksburg. She couldn't deny she was happy for Joe, even as her heart hung heavy in her chest because it apparently was regaining another member of his family that had brought the contentment to Joe's face, not her.

"Why didn't you bring her here?" Mary Elizabeth asked.

Joe shook his head. "Unlike you and Seth, she has a family; parents who love her. I couldn't take her away from that when she has no memory of us or her life before the Millers."

"Well, that's just dandy," her daddy said with a nod. "Seems to me you've done a fine job by your family, Joe, even if it has taken you a while."

Joe's face fell as he looked from Seth to Mary Elizabeth. "I wasn't there when they needed me most."

"Nonsense," Mary Elizabeth argued, reaching out to put her hand on his arm. "You are our brother, not our parents. Paw could have died later, after you'd gone to find a job and we would have been in the same fix. As it is, you rescued us when we needed you most. And you would have saved Jessica if she had needed it." She paused then added, "Sometimes you have to live with what you *have* and not dwell on what might have been." She lifted Joey from his highchair and cuddled him close. "I'm not proud of what happened to me, but I wouldn't change a thing if it meant I didn't have my baby."

The men, uncomfortable with the emotion that hung heavy over the room, rapidly excused themselves. Mary Elizabeth left shortly after, holding Joey away from her and wrinkling her nose, and Sky needed no further explanation.

In silence, she sipped her coffee and pondered her fate. She was doomed to love a man who was all about family, just not about starting a family with her. It seemed every time she *thought* she had him right where she wanted him, something interfered. How did he not see what was right in front of his face? What would it take to finally…?

"Sweet heavens," she cried, her coffee cup clattering to the saucer as she bolted up from the table. In her happiness to finally have him home she had forgotten all about her trip to the Kickapoo reservation. Last night, their passion had wiped everything from her mind. If it took finding every last member of his family before Joe relinquished his quest, she only hoped she held the key to the final mystery.

* * *

"I don't understand why you had to go to town today," Joe commented as they bounced along the dirt road in the wagon, his horse tied to the end gate. "I just got back and really didn't need to be away from the ranch at the moment."

"There's nothing that can't wait another day. The cattle have been sold, the yearlings are at pasture and the corrals have all been repaired." There was always work to be done on a ranch, but she had played her ace to get Joe to go along with her, without telling him about their final destination. "Besides, you're the one who said you'd go when you heard me tell daddy I was heading that way."

"Yes, because you have no business going alone."

This was exactly why she had talked to her father when in Joe's hearing. "I always went alone before you were here."

"Only because you're spoiled and your father can deny you nothing." There was no heat in his words and Sky didn't think he really believed that, so for the moment let it pass.

"The weather's changing." She switched subjects, snuggling closer to him and tucking her arm through his.

He gave her a sidelong glance, but reached over and turned up the collar of her sheepskin jacket. "Yet another reason not to be out. The weather this time of year is unpredictable and those clouds don't look inviting." He nodded to the distant mountains, where dark, thick clouds were forming.

"We can always hope to get stranded at the line shack." She shot him her most winsome smile.

He laughed out loud. "What am I to do with you?" In answer to his own question, he pulled the team to a stop and took her in his arms. His kiss was warm and tender, not like the passionate ravishment of last night, but just as arousing. When she would have hoped he would deepen the embrace, he lifted his head and gazed at her. "God, how I missed you." Before she could answer in kind, he turned and picked up the reins, clucking to get the horses moving again.

It would have been much easier if she had just told Joe what she knew about the twin boys living at the reservation, but she was so afraid she was wrong. While she could bear the disappointment, she didn't want it for Joe until every stone had been turned.

They rode in companionable silence for the remainder of the trip. Patch had given her a supply list as there would be more hungry mouths to feed when the remainder of the crew returned. And, as Joe had said, the weather was unpredictable, so she would load up supplies for the ranch to see them through winter months if need be. As long as she was going, she also wanted to get more staples for the Kickapoo, for although the braves would hunt throughout the winter, they wouldn't have things such as flour and grain to see them through.

While Joe saw to the supplies, she strolled through the mercantile for material and thread for new clothes for Joey, who was growing faster than they could keep up with. She also picked out some bright calico for Mary Elizabeth, whose clothes hung on her now that she had slimmed down after the baby. She chose a new stuffed pony for Joey along with books and peppermints for the children. She then added a tin of chocolates—Joe's favorites—which she would use to bribe him if necessary.

Once the supplies were loaded and Mr. McGuffy carefully wrapped her materials and notions, she quickly climbed up on the seat before Joe and grabbed the reins.

When he gave her a look, she smiled. "I do know how to handle a team."

He chuckled, climbing up beside her. His good humor lasted only as long as it took to leave town. When Sky veered west instead of southeast, he reached over and grabbed the reins.

"Sky?" There was a wealth of questions in that one word.

She sighed. "As long as we're this close, I thought we would take some supplies to the Kickapoo." When he scowled she quickly added, "Daddy knows that was my plan."

He wasn't placated. "*I* didn't know that was the plan. Were you going to tell me, or was I to assume all that extra flour was in case Patch couldn't teach Seth to cook without burning the biscuits?" When she didn't answer right away, he continued. "Sky, you know how I feel about your visits to the reservation."

She turned to him with a frown. "No, Joe, I really don't."

His sigh hung between them. "I don't have anything against the Kickapoo. I just don't want to get in the middle of their problems with the government. And I don't want you in the middle either. The Kickapoo have their place on the other side of the Rio Grande. We have ours here."

He tried to wrest the reins away, but she held tight. "There are chocolates in the back. Indulge yourself."

He didn't budge, his hand tight on hers. With a heartfelt sigh, she released her grip but before he could turn the team, she blurted out her secret.

"There are twins—boys—at the reservation."

Joe stilled immediately, staring at her as though she had spouted that the sky was green.

When he didn't speak, she began rambling, "I've seen them before but never thought much about it because I didn't know your story. When I went the last time, they were off fishing so I couldn't ask them any questions. I spoke of them to Black Thunder, and...."

"More than one woman has given birth to twins in this world," Joe interrupted her. Then, almost to himself, he added, "It couldn't be so simple, that they were this close and I never found them." He scowled at her, anger evident in his voice. "Besides, they are Indian."

"Living with the Indians," Sky corrected, gently placing a hand over his clenched ones. "Brown haired children…with blue eyes."

Chapter Twenty-One

"Why didn't you tell me?" Joe slapped the reins against the horses' backs. "Were you ever going to tell me?"

Sky grabbed the iron rail at the edge of the seat to keep from being thrown as the horses took off at a wild canter. One wagon wheel hit a rut, throwing her against Joe, but he didn't seem to notice.

When she was steady enough to look around, she realized that he had not turned the horses back toward town, but was heading, at an alarming rate, toward the reservation.

"Slow down," she said, tugging on his arm, then added, "Please." It seemed forever before her request registered, but finally he pulled back on the reins, bringing the horses to a walk. When she kept her gaze on him, his jaw tight and his eyes straight ahead, her heart broke. She had thought helping him find the remainder of his family would release him from his obligations so he would be free to love her like she loved him instead of always searching, wondering. Instead, he seemed to blame her for his problems.

"How long have you known?" His curtly spoken question confirmed her worst suspicions.

"I don't *know*," she started but when he shot her a narrow glare, she quickly added, "not for sure. That's why I needed you to come with me." She told him what little she had gathered about the twins. "And I only began to put it all together the very last time I was there, while you were gone," she concluded.

Joe's scowl softened, although the afternoon light still glinted off the flint in his eyes. "The time frame might be right, but why in the world would the Kickapoo keep them? Why not take them to Fort Duncan?"

It was a question Sky hadn't thought to ask Black Thunder, so she shrugged and offered an opinion. "Perhaps because the soldiers would never have believed the Indians accidentally found the children. And because the boys were found on the east side of the Rio."

"Texas land?" Joe asked and at her nod, he added what she hadn't. "So the soldiers might think the Indians had killed the parents in a raid."

She waited, wanting Joe to believe her, to believe in her friends, the Kickapoo. She wasn't hesitant about taking him to the reservation. She trusted him implicitly, knowing that even though he had once fought Indians as a Texas Ranger, it was no longer his job. Besides, he said he had nothing against this particular tribe, most of whom had migrated to Mexico on their own. Now that she had told him her suspicions, he seemed reluctantly anxious.

Even so, he pulled the team to a stop just after they crossed the river. At first, Sky thought he meant to water them, but he didn't move to get down. Instead, he wrapped the reins around the brake and turned to her. He placed both hands on her shoulders, drawing her forward until their lips all but touched.

"Thank you for what you've done for Seth and Mary Elizabeth; for what you're doing now," he whispered. Then his lips touched hers so tenderly tears welled in her eyes. "Do you know how much I love you for helping put my family back together?"

They should have been words she had longed to hear from him, so why did her heart feel as though it were shattered in a million pieces? Did he not know *she* wanted to be his family? Suddenly angry at his thick-headedness, she struggled to push him aside. "You are the most stubborn, ignorant...."

"Shh." He went strangely still. "We're being watched," he said softly. While his head never turned, his eyes shifted from side to side, surveying the terrain.

She wiggled until he let her go, and although she looked around, too, she couldn't see anyone. That didn't surprise her, but she knew they were out there and also knew exactly where they would make their presence known.

She reached over Joe and unwound the reins, clucking the horses into a walk. Joe shifted on the seat, straightening, shoulders back as though he were expecting a fight, but he didn't say another word as they continued away from the river. They were met three miles from the reservation, where the foothills began a gradual curve to the northeast. Only then did three braves ride toward them.

"They're an escort, and they know me," Sky stated in a low voice hoping to reassure Joe. When she saw his hand slide up his thigh toward his holstered gun, she whispered urgently, "Don't you dare cause trouble."

Joe swiveled his gaze to her and frowned. "You're the trouble maker." But he did relax, bracing his elbows on his knees and letting his hands dangle between his legs.

Sky made a face as she clucked the horses into a trot, closing the distance between them and the braves. She hadn't sent word that they were coming, but Two Feathers always had braves scouting the area.

She exchanged a few words in Kickapoo, gesturing between Joe and the braves.

"They have already sent someone back to the village to tell Black Thunder we are here. He is waiting for us at his lodge. Red Hawk, Wild Dog, and Running Pony will escort us." This she said loud enough for the braves to hear.

She then leaned closer to Joe before adding, "They are leery of your presence but I explained you are looking for your brothers. The Kickapoo have a great sense of family, so your quest is important to them. That's probably the only reason they will let you come with me." She grinned at his narrowed gaze and added, "Especially since you counted coup on Red Hawk the last time you met."

Joe would have liked to argue with her. The hair on the back of his neck bristled as the one called Red Hawk stared at him for endless minutes. Joe stared right back, determined not to show fear, even if he was outnumbered. He wanted to pull Sky out and take her home, but regardless of what he would rather do, he knew he had to trust her. To her questioning look, he gave a curt nod. The braves silently turned and rode away, expecting them to follow.

All Joe's senses were alert as they entered the village. Women came away from their cooking fires and stared as they rode slowly between lodges. Young children ran after, yelling words like *"chepi"* that Joe didn't understand. Sky laughed at the children, replying cheerfully in their tongue as they rode deeper into the camp.

When she brought the wagon to a stop and got down, he stayed where he was at her request. She reached into one of the bags in the bed of the wagon and withdrew books which the children eagerly grabbed from her hands, chatting in a mixture of English and Kickapoo. Then she gestured to the other supplies in the back half of the wagon as she spoke to the women, and Joe realized exactly why she had divided the supplies she had purchased in town. What he had always mistaken for overindulgence when she asked her father for more money was in fact generosity. She didn't spend her pin money on silks and parasols, but rather on flour and calico for the Indians. She reached deeper into the bag. She didn't buy herself jewelry and bric-à-brac; she got colorful beads and spinning tops for the children.

He scanned the faces of the children as they laughed at her presents. Would he even recognize Matthew or Michael? How much did a child change in seven years—a lifetime? In the innocent young faces, he saw no fear. Matthew and Michael would be nine now—young but far from innocent. Would they remember him?

Joe would have preferred beginning his search right away but Sky insisted they must follow ceremony, and that meant greeting the old chief first. As they were led toward the largest lodge, Joe continued to survey the children. It shouldn't have been hard to find two identical boys among the brown skinned Indian children, but when Joe tried to form a mental picture of his brothers, all he saw were black haired, barefoot boys in breechcloth.

His heart ached for the conditions under which these Indians were living. The ground in this part of Mexico was dry and barren, and even though it was bordered by the Rio Grande, he wondered how the Indians managed. Few ranchers or settlers would care about the plight of a tribe on the other side of the river, even if it had been their own government that forced them there. When Sky took his hand in hers to lead him toward the lodge, he couldn't help but lift it to his lips and kiss it for what her family did to help. She gave him a sweet, if somewhat sad, smile.

Joe had to curb his curiosity when they stepped inside the chief's lodge, for he knew he couldn't just blurt out with his questions. Instead, he tried to follow Sky's lead. Again he was amazed at her ability to communicate with these people. She nodded politely to the old chief, said a few words that Joe didn't understand, and then gestured to Joe.

"This is my friend, Joe Dawson." To him, she said softly, "Just a slight incline of your head to acknowledge him. Don't try to shake his hand."

Joe cocked an eyebrow. "Am I allowed to speak at all?"

With a completely serious expression, she said, "Not if you know what's good for you."

The old chief laughed and Joe realized he understood English, especially because for the next hour, the chief expounded on what was happening with his people. And Joe finally understood—he really did—although as a lone cowboy there was little he could do.

The chief's last words were to Sky, and in Kickapoo. She looked at Joe before answering the chief in his native tongue.

When they were finally dismissed, Joe had to ask, "What did Black Thunder say when you gave me that strange look?"

"What look?" Sky skirted the cook fire positioned right outside the lodge.

"You know. When you had that *scared rabbit* look like you wondered if I was going to jump up and do something."

Sky shrugged. "He was talking about the soldiers forcing them to remain on this land that doesn't support them, forcing them to forget the old ways."

"And why would that make me angry?"

"Because he doesn't acknowledge any difference between soldiers and the law, like a sheriff or the Rangers. He knows you were a Ranger."

"All that happened before I was even born."

She had the grace to look embarrassed. "Well, I know. But I wasn't sure how you would react."

"I'm not crazy enough to try something surrounded by the enemy."

"They are not the enemy."

"I'm sorry. You're right." He rubbed a hand over his face. "Now can we look for the twins?"

She turned away, a slight blush to her cheeks.

He grabbed her arm. "You did tell him why we were here?"

"Yes, of course, but the Kickapoo are high on ceremony so we have to wait for tonight."

"Tonight?" He looked toward the west where the sun could barely be seen. "Why?" he asked, although it really didn't matter. He had hoped to make it back to town before nightfall, but it was already too late for that.

"We happened to come on the Day of the Children. It's a very important ceremony where the children of the tribe are celebrated and the older ones are introduced to the tribe as adults."

Joe sighed. He had come so far and now he had to wait even longer. Sky seemed to sense his unrest because she took him by the hand and led him back behind the lodge to a small grove of trees. They sat behind one of the larger to block the wind, their backs against the trunk.

Sky rested her head on his shoulder. "What will you do if these boys aren't your brothers?"

Joe's heart pounded. "I don't know. Keep looking, I guess." He had thought he had finally let go of his quest, but then he found Jessica. And while he was happy that she had loving parents to take care of her, it had made him more anxious about the others. He hoped the twins had happy lives like Jessica and had not gone through the hell which Seth and Mary Elizabeth had been subjected. Besides, it was time he took hold of his own future and settled down with Sky. Perhaps when they had a family of their own, the aching hole in his heart would heal.

He started to speak his thoughts out loud, to finally tell her how he felt, but when he turned, her head fell onto his chest and he realized she was asleep. Gently, he curled an arm around her shoulders and closed his eyes.

The distant beat of drums awakened them and as Joe stood, he realized it was pitch black. He still felt uneasy, staying overnight with the tribe, but refused to show it as Sky excitedly led him back toward a huge bonfire in the middle of the circle of lodges.

"Hurry. The Kickapoo try very hard to carry on the traditions of their ancestors, and this ceremony is so moving, so...." She seemed to be at a loss for words, and Joe understood why.

As they sat on the outer edge of the circle, drums began beating, the rhythm compelling. It didn't take long before Joe felt the beat in his blood, in his very heart and soul. Over and over, the powerful beat and the movements of the dancers as they circled the fire spoke of some hidden meaning.

Sky reached for his hand and when he glanced her way, her eyes sparkled in the firelight. Her skin glowed and her head bobbed ever so slightly with the beat. Then she jutted her chin, wanting him to turn back to the dance.

Older dancers, a mixture of braves and women, snaked out of a break in the circle and then quickly returned with the children, who entered from the oldest to the very smallest, barely waddling as he clasped the hand of the one in front of him. Joe tried to scan the faces of the boys, but between the flickering fire and the weaving, circling of the dancers, it was impossible to focus on any one face.

The adults left the circle, and the children began chanting as they danced, shaking strings of bells and clanking hollow wooden rods together.

But above it all was the pounding, pounding of the drums, their sound swelling until the very air vibrated. It called to him across the distance, but even stronger was the touch of Sky's hot hand in his. He turned to watch as she, too, was carried away with the strange music. Her eyes were glazed, her upper body swayed, undulating like a primal animal among nature. He ached to capture the image before his eyes, yet that essence was part of the night and would disappear with the wood smoke.

Instead of a mystical creature, Joe wanted the real Sky. He tugged on her hand until she looked from the dancers to him. He turned until they were facing and he captured her other hand. He brought both to his mouth, kissing one then the other.

"Marry me."

Her eyes widened; her mouth opened in a small "oh", and her hands begin to shake beneath his.

"But your brothers," she stammered.

Joe shook his head. "They may be here or they may not be. Seth, Mary Elizabeth, Jessica and little Joey—they are my kin." He squeezed her hands, trying to tell her how he felt. "But you are my *life*. I love you with everything I am."

Sky flung herself into his arms so quickly she knocked Joe onto his back, with herself on top of him. She kissed him with such ardor Joe felt his manhood responding and only managed to set her aside because the beat of the drum still echoed in his head, reminding him of their audience.

She took his hand and led him away from the fire, explaining as they entered a small lodge off to the side of the chief's, "I often stay when I come to see my friends. This was Black Thunder's eldest daughter's lodge, but she has married and moved on with her husband."

As soon as the deerskin flap fell behind them, she laughed and launched herself into his arms. "Tell me again."

"Skyla Tate, are you going to be a nag of a wife?" His own humor was high, until he realized that she hadn't said yes. His mouth turned down into a frown. "Actually, you didn't answer my proposal."

She strutted away from him, then turned, very slowly undoing her blouse, one button at a time. "*Actually*," she mimicked, "you didn't propose, you commanded—*marry me.*"

"Well, I never asked anyone before and...." Joe was having trouble with his thoughts because Sky threw off her blouse, followed by her chemise, and was toeing out of her boots. Hopping from foot to foot made her breasts jiggle and Joe swallowed, hard.

"Do you really love me?" She stood before him naked, a glorious goddess, and he was humbled to think that she loved him.

"I think I have loved you all my life. You have the spirit of a wild mustang, the beauty of a cactus flower, and a heart as pure as the Texas sky is blue."

His words made her cry, which was certainly not his intent. He gathered her in his arms and they sank to the soft furs strewn across the dirt floor. He told her again and again of his love, finally able to release his heart into her safekeeping, where it belonged. And deep in the night, just as he fell asleep, she snuggled close and whispered *"yes"* in his ear.

* * *

"We've been summoned," Sky said softly as she shook his shoulder.

Joe opened gritty eyes and saw a shadow slipping out past the sliver of light as the deerskin flap fell back in place. He groaned as he rolled over, reaching in vain for Sky, who was already up and dressing.

The smell of wood smoke from the fire the night before still hung on the air; the drums continued to echo his heartbeat. But foremost in his mind was the image of Sky, loving him in the dark of night.

"Did you really say yes?" he asked, leaning on an elbow, reluctant to leave the warmth of the furs and skins.

She paused, one leg in her Levi's, her hands gripping the waist. "Why wouldn't I?"

In the heat of last night's passion, Joe had been honest with his heart and his yearnings, but in the hazy light of morning, his mind jumbled with doubt. He got up, turning his back as he started to dress. "Maybe because I have nothing to offer you. I'm a cowboy, with no land, no herd of cattle. Hell, I don't even have the wild mustangs that Seth managed to rope on the trail."

Before he donned his shirt, her hands slid around his waist and splayed against his chest. Her breath was warm on his back, then her lips peppered his taut muscles with kisses.

"Do you think that is more important than your integrity, your loyalty; your gentleness?"

She slid under one arm to face him. "I love all that makes you who you are, Joe Dawson. And that has nothing to do with material goods."

In her glittering gaze he saw his future, and whatever today held, he knew she would always be by his side.

"Okay, then. Let's go see what the old chief has to say."

Hand in hand, they exited the lodge and turned toward Black Thunder's. When they were bid entrance, Joe stopped short just inside. Seated to the right of the chief was Two Feathers, his son, but Joe's gaze was riveted on those to the left. Red Hawk sat cross-legged and scowling, and to his left were two young boys.

"So you have chosen?" Two Feathers asked the minute they were seated across the low fire. Joe looked from the brave to Sky, wondering if there was more history between the two than she had ever told him.

227

"He is *nuttah*, my heart," she replied softly, placing her hand over her heart for emphasis.

Before the brave said more, Black Thunder raised a hand in silence. "It is for another reason I have called you here, *Oota Dabun*, although I am pleased to see you are happy." His gaze moved to Joe, who held it steadily with his own.

"You have questions, but perhaps first you must tell us your story of how you came to lose your family."

Joe glanced at Sky, sure she had already told the old man what she knew, but at her slight nod, he began. Even now, when he had found most of his kin, his voice caught with emotion at the retelling. The lodge was quiet except for his voice, and when he was done, his gaze swept the boys, who had sat as still as statues throughout it all.

"I do not belong to this man, this paleface," said one of the youngsters in anger.

"Angry Dog, it is not your place to speak," Red Hawk said softly, and Joe was surprised at the affection in the brave's voice. Then he turned his gaze to Joe and suddenly he understood.

"You are their father," he stated, and it was not a question.

"I found them four summers ago. They became my responsibility."

Although Joe didn't understand the Kickapoo culture, he did understand propriety. "May I ask them questions?" he respectfully asked Red Hawk, then swung his gaze to include Black Thunder. When the men acquiesced, he turned to the boys.

"Do either of you remember any of your time before you came to live with the Kickapoo? Are the names Matthew or Michael familiar to you?"

The one named Angry Dog rapidly shook his head, but the other one tilted his head, his eyes wide. He started to speak but his brother grabbed his arm and spoke rapidly in Kickapoo.

"Let him speak," reprimanded Red Hawk gently. "We will know the true story."

"We were five summers old. Our parents were traveling to Old Mexico, but the river was swollen with rain. Our father left us on the bank as he tried to drive the team across but the wagon tipped. Our mother went into the river after him and soon, they were both lost."

Joe sat still, waiting for more. Their story was what Sky had told him, but it still didn't make them his brothers.

"And your names before the Kickapoo?" He held his breath.

One boy looked at the other, but it was the reticent one who answered. "I am Michael, now known as Little Fox. My brother is Matthew."

"I am Angry Dog, son of Red Hawk!" The other boy exploded. "One day I will be a great warrior as my father and his father before him." Regardless of the respect due to the old chief, the youngster surged to his feet and ran from the lodge.

In the silence that followed, Joe's heart beat so furiously he could not have spoken. Four years with the Indians had effectively wiped one child's memory of all that had come before. As he looked over at the remaining boy, he still could find no resemblance between this youth and the toddler he had once held through a bout with a fever.

To confirm his remaining doubts, he reached beneath his shirt and pulled out the concho, lifting the leather thong over his head. He held it out to the child, whose blue eyes grew wide. Slowly, hesitant, he too removed a string of sinew, at the end of which hung an identical silver button.

Sky gasped, but Joe saw nothing except the young child, and only through tears clouding his vision. He made no effort to hide his emotions. In the background Red Hawk spoke rapidly in Kickapoo, his concerns answered in soft tones by Sky or the old chief. And all the while, Michael's gaze never wavered from Joe's face.

"In dreams, I see a tall man holding me, and a red-haired girl wiping my face with cool water. I hear a promise, but the shaman says perhaps it was from another life."

Joe shook his head. "No, no. You had a fever. Mary Elizabeth and I took care of you."

"She is your wife?" Red Hawk asked this, looking between him and Sky with a scowl.

"No, she is my sister, and sister to Michael and Matthew." His voice broke as he tried to explain. "I promised to come back for them." He looked directly at Michael. "I searched for you. I swear I did. I have been looking for seven years." Joe's emotions were hard to check, and he tried not to be too eager as he spoke to Black Thunder. "These two are my brothers, my family. I would like to take them home with me. We have been apart for too long."

No one said anything for a time and Joe wondered if he had overstepped. When Black Thunder made a gesture, Sky lightly touched his arm and stood. "We have to go."

Joe wanted to refuse, wanted to threaten that he would get Fort Duncan soldiers. Instead, he followed her out of the lodge and into the crisp air of a sunny autumn morning.

"They can't keep them," he said as he paced.

"They haven't said that they would," Sky countered. Her worried voice had Joe turning toward her and she grabbed his hands to hold him still. "Joe, they were two years of age when you left. They apparently had parents for three years, and now they have had four years with the Kickapoo. They appear to be happy children, and I could see the affection Red Hawk has for them."

At his protest, she held up a hand. "Tell me, would it be any different than when you left Jessica with the Millers?"

He scowled at her, even if somewhere in his mind he knew she had a point. Still, he wouldn't accept that ending until he had begged, if necessary. He didn't have a chance as Two Feathers exited the lodge and came to them.

His face was a mask that Joe couldn't read, but shouldn't have been surprised at the words he spoke, "My father has heard your story. He will speak with Angry Dog and Little Fox and he will make his decision."

Joe started to protest but Two Feathers held up a hand. "Regardless of your laws, you are on Kickapoo land and must abide by our laws." He turned to Sky. "Take your friend home, *Numees*. There is no more for you to do here."

Epilogue

Fall turned to winter, and although there was no snow, the days were cold and windy. Still, the herd had to be looked after and the horses fed, so cowboys bundled up, oftentimes exchanging their favorite wide-brimmed hat for a knitted hat and scarf.

Joe was no exception, Sky noted, as he pulled on a cap before he left Bonita's kitchen where they more often than not ate their meals now that the weather had changed. The dining room had no fireplace, and Bonita usually kept the stove stoked. Besides, the kitchen was roomy enough for all of them, and small enough to make it feel like family.

When Joe stopped to give Sky a kiss, she tugged the cap lower over his ears. "I like that on you," she said of the bright colors.

"It's a good thing my sister knows how to knit," he teased, tweaking her nose before dropping another kiss exactly there.

"There are things I know how to do," she replied, and at the lift of his eyebrow and smirk on his lips, she blushed. "Besides that," she whispered. With a great laugh, he swept her off her feet into a fierce hug.

Mary Elizabeth laughed behind her, and Seth groaned as he excused himself from the table. At thirteen, any display of affection embarrassed him beyond measure. But ever since their return from the reservation, Joe had been open about courting her.

Her daddy had been thrilled when they announced they were to marry, and he insisted they have the wedding at the ranch in the spring. Sky told him she couldn't wait, and hence she, Mary Elizabeth and Bonita were deep into plans for a Christmas wedding. They had invited neighboring ranchers and friends from town, and she hoped the weather would cooperate. Regardless of who showed up, she would not be deterred from that date, only a few short weeks away.

Sky felt the quickening low in her abdomen and placed a hand there, at once excited and scared to death that she was with child. She thought to ask Mary Elizabeth what to expect, but since she had yet to tell Joe, she kept the secret as best she could. At the rate she was eating, though, she would soon be the size of a horse. She looked forlornly at the jam tarts on a pretty china plate in the center of the table. Just as she reached out to pinch off a small piece, the door opened and Joe stuck his head back in.

"I won't be home for supper," he said, then he was gone again.

Sky looked at Mary Elizabeth, who reached a hand over to squeeze hers. They both knew what that meant. For the past two months, since Joe had discovered the twins, he made weekly trips out to the reservation. He didn't ask her to go with him, but she assumed Black Thunder had agreed to this, otherwise the visits would have ended with the first.

He rarely spoke of what occurred there, although he wasn't secretive as to where he went. Once he had taken Seth with him, the boy could not keep his mouth closed about it. In fact, Seth appeared to be in awe of the Kickapoo and the fact that one of his brothers, Michael, was studying with the shaman.

"To be a doctor," Seth had told her, although she already knew what it meant.

He had refused to take Mary Elizabeth, stating the long ride would be too much for her and she needed to stay with Joey. She seemed all right with that, although she often was the one with the questions. Like now, when she asked the question on everyone's mind, "Do you think they will ever allow the boys to come here? There can't be much for them *out there*." Having never been to the reservation, Mary

Elizabeth waved a hand vaguely to encompass everything beyond the ranch.

Sky shrugged. "The Kickapoo, like so many of their kind, are trying hard to preserve their way of life, which includes being self-sustaining even in the most difficult of times. They want their children to know the old ways, to understand who they are and where they have come from." At Mary Elizabeth's look, she added, "The boys are considered their children, therefore Kickapoo."

Joe did speak of his visit the next night when he came in for supper. "I have been trying to talk Michael and Matthew into coming to the ranch. Seeing them in the midst of the tribe, it appears that they belong, but only Matthew *wants* to be there." He shook his head. "He well fits his name of Angry Dog, because every time I so much as approach the two of them, he shouts words I don't understand and runs off."

"Guess you can't blame him," her daddy said. "A way of life gets ingrained in a body, even if it's not the same life as others have, or want."

Sky followed his look around the table, understanding what he was saying. Joe, lost as a boy, had been lucky to find his way to the ranch and to be taken under her father's wing. Seth could well have become an outlaw, and Mary Elizabeth? Only the good Lord had protected her from further damage.

"Won't Michael come, even if Matthew doesn't?" Mary Elizabeth asked.

Joe shook his head. "I asked."

"But we're family," Mary Elizabeth protested.

Joe gave her a smile. "I think he understands that, and our story, because I have told him over and again what happened. But Matthew is his twin. He won't leave his brother."

* * *

It was the night before her wedding, and although Sky had told Joe he wasn't to see her before the ceremony, he didn't seem inclined to leave her bed. Instead, he continued to express his gratitude in the most charming ways, such as kissing behind her knee where her skin was so sensitive.

"That is for agreeing to marry me," he whispered as he nibbled a trail from her knee up her thigh to her belly. His tongue snaked out to tickle her belly button before he planted a kiss there, too. "And that is for inviting the Millers to the wedding."

Sky hadn't been sure her letter would reach them in time, but they had arrived that afternoon and everyone had been delighted. Mister and Missus Miller said they had explained about Isabelle's family on the ride there, and the girl had been overcome with excitement to learn she had brothers and sisters. She was a miniature Mary Elizabeth with her bright red hair and braids and she became Sky's daddy's favorite within minutes.

As Joe's lips meandered up her body toward her breasts, Sky forgot everything except the exquisite passion he always evoked. But when he cupped her tender breasts in his large hands and squeezed, she groaned.

He stopped, leaning back to gaze at her. When she didn't say anything, he lifted one breast as though testing the weight of it in his hand. Still with his gaze on her, he slid his hand down to her belly, which was only slightly swollen. His eyes narrowed, slate gray turning silvery in the moonlight. One dark eyebrow lifted, a trait she normally loved but which at the moment made her nervous. What if he didn't want children?

"That is because you love me." She lifted her head to meet his lips, pouring all her love into her kiss.

* * *

Joe anxiously dragged a finger beneath the scratchy collar of the white shirt, trying to loosen the strangle hold it had on his neck. He peered into the mirror over the basin, the man gazing back in a brown suit and string tie unknown to him. He had bought the suit on one of his trips to town, not wanting to disappoint Sky by showing up at their

235

wedding all in black, his preferred color until recently. Perhaps because his heart was full, he was more easily persuaded to wear the soft blues and brown plaids she had picked for him.

There didn't seem to be much that could disappoint her, he thought as he brushed his wayward hair. After all, she had agreed to marry him, a cowboy with little money and few prospects. *But we have family,* she had whispered to him last night, *and that's all that really matters.*

When the true meaning of Sky's words had seeped in—that *they* would be a family—he awoke that morning with a feeling of contentment, something that had eluded him all his life. He wouldn't have thought he could be any happier, having found his kin, scattered though they were. At least they were all healthy and happy. But the thought of being a father, of teaching a child of his very own right from wrong and how to be a man both terrified and excited him.

A commotion down the hall had Joe looking at the clock on the table, assuring himself he was not late for his own wedding. Raised voices—one feminine shriek in particular—came to him through the partly open door, and regardless of the propriety of not seeing his bride before the ceremony, he hurried out of the room.

"Hurry, Joe," Mary Elizabeth screamed at him from where she stood at the open doorway, only one of several women trying to see what was happening and stay behind the protection of the walls at the same time. Joe bolted out the front door, reaching for his sidearm, which of course was back in his room.

Every cowboy on the ranch was lined up in front of the porch, backs to him, rifles at the ready. Many of the male guests spread out along the porch rail, and unlike Joe, each had a gun, unholstered.

Sky, a vision in cream lace, her hair blown by the breeze, struggled to break through the line of men. Her father, alarm registering in the dark planes of his face, tried to hold her back.

236

Joe looked just beyond them and his heart dropped at the cause of the commotion. Riding into the yard were the Kickapoo, or at least those of the tribe who were the fiercest—a dozen or more warriors, regaled in full ceremonial headdress and deerskin. They pulled their horses to a stop only a few yards from the men, and for a minute, not a sound could be heard on that clear Christmas morning.

Joe was the first to move, stepping down from the porch and tugging off his jacket, slipping it over Sky's shoulders. "You'll catch your death," he said softly as the cold air seeped through the wool of his shirt.

"Cooper Tate," Two Feathers called out.

When Sky's father stepped forward, straight and tall, one of the braves, Red Hawk, swung down from his horse. Joe heard rifles being cocked behind him and quickly put up a hand. His own heart pounded, but not in fear. The brave motioned, and two riders from behind swung down and stepped forward, one on either side of Red Hawk.

Matthew and Michael.

"My father, Black Thunder, knows you as a friend, one who has shared with the Kickapoo," Two Feathers spoke. "A good man who has raised a daughter as generous and kind as he; who befriended a lost youth and raised him like a son."

Sky was shaking, and Joe tightened his grip on her shoulders, otherwise, he was sure he would have rushed forward and grabbed the twins.

Two Feathers continued, "My father knows the times are changing, that our way of life is not as we have known. He has spoken. The boys, though they are Kickapoo in their hearts, must learn the white man's ways. He believes as they grow and learn, they will find a way to help the Kickapoo."

Red Hawk raised his head from where he had been speaking softly to the twins. He looked directly at Joe. "You have shown much spirit and bravery in your quest. I would have my sons learn those traits and more."

237

Before Joe could gather his wits, Red Hawk remounted and together he and Two Feathers turned and rode away, the other braves close behind.

And so, with his five brothers and sisters close behind him, with neighbors and friends as witness, Joe pledged his love to Sky, who had always held his heart.

The End

Also by Barbara Baldwin from Books We Love

Lost Knight of Arabia
Spinning Through Time
A Game of Love
Always Believe
Prospecting for Love
If Wishes Were Magic
Love in Disguise

Barbara was born in California and now resides in the Midwest. She loves to travel and explore new places, which usually means each of her novels is set in a different locale. She has been published in formats from poetry and short stories to full-length fiction. She really loves writing romance, whether it is contemporary, historical or time travel. She has an MA in Communication and has taught every grade from Kindergarten to college. Visit her website at http://www.authorsden.com/barbarajbaldwin.

www.ingramcontent.com/pod-product-compliance
Lightning Source LLC
Chambersburg PA
CBHW051642260626
47170CB00004B/1288